Praise for *Wicked Wonders*

"A shimmering cornucopia of language, emotion, and surprises rich with meaning. No one gives us the terrible innocence and longings of childhood better than Ellen Klages. These stories are fabulous, in every sense of that multi-faceted word."
—Nancy Kress, author of *After the Fall, Before the Fall, During the Fall*

"*Wicked Wonders* will realign disparate parts of your heart into quantum sympathy. Read it. Read it now."
—William Alexander, National Book Award–winning author of *Goblin Secrets*

"Delightful. Disturbing. Delicious. And always, her prose is gorgeous. Klages is one of my favourite authors."
—Nalo Hopkinson, author of *The Salt Roads* and *Falling in Love with Hominids*

"Whenever I start to read a new story by the incomparable Ellen Klages, I feel as if I'm on the edge of my seat in the front row of the theater: keen-eyed and determined, this time, to pay close attention to the entire performance and figure out how she does it. I never do figure it out—her hands are too quick, too deft, and she seems to be everywhere at once. But that's OK, the magic happens anyway, and bits of it still glitter on my shoulders as I re-enter my life, dazed and exhilarated, wiser and richer for the experience."
—Andy Duncan, author of *The Night Cache* and *The Pottawatomie Giant*

"Stunning. She draws your eye to the waves at the shore then gathers the tide behind your back. Bradbury, Dahl, Jackson? No— simply incomparable Klages."
—Karen Lord, author of *The Galaxy Game* and *The Best of All Possible Worlds*

"Smart, often funny, and satisfyingly strange, these wicked stories will delight."
—Jenny Blackford, author of *Duties to My Cat* and *The Princess and the Slave*

"If you enjoy strong or subversive female protagonists in speculative fiction, this collection is for you!"
—*Read Well Reviews*

Praise for *Portable Childhoods*

"Klages, whose debut novel, *The Green Glass Sea* (2006), won the Scott O'Dell Award for Historical Fiction, demonstrates both superior writing skill and a wide range in an impressive short-story collection that defies easy categorization."
—*Publishers Weekly*, starred review

"Ellen Klages believes books can be magic, and now she's delivered the proof: this spell-weaving collection of her short stories."
—Connie Willis, author of *Doomsday Book*

"Consistently well written and emotionally stimulating, the book is one of the loveliest you'll find."
—*School Library Journal*

"Klages creates wonder-filled and beautiful worlds in her short stories, making this a tremendously satisfying collection."
—*Booklist*

"Klages has the true storyteller's gift."
—Charles de Lint, *The Magazine of Fantasy & Science Fiction*

WICKED WONDERS

ELLEN KLAGES

TACHYON | SAN FRANCISCO

Tachyon Publications LLC
1459 18th Street #139
San Francisco, CA 94107
(415) 285-5615
www.tachyonpublications.com
tachyon@tachyonpublications.com

Series Editor: Jacob Weisman
Project Editor: Rachel Fagundes

ISBN 13: 978-1-61696-261-6

Printed in the United States by Worzalla
First Edition: 2017

9 8 7 6 5 4 3 2 1

To Gary and Jonathan, boon companions.
The next round's on me.

CONTENTS

INTRODUCTION
BY KAREN JOY FOWLER

I once saw Ellen Klages in a chicken suit.

This is something I can't truthfully say about any other friend I have. (Nor can it be said about me. At least not yet.) A still more startling fact: I'm not the only one who saw this; there are a great many of us. We are legion. "Remember that time Ellen wore the chicken suit?" we say when we gather together in our great numbers. Ellen Klages sure rocked that chicken suit.

I've known Ellen for many years now, so many that I've lost count. I met her before I read her, back when she was just a sprig. This was a few years before she'd written any of that body of fiction for which she's now known.

I've seen her with hair and without. I've seen her at the poker table (where she is terrifying). I've seen her on panels and at readings (where she is brilliant). I've seen her doing her stand-up routine for the auction that supports the James Tiptree, Jr. Award (where she is hilarious).

I've been in her living room many times, with its motley and somewhat disturbing collection of ephemera, and she's made me onion soup, which I've eaten at her kitchen table and gone back for seconds. She is, in short, a very good friend.

She's the kind of friend you might take a road trip with, and I've done that, too, more than once. On a particularly memorable occasion, I passed through Kansas with the amazing Kelly Link in the back seat and the amazing Ellen at the wheel. For hours, an Oz-like tornado paced us on the right. I watched it from the passenger window, a green and boiling sky from which lightning emerged in fantastic cracks and sheets. It was incredible, an awesome display that lasted for many, many miles.

As we drove, we heard twister warnings on the radio, always for some town we had only just passed through. The storm seemed to be behind as well as beside us. I remember how magical it all felt—the strange, theatrical sky, like nothing I have ever seen before or since; random bits of trash and torn-off nature whirling about us. And our small band of adventurers, often the only car on the road, repeatedly being told to stop driving immediately, to find a safe hole somewhere, which we eventually did, although that safety ended the magic instantly, so it's a decision I can't help but regret. How long might we have been able to continue driving alongside, but never *into*, danger?

Somewhere in the middle of that carefully curated memory is a useful metaphor for thinking about Ellen's fiction. There is something powerfully strange and strangely powerful, but it is off to the side or coming up behind you. You'll sense it in the small, particular details at which Ellen excels—the way a woman folds a piece of paper, the expanding X's of an elevator door as it closes, the line of descant in a camp sing-along, the last leaf falling from dying tree, the mathematical patterns on the shell of a tortoise.

Ellen has long been acknowledged for her extraordinary gift at evoking the ordinary, but potent magic of childhood. Here, as in her other collection, much of her fiction takes place beyond adult supervision, in those spaces where a childhood actually happens.

This might be a lake or a cabin, a closet or an elevator. You'll find yourself in secret houses and secret streets, basements, and space ships. There may be trapdoors or traps, chutes or ladders.

Ellen's young protagonists are both tough and sensitive. Like so many of us, they don't quite fit in. So they're always looking for the chance, unavailable in their homes and schools and communities, to be their true selves. This desire to live authentically, to speak with one's true voice, is where Ellen's work cuts the deepest. In her childhood stories, she balances like an acrobat between two contradictory truths—that 1) a young person suffers from having no power in the adult world and 2) growing up is something to be avoided as long as possible. Families must be escaped, but childhood is the kingdom from which you are expelled.

In general, Ellen is sympathetic to children (as they deserve) and suspicious of adults (as likewise). But several of these stories do involve older women, women who've achieved a thrilling competence, for good or ill. Some of these women may be people you already know. But young or old, benign or malevolent, these stories all have the ring of someone speaking in their own true voice.

The Ellen you meet in the world and the Ellen you meet in her stories are not exactly the same person. Ask anyone who knows her and the first thing they will say is how funny she is. You'll get a sense of this from "The Scary Ham" in this collection, which got its start as an oral tale and represents pretty accurately what it's like to spend an evening with her.

The other stories are more likely to make you cry than laugh. In the written form, Ellen is more tender than humorous. You feel how much she cares for her protagonists, how much she wishes them well. People who deserve a come-uppance will get that, but people who don't won't. They'll be given instead an ending you'll believe that they are tough enough to survive. It might even be a happy one. Sometimes it is.

In terms of genre, these stories are range-free. There is the out-and-out high fantasy of "Sponda the Suet Girl" and the contemporary fantasies of "Echoes of Aurora" and "The Education of a Witch." Science fiction is represented with "Amicae Aeternum" and "Goodnight Moons." Historical fantasies with "Hey, Presto!" and "Caligo Lane." Metafiction with "Household Management" and "Mrs. Zeno's Paradox."

It doesn't do, of course, to have favorites, but to me "Woodsmoke" shows all of Ellen's great gifts brought together to perfect purpose. It's just a remarkable piece of work, managing to take the reader both back to childhood, and also out into the larger, confusing world adults have made. There is no fantastical element in this story at all; you never know what you are going to get in a Klages story.

There may be supernatural events or powers, but often there are not. There may be fairies or magicians, or there may only be parents and camp counselors. There may be spells, or there may be math. The only thing you can depend on is magic. However sober and quotidian the world, Ellen always brings the magic.

THE EDUCATION OF A WITCH

1.

Lizzy is an untidy, intelligent child. Her dark hair resists combs, framing her face like thistles. Her clothes do not stay clean or tucked in or pressed. Some days, they do not stay on. Her arms and face are nut-brown, her bare legs sturdy and grimy.

She intends to be a good girl, but shrubs and sheds and unlocked cupboards beckon. In photographs, her eyes sparkle with unspent mischief; the corner of her mouth quirks in a grin. She is energy that cannot abide fences. When she sleeps, her mother smooths a hand over her cheek, in affection and relief.

Before she met the witch, Lizzy was an only child.

The world outside her bedroom is an ordinary suburb. But the stories in the books her mother reads to her, and the ones she is learning to read herself, are full of fairies and witches and magic.

She knows they are only stories, but after the lights are out, she lies awake, wondering about the parts that are real. She was named after a princess, Elizabeth, who became the queen of England. Her father has been there, on a plane. He says that a man's house is his castle, and when he brings her mother flowers, she smiles and proclaims, "You're a prince, Jack Breyer." Under the sink—where she is not supposed to look—many of the cans say M-A-G-I-C in big letters. She watches very carefully when her mother sprinkles the powders onto the counter, but has not seen sparkles or a wand. Not yet.

2.

Lizzy sits on the grass in the backyard, in the shade of the very big tree. Her arms are all over sweaty and have made damp, soft places on the newsprint page of her coloring book. The burnt umber crayon lies on the asphalt driveway, its point melted to a puddle. It was not her favorite. That is purple, worn down to a little stub, almost too small to hold.

On the patio, a few feet away, her parents sit having drinks. The ice cubes clink like marbles against the glass. Her father has loosened his tie, rolled up the sleeves of his white go-to-the-office shirt. He opens the evening paper with a crackle.

Her mother sighs. "I wish this baby would hurry up. I don't think I can take another month in this heat. It's only the end of June."

"Can't rush Mother Nature." More crackle, more clinks. "But I *can* open the windows upstairs. There's a Rock Hudson movie at the drive-in. Should be cool enough to sleep when we get back."

"Oh, that would be lovely! But, what about—" She drops her voice to a whisper. "Iz-ee-lay? It's too late to call the sitter."

Lizzy pays more attention. She does not know what language that is, but she knows her name in most of the secret ways her parents talk.

"Put her in her jammies, throw the quilt in the back of the station wagon, and we'll take her along."

"I don't know. Dr. Spock says movies can be very frightening at her age. *We* know it's make-believe, but—"

"The first show is just a cartoon, one of those Disney things." He looks back at the paper. "*Sleeping Beauty.*"

"Really? Well, in that case; she loves fairy tales."

Jammies are for after dark, and always in the house. It is confusing, but exciting. Lizzy sits on the front seat, between her parents, her legs straight out in front of her. She can feel the warm vinyl through thin cotton. They drive down Main Street, past the Shell station—S-H-E-L-L—past the dry cleaners that give free cardboard with her father's shirts, past the Methodist church where she goes to Nursery School.

After that, she does not know where they are. Farther than she has ever been on this street. Behind the car, the sun is setting, and even the light looks strange, glowing on the glass and bricks of buildings that have not been in her world before. They drive so far that it is country, flat fields and woods so thick they are all shadow. On either side of her, the windows are rolled down, and the air that moves across her face is soft and smells like grass and barbecue. When they stop at a light, she hears crickets and sees a rising glimmer in the weeds beside the pavement. Lightning bugs.

At the Sky View Drive-In they turn and join a line of cars that creep toward a lighted hut. The wheels bump and clatter over the gravel with each slow rotation. The sky is a pale blue wash now, streaks of red above the dark broccoli of the trees. Beyond the hut where her father pays is a parking lot full of cars and honking and people talking louder than they do indoors.

Her father pulls into a space and turns the engine off. Lizzy wiggles over, ready to get out. Her mother puts a hand on her arm. "We're going to sit right here in the car and watch the movie." She points out the windshield to an enormous white wall. "It'll be dark in just a few minutes, and that's where they'll show the pictures."

"The sound comes out of this." Her father rolls the window halfway up and hangs a big silver box on the edge of the glass.

The box squawks with a sharp, loud sound that makes Lizzy put her hands over her ears. Her father turns a knob, and the squawk turns into a man's voice that says ". . . concession stand right now!" Then there is cartoon music.

"Look, Lizzy." Her mother points again, and where there had been a white wall a minute before is now the biggest Mickey Mouse she has ever seen. A mouse as big as a house. She giggles.

"Can you see okay?" her father asks.

Lizzy nods, then looks again and shakes her head. "Just his head, not his legs." She smiles. "I could sit on Mommy's lap."

"'Fraid not, honey. No room for you until the baby comes."

It's true. Under her sleeveless plaid smock, her stomach is very big and round and the innie part of her lap is outie. Lizzy doesn't know how the baby got in there, or how it's going to come out, but she hopes that will be soon.

"I thought that might be a problem." Her father gets out and opens the back door. "Scoot behind the wheel for a second."

Lizzy scoots, and he puts the little chair from her bedroom right on the seat of the car. Its white painted legs and wicker seat look very wrong there. But he holds it steady, and when she climbs up and sits down, it *feels* right. Her feet touch flat on the vinyl, and she can see *all* of Mickey Mouse.

"Better?" He gets back in and shuts his door.

"Uh-huh." She settles in, then remembers. "Thank you, Daddy."

"What a good girl." Her mother kisses her cheek. That is almost as good as a lap.

Sleeping Beauty is Lizzy's first movie. She is not sure what to expect, but it is a lot like TV, only much bigger, and in color. There is a king and queen and a princess who is going to marry the prince, even though she is just a baby. That happens in fairy tales.

Three fairies come to bring presents for the baby. Not very good ones—just beauty and songs. Lizzy is sure the baby would rather have toys. The fairies are short and fat and wear Easter colors. They have round, smiling faces and look like Mrs. Carmichael, her Sunday School teacher, except with pointy hats.

Suddenly the speaker on the window booms with thunder and roaring winds. Bright lightning makes the color pictures go black-and-white for a minute, and a magnificent figure appears in a whoosh of green flames. She is taller than everyone else, and wears shiny black robes lined with purple.

Lizzy leans forward. "Oooh!"

"Don't be scared." Her mother puts a hand on Lizzy's arm. "It's only a cartoon."

"I'm not." She stares at the screen, her mouth open. "She's *beautiful.*"

"No, honey. She's the witch," her father says.

Lizzy pays no attention. She is enchanted. Witches in books are old and bent over, with ugly warts. The woman on the screen has a smooth, soothing voice, red, red lips, and sparkling eyes, just like Mommy's, with a curving slender figure, no baby inside.

She watches the story unfold, and clenches her hands in outrage for the witch, Maleficent. If the whole kingdom was invited to the party, how could they leave *her* out? That is not fair!

Some of this she says a little too out loud, and gets *Shhh!* from both her parents. Lizzy does not like being shh'd, and her lower lip juts forward in defense. When Maleficent disappears, with more wind and green flames, she sits back in her chair and watches to see what will happen next.

Not much. It is just the fairies, and if they want the baby princess, they have to give up magic. Lizzy does not think this is a good trade. All they do is have tea, and call each other "dear," and talk about flowers and cooking and cleaning. Lizzy's chin drops, her hands lie limp in her lap, her breathing slows.

"She's out," her father whispers. "I'll tuck her into the back."

"No," Lizzy says. It is a soft, sleepy no, but very clear. A few minutes later, she hears the music change from sugar-sweet to pay-attention-now, and she opens her eyes all the way. Maleficent is back. Her long slender fingers are a pale green, like cream of grass, tipped with bright red nails.

"Her hands are pretty, like yours, Mommy," Lizzy says. It is a nice thing to say, a compliment. She waits for her mother to pat her arm, or kiss her cheek, but hears only a soft *pfft* of surprise.

For the rest of the movie, Lizzy is wide, wide awake, bouncing in her chair. Maleficent has her own castle, her own mountain! She can turn into a dragon, purple and black, breathing green fire! She fights off the prince, who wants to hurt her. She forces him to the edge of a cliff and then she—

A tear rolls down Lizzy's cheek, then another, and a loud sniffle that lets all the tears loose.

"Oh, Lizzy-Lou. That was a little *too* scary, huh?" Her mother wipes her face with a tissue. "But there's a happy ending."

"Not. Happy." Lizzy says between sobs. "He *killed* her."

"No, no. Look. She's not dead. Just sleeping. Then he kisses her, and they live happily ever after."

"Noooo," Lizzy wails. "Not her. *Mel*ficent!"

They do not stay for Rock Hudson.

3.

"Lizzy? Put your shoes back on," her mother says.

Her father looks up over *Field and Stream*. "Where are you two off to?"

"Town and Country. I'm taking Lizzy to the T-O-Y S-T-O-R-E."

"Why? Her birthday's not for months."

"I know. But everyone's going to bring presents for the baby, and Dr. Spock says that it's important for her to have a little something too. So she doesn't feel left out."

"I suppose." He shrugs and reaches for his pipe.

When her mother stops the car right in front of Kiddie Korner, Lizzy is so excited she can barely sit still. It is where Christmas happens. It is the most special place she knows.

"You can pick out a toy for yourself," her mother says when they are inside. "Whatever tickles your fancy."

Lizzy is not sure what part of her is a fancy, but she nods and looks around. Kiddie Korner smells like cardboard and rubber and dreams. Aisle after aisle of dolls and trucks, balls and blocks, games and guns. The first thing she sees is Play-Doh. It is fun to roll into snakes, and it tastes salty. But it is too ordinary for a fancy.

She looks at stuffed animals, at a doll named Barbie who is not a baby but a grown-up lady, at a puzzle of all the United States. Then she sees a *Sleeping Beauty* coloring book. She opens it to see what pictures it has.

"What fun! Shall we get that one?"

"Maybe."

It is too soon to pick. There is a lot more store. Lizzy puts it back on the rack and turns a corner. *Sleeping Beauty* is everywhere. A Little Golden Book, a packet of View-Master reels, a set of to-cut-out paper dolls, a lunchbox. She stops and considers each one. It is hard to choose. Beside her, she hears an impatient puff from her mother, and knows she is running out of time.

She is about to go back and get the coloring book when she sees a shelf of bright yellow boxes. Each of them says P-U-P-P-E-T in large letters.

"Puppets!" she says, and runs over to them.

"Oh, look at those! Which one shall we get? How about the princess? Isn't she pretty!"

Lizzy does not answer. She is busy looking from one box to the next, at the molded vinyl faces that peer out through cellophane windows. Princess, princess, princess. Prince. King.

19

Fairy, fairy, prince, fairy, princess—and then, at the end of the row, she sees the one that she has not quite known she was looking for. Maleficent!

The green face smiles down at her like a long-lost friend.

"That one!" Lizzy is not tall enough to grab the box; she points as hard as she can, stretching her arm so much it pulls her shoulder.

Her mother's hand reaches out, then stops in mid-air. "Oh." She frowns. "Are you sure? Look, here's Flora, and Fauna, and—" She pauses. "Who's the other one?"

"Merryweather," Lizzy says. "But I want *her!*" She points again to Maleficent.

"Hmm. Tell you what. I'll get you all *three* fairies."

That is tempting. But Lizzy knows what she wants now, and she knows how to get it. She does not yell or throw a tantrum. She shakes her head slowly and makes her eyes very sad, then looks up at her mother and says, in her quiet voice, "No thank you, Mommy."

After a moment, her mother sighs. "Oh, *all* right," she says, and reaches for the witch.

Lizzy opens the box as soon as they get in the car. The soft vinyl head of the puppet is perfect—smiling red lips, yellow eyes, curving black horns. Just as she remembers. Beneath the pale green chin is a red ribbon, tied in a bow. She cannot see anything more, because there is cardboard.

It takes her a minute to tug that out, and then the witch is free. Lizzy stares. She expected flowing purple and black robes, but Maleficent's cotton body is a red plaid mitten with a place for a thumb on each side.

Maybe the black robes are just for dress-up. Maybe this is her bathrobe. Lizzy thinks for a few minutes, and decides that is true. Plaid is what Maleficent wears when she's at home, in her castle, reading the paper and having coffee. It is more comfortable than her work clothes.

4.

On Saturday, Lizzy and her mother go to Granny Atkinson's house on the other side of town. The women talk about baby clothes and doctor things, and Lizzy sits on the couch and plays with her sneaker laces. Granny gets out a big brown book, and shows her a picture of a fat baby in a snowsuit. Mommy says *she* was that baby, a long time ago, but Lizzy does not think that could be true. Granny laughs and after lunch teaches Lizzy to play gin rummy and lets her have *two* root beers because it is so hot.

When they pull into their own driveway, late in the afternoon, Lizzy's mother says, "There's a big surprise upstairs!" Her eyes twinkle, like she can hardly wait.

Lizzy can't wait either. She runs in the front door and up to her room, which has yellow walls and a window that looks out onto the driveway so she can see when Daddy comes home. She has slept there her whole life. When she got up that morning, she made most of her bed and put Maleficent on the pillow to guard while she was at Granny's.

When she reaches the doorway, Lizzy stops and stares. Maleficent is gone. Her *bed* is gone. Her dresser with Bo Peep and her bookcase and her toy chest and her chair. All gone.

"Surprise!" her father says. He is standing in front of another room, across the hall, where people sleep when they are guests. "Come and see."

Lizzy comes and sees blue walls and brown heavy curtains. Her bed is next to a big dark wood dresser with a mirror too high for her to look into. Bo Peep is dwarfed beside it, and looks as lost as her sheep. The toy chest is under a window, Maleficent folded on top.

"Well, what do you think?" Her father mops his face with a bandana and tucks it between his blue jeans and his white t-shirt.

"I *liked* my room," Lizzy says.

"That's where the baby's going to sleep, now." Her mother gives her a one-arm hug around the shoulders. "*You* get a big-girl room." She looks around. "We will have to get new curtains. You can help me pick them out. Won't that be fun?"

"Not really." Lizzy stands very still in the room that is not her room. Nothing is hers anymore.

"Well, I'll let you get settled in," her father says in his glad-to-meet-you voice, "and get the grill started." He ruffles his hand on Lizzy's hair. "Hot dogs tonight, just for you."

Lizzy tries to smile, because they are her favorite food, but only part of her mouth goes along.

At bedtime, her mother hears her prayers and tucks her in and sings the good-night song in her sweet, soft voice. For that few minutes, everything is fine. Everything is just the way it used to be. But the moment the light is off and the door is closed—not all the way—that changes. All the shadows are wrong. A streetlight is outside one window now, and the very big tree outside the other, and they make strange shapes on the walls and the floor.

Lizzy clutches Maleficent under the covers. The witch will protect her from what the shapes might become.

5.

"When do you get the baby?" Lizzy asks. They are in the yellow bedroom, Lizzy's real room. Her mother is folding diapers on the new changing table.

"Two weeks, give or take. I'll be gone for a couple of days, because babies are born in a hospital."

"I'll go with you!"

"I'd like that. But this hospital is only for grown-ups. You get to stay here with Teck."

Teck is Lizzy's babysitter. She has a last name so long no one can say it. Lizzy likes her. She has white hair and a soft, wrinkled face and makes the *best* grilled cheese sandwiches. And she is the only person who will play Candy Land more than once.

But when the baby starts to come, it is ten days too soon. Teck is away visiting her sister Ethel. Lizzy's father pulls into the driveway at two in the afternoon with Mrs. Sloupe, who watches Timmy Lawton when his parents go out. There is nothing soft about her. She has gray hair in tight little curls, and her lipstick mouth is bigger than her real one.

"I'll take your suitcase upstairs," he tells her. "You can sleep in our room tonight."

Her mother sits in a chair in the living room. Her eyes are closed, and she is breathing funny. Lizzy stands next to her and pats her hand. "There there, Mommy."

"Thank you, sweetie," she whispers.

Daddy picks her up and gives her a hug, tight and scratchy. "When you wake up in the morning, you're going to be a big sister," he says. "So I need you to behave for Mrs. Sloupe."

"I'll be very hāve," Lizzy says. The words tremble.

He puts her down and Mommy kisses the top of her head. Then they are gone.

Mrs. Sloupe does not want to play a game. It is time for her stories on TV. They can play after dinner. Dinner is something called chicken ala king, which is yellow and has peas in it. Lizzy only eats two bites because it is icky, and her stomach is scared.

Lizzy wins Candy Land. Mrs. Sloupe will not play again. It is bedtime. But she does not know how bedtime works. She says the now-I-lay-me prayer with the wrong words, and tucks the covers too tight.

"Playing fairy tales, were you?" she says, reaching for Maleficent. "I'll put this ugly witch in the toy chest, where you can't see it. Don't want you having bad dreams."

"No!" Lizzy holds on to the puppet with both arms.

"Well, aren't you a queer little girl?" Mrs. Sloupe says. "Suit yourself." She turns off the light and closes the door, all the way, which makes the shadows even more wrong. When Lizzy finally falls asleep, the witch's cloth body is damp and sticky with tears.

Her father comes home the next morning, unshaven and bleary. He picks Lizzy up and hugs her. "You have a baby sister," he says. "Rosemary, after your mother's aunt." Then he puts her down and pats her behind, shooing her into the living room to watch *Captain Kangaroo*.

Lizzy pauses just beyond the hall closet and before he shuts the kitchen door, she hears him tell Mrs. Sloupe, "She was breech. Touch and go for a while, but they're both resting quietly, so I think we're out of the woods."

He takes Mrs. Sloupe home after dinner, and picks her up the next morning. It is three days before Teck arrives to be the real babysitter, and she is there every day for a week before he brings Mommy and the baby home.

"There's my big girl," her mother says. She is sitting up in bed. Her face looks pale and thinner than Lizzy remembers, and there are dark places under her eyes. The baby is wrapped in a pink blanket beside her. All Lizzy can see is a little face that looks like an old lady.

"Can we go to the playground today?"

"No, sweetie. Mommy needs to rest."

"Tomorrow?"

"Maybe next week. We'll see." She kisses Lizzy's cheek. "I think there's a new box of crayons on the kitchen table. Why don't you go look? I'll be down for dinner."

Dinner is a sack of hamburgers from the Eastmoor Drive-In. Then at bedtime, Mommy comes in and does all the right things. She sings *two* songs, and Lizzy falls asleep smiling. But she has a bad dream, and when she goes to crawl into bed with Mommy and Daddy, to make it all better, there is no room. The baby is asleep between them.

For days, the house is full of grown-ups. Ladies and aunts

come in twos and threes and bring casseroles and only say hi to Lizzy. They want to see the baby. They all make goo-goo sounds and say, "What a little darling!" At night, some men come, too. They look at the baby, but just for a minute, and do not coo. They go out onto the porch and have beers and smoke.

The rest of the summer, all any grown-up wants to do is hold the baby or feed the baby or change the baby. Lizzy doesn't know why; that is *very* stinky. She tries to be more interesting, but no one notices. The baby cannot do a somersault, or say the Pledge of Allegiance or sing "Fairy Jocka Dormy Voo." All she can do is lie there and spit up and cry.

And sleep. The baby sleeps all the time, and every morning and every afternoon, Mommy naps with her. The princess is sleeping, so the whole house has to stay quiet. Lizzy cannot play her records, because it will wake the baby. She can't jump on her bed. She can't even build a tall tower with blocks because if it crashes, it will wake the baby. But when the baby screams, which is a lot, no one even says *Shhh!*

Lizzy thinks they should give the baby back.

"Will you read to me?" she asks her mother, when nothing else is happening.

"Oh—not now, Lizzy-Lou. I've got to sterilize some bottles for Rosie. How 'bout you be a big girl, and read by yourself for a while?"

Lizzy is tired of being a big girl. She goes to her room but does not slam the door, even though she wants to, because she is also tired of being yelled at. She picks up Maleficent. The puppet comes to life around her hand. Maleficent tells Lizzy that she is very smart, very clever, and Lizzy smiles. It is good to hear.

Lizzy puts on her own bathrobe, so they match. "Will you read to me?" she asks. "Up here in our castle?"

Maleficent nods, and says in a smooth voice, "Of course I will. That would be lovely," and reads to her all afternoon. Even though she can change into anything she wants—a dragon, a ball of green fire—her eyes are always kind, and every time Lizzy comes into the room, she is smiling.

On nights when Mommy is too tired, and Daddy puts Lizzy to bed, the witch sings the good-night song in a sweet, soft voice. She knows all the words. She whispers, "Good night, Lizzy-Tizzy-Toot," the special, only-at-bedtime, good-dreams name.

Maleficent loves Lizzy best.

6.

Lizzy is glad when it is fall and time for nursery school, where they do not allow babies. Every morning Mrs. Breyer and Mrs. Huntington and Mrs. Lawton take turns driving to Wooton Methodist Church. When her mother drives, Lizzy gets to sit in the front seat. Other days she has to share the back with Tripper or Timmy.

She has known Timmy her whole life. The Lawtons live two doors down. They have a new baby too, another boy. When they had cocktails to celebrate, Lizzy heard her father joke to Mr. Lawton: "Well, Bob, the future's settled. My two girls will marry your two boys, and we'll unite our kingdoms." Lizzy does not think that is funny.

Timmy is no one's handsome prince. He is a gangly, insubstantial boy who likes to wear sailor suits. His eyes always look as though he'd just finished crying because he is allergic to almost everything, and is prone to nosebleeds. He is not a good pick for Red Rover.

The church is a large stone building with a parking lot and a playground with a fence around it. Nursery school is in a wide, sunny room on the second floor. Lizzy climbs the steps as fast as she can, hangs up her coat on the hook under L-I-Z-Z-Y, and tries to be the first to sit down on the big rug in the middle of the room, near Mrs. Dickens. There are two teachers, but

Mrs. Dickens is her favorite. She wears her brown hair in braids wrapped all the way around her head and smells like lemons.

Lizzy knows all the color words and how to count up to twenty. She can write her whole name—without making the Zs backward—so she is impatient when the other kids do not listen to her. Sometimes she has to yell at them so she can have the right color of paint. The second week of school, she has to knock Timmy down to get the red ball at recess.

Mrs. Dickens sends a note home, and in the morning, the next-door neighbor comes over to watch the baby so Lizzy's mother can drive her to school, even though it is not her turn.

"Good morning, Lizzy," Mrs. Dickens says at the door. "Will you get the music basket ready? I want to talk to your mother for a minute."

Lizzy nods. She likes to be in charge. But she also wants to know what they are saying, so she puts the tambourine and the maracas in the basket very quietly, and listens.

"How are things at home?" Mrs. Dickens asks.

"A little hectic, with the new baby. Why?"

"New baby. Of course." Mrs. Dickens looks over at Lizzy and puts a finger to her lips. "Let's continue this out in the hall," she says, and that's all Lizzy gets to hear.

But when they make Circle, Mrs. Dickens pats the right side of her chair, and says, "Come sit by me, Lizzy." They sing the good-morning song and have Share and march to a record and Lizzy gets to play the cymbals. When it is time for Recess, Mrs. Dickens rings the bell on her desk, and they all put on their coats and hold hands with their buddies and walk down the stairs like ladies and gentlemen. For the first time, Mrs. Dickens is Lizzy's buddy, and no one gets knocked down.

On a late October morning, Lizzy's mother dresses her in a new green wool coat, because it is cold outside. It might snow. She runs up the stairs, but the coat is stiff and has a lot of buttons, and by the time she hangs it up, Anna von Stade is sitting in *her* place in the circle. Lizzy has to sit on the other side of Mrs. Dickens and is not happy. Timmy sits down beside her, which does not help at all.

"Children! Children! Quiet now. Friday is a holiday. Who knows what it is?"

Lizzy's hand shoots straight up. Mrs. Dickens calls on Kevin.

"It's Halloween," he says.

"Very good. And we're going to have our *own* Halloween party."

"I'm going to be Pinocchio!" David says.

"We raise our hand before speaking, David." Mrs. Dickens waggles her finger at him, then waits for silence before she continues. "That will be a good costume for trick-or-treating. But for *our* party, I want each of you to come dressed as who you want to be when you grow up."

"I'm going to be a fireman!"

"I'm going to be a bus driver!"

"I'm going—"

Mrs. Dickens claps her hands twice. "Children! We do not talk out of turn, and we do not talk when others are talking."

The room slowly grows quiet.

"But it is good to see that you're all *so* enthusiastic. Let's go around the circle, and everyone can have a chance to share." She looks down to her right. "Anna, you can start."

"I'm going to be a ballerina," Anna says.

Lizzy does not know the answer, and she does not like that. Besides, she is going to be last, and all the right ones will be gone. She crosses her arms and scowls down at the hem of her plaid skirt.

"I'm going to be a doctor," Herbie says.

Fireman. Doctor. Policeman. Teacher. Mailman. Nurse. Baseball player. Mommy. Lizzy thinks about the lady jobs. Nurses wear silly hats and have to be clean all the time, and she is not good at that. Teacher is better, but two people have already said it. She wonders what else there is.

Tripper takes a long time. Finally he says, "I guess I'll be in sales."

"Like your father? That's nice." Mrs. Dickens nods. "Carol?"

Carol will be a mommy. Bobby will be a fireman.

Timmy takes the longest time of all. Everyone waits and fidgets. Finally he says he wants to drive a steam shovel like Mike Mulligan. "That's fine, Timmy," says Mrs. Dickens.

And then it is her turn.

"What are *you* going to be when you grow up, Lizzy?"

"Can I see the menu, please?" Lizzy asks. That is what her father says at the Top Diner when he wants a list of answers.

Mrs. Dickens smiles. "There isn't one. You can be anything you want."

"Anything?"

"That's right. You heard Andrew. He wants to be president someday, and in the United States of America, he can be."

Lizzy doesn't want to be president. Eisenhower is bald and old. Besides, that is a daddy job, like doctor and fireman. What do ladies do besides mommy and nurse and teacher? She thinks very hard, scrunching up her mouth—and then she knows!

"I'm going to be a witch," she says.

She is very proud, because no one has said that yet, no one in the whole circle. She looks up at Mrs. Dickens, waiting to hear, "Very good. Very creative, Lizzy," like she usually does.

Mrs. Dickens does not say that. She shakes her head. "We are not using our imaginations today. We are talking about real-life jobs."

"I'm going to be a witch."

"There is no such thing." Mrs. Dickens is frowning at Lizzy now, her face as wrinkled as her braids.

"Yes there is!" Lizzy says, louder. "In Hansel and Gretel, and Snow White and Sleeping—"

"Elizabeth? You know better than that. Those are only stories."

29

"Then stupid Timmy can't drive a steam shovel because Mike Mulligan is only a story!" Lizzy shouts.

"That's *enough!*" Mrs. Dickens leans over and picks Lizzy up under the arms. She is carried over to the chair that faces the corner and plopped down. "You will sit here until you are ready to say you're sorry."

Lizzy stares at the wall. She is sorry she is sitting in the dunce chair, and she is sorry that her arms hurt where Mrs. Dickens grabbed her. But she says nothing.

Mrs. Dickens waits for a minute, then makes a *tsk* noise and goes back to the circle. For almost an hour, Lizzy hears Nursery School happening behind her: blocks clatter, cupboards open, Mrs. Dickens gives directions, children giggle and whisper. This chair does not feel right at all, and Lizzy squirms. After a while she closes her eyes and talks to Maleficent without making any sound. Out of long repetition, her thumb and lips move in concert, and the witch responds.

Lizzy is asking when she will learn to cast a spell, how that is different from spelling ordinary W-O-R-D-S, when the Recess bell rings behind her. She makes a disappearing puff with her fingers and opens her eyes. In a moment, she feels Mrs. Dickens's hand on her shoulder.

"Have you thought about what you said?" Mrs. Dickens asks.

"Yes," says Lizzy, because it is true.

"Good. Now, tell Timmy you're sorry, and you may get your coat and go outside."

She turns in the chair and sees Timmy standing behind Mrs. Dickens. His hands are on his hips, and he is grinning like he has won a prize.

Lizzy does not like that. She is not sorry.

She is *mad.*

Mad at Mommy, mad at the baby, mad at all the unfair things. Mad at Timmy Lawton, who is right there.

Lizzy clenches her fists and feels a tingling, all over, like goosebumps, only deeper. She glares at Timmy, so hard that she can feel her forehead tighten, and the anger grows until it surges through her like a ball of green fire.

A thin trickle of blood oozes from Timmy Lawton's nose. Lizzy stares harder and watches blood pour across his pale lips and begin to drip onto his sailor shirt, red dots appearing and spreading across the white stripes.

"Help?" Timmy says.

Mrs. Dickens turns around. "Oh, dear. Not again." She sighs and calls to the other teacher. "Linda? Can you get Timmy a washcloth?"

Lizzy laughs out loud.

In an instant, Lizzy and the chair are off the ground. Mrs. Dickens has grabbed it by the rungs and carries it across the room and out the classroom door. Lizzy is too startled to do anything but hold on. Mrs. Dickens marches down the hall, her shoes like drumbeats.

She deposits Lizzy with a thump in the corner of an empty Sunday School room, shades drawn, dim and chilly with brown-flecked linoleum and no rug.

"You. Sit. There," Mrs. Dickens says in a voice Lizzy has not heard her use before.

The door shuts and footsteps echo away. Then she is alone and everything is very quiet. The room smells like chalk and furniture polish. She lets go of the chair and looks around. On one side is a blackboard, on the other a picture of Jesus with a hat made of thorns, like the ones Maleficent put around Sleeping Beauty's castle.

Lizzy nods. She kicks her feet against the rungs of the small chair, bouncing the rubber heels of her saddle shoes against the wood. She hears the other children clatter in from Recess. Her stomach gurgles. She will not get Snack.

But she is not sorry.

It is a long time before she hears cars pull into the parking lot, doors slamming and the sounds of many grown-up shoes on the wide stone stairs.

She tilts her head toward the door, listens.

"—Rosemary? Isn't she adorable!" That is Mrs. Dickens.

And then, a minute later, her mother, louder. "Oh, dear, *now* what?"

Another minute, and she hears the click-clack of her mother's shoes in the hall, coming closer.

Lizzy turns in the chair, forehead taut with concentration. The tingle begins, the green fire rises inside her. She smiles, staring at the doorway, and waits.

AMICAE AETERNUM

It was still dark when Corry woke, no lights on in the neighbors' houses, just a yellow glow from the streetlight on the other side of the elm. Through her open window, the early summer breeze brushed across her coverlet like silk.

Corry dressed silently, trying not to see the empty walls, the boxes piled in a corner. She pulled on a shirt and shorts, looping the laces of her shoes around her neck and climbed from bed to sill and out the window with only a whisper of fabric against the worn wood. Then she was outside.

The grass was chill and damp beneath her bare feet. She let them rest on it for a minute, the freshly-mowed blades tickling her toes, her heels sinking into the springy-sponginess of the dirt. She breathed deep, to catch it all—the cool and the green and the stillness—holding it in for as long as she could before slipping on her shoes.

A morning to remember. Every little detail.

She walked across the lawn, stepping over the ridge of clippings along the verge, onto the sidewalk. Theirs was a corner lot. In a minute, she would be out of sight. For once, she was up before her practical, morning-people parents. The engineer and the physicist did not believe in sleeping in, but Corry could count on the fingers of one hand the number of times in her eleven years that she had seen the dawn.

No one else was on the street. It felt solemn and private, as if she had stepped out of time, so quiet she could hear the wind ruffle the wide canopy of trees, an owl hooting from somewhere behind her, the diesel chug of the all-night bus two blocks away. She crossed Branson St. and turned down the alley that ran behind the houses.

A dandelion's spiky leaves pushed through a crack in the cement. Corry squatted, touching it with a finger, tracing the jagged outline, memorizing its contours. A weed. No one planted it or planned it. She smiled and stood up, her hand against a wooden fence, feeling the grain beneath her palm, the crackling web of old paint, and continued on. The alley stretched ahead for several blocks, the pavement a narrowing pale V.

She paused a minute later to watch a cat prowl stealthily along the base of another fence, hunting or slinking home. It looked up, saw her, and sped into a purposeful thousand-leg trot before disappearing into a yard. She thought of her own cat, Mr. Bumble, who now belonged to a neighbor, and wiped at the edge of her eye. She distracted herself by peering into backyards at random bits of other people's lives—lawn chairs, an overturned tricycle, a metal barbecue grill, its lid open.

Barbecue. She hadn't thought to add that to her list. She'd like to have one more whiff of charcoal, lit with lighter fluid, smoking and wafting across the yards, smelling like summer. Too late now. No one barbecued their breakfast.

She walked on, past Remington Rd. She brushed her fingers over a rosebush—velvet petals, leathery leaves; pressed a hand against the oft-stapled roughness of a telephone pole, fringed with remnants of garage-sale flyers; stood on tiptoe to trace the red octagon of a stop sign. She stepped from sidewalk to grass to asphalt and back, tasting the textures with her feet, noting the cracks and holes and bumps, the faded paint on the curb near a fire hydrant.

"Fire hydrant," she said softly, but aloud, checking it off in her mind. "Rain gutter. Lawn mower. Mailbox."

The sky was just beginning to purple in the east when she reached Anna's back gate. She knew it as well as her own. They'd been best friends since first grade, had been in and out of each other's houses practically every day. Corry tapped on the frame of the porch's screen door with one knuckle.

A moment later, Anna came out. "Hi, Spunk," she whispered.

"Hi, Spork," Corry answered. She waited while Anna eased the door closed so it wouldn't bang, sat on the steps, put on her shoes.

Their bikes leaned against the side of the garage. Corry had told her mom that she had given her bike to Anna's sister Pat. And she would, in an hour or two. So it hadn't really been a lie, just the wrong tense.

They walked their bikes through the gate. In the alley, Corry threw a leg over and settled onto the vinyl seat, its shape molded to hers over the years. Her bike. Her steed. Her hands fit themselves around the rubber grips of the handlebars and she pushed off with one foot. Anna was a few feet behind, then beside her. They rode abreast down to the mouth of the alley and away.

The slight grade of Thompson St. was perfect for coasting, the wind on their faces, blowing Corry's short dark hair off her forehead, rippling Anna's ponytail. At the bottom of the hill, Corry stood tall on her pedals, pumping hard, the muscles in her calves a good ache as the chain rattled and whirred as fast and constant as a train.

"Trains!" she yelled into the wind. Another item from her list.

"Train whistles!" Anna yelled back.

They leaned into a curve. Corry felt gravity pull at her, pumped harder, in control. They turned a corner and a moment later, Anna said, "Look."

Corry slowed, looked up, then braked to a stop. The crescent moon hung above a gap in the trees, a thin sliver of blue-white light.

Anna began the lullaby her mother used to sing when Corry first slept over. On the second line, Corry joined in.

I see the moon, and the moon sees me.
The moon sees somebody I want to see.

The sound of their voices was liquid in the stillness, sweet and smooth. Anna reached out and held Corry's hand across the space between their bikes.

God bless the moon, and God bless me,
And God bless the somebody I want to see.

They stood for a minute, feet on the ground, still holding hands. Corry gave a squeeze and let go. "Thanks."

"Any time," said Anna, and bit her lip.

"I know," Corry said. Because it wouldn't be. She pointed. The sky was lighter now, palest blue at the end of the street shading to indigo directly above. "Let's get to the park before the sun comes up."

No traffic, no cars. It felt like they were the only people in the world. They headed east, riding down the middle of the street, chasing the shadows of their bikes from streetlight to streetlight, never quite catching them. The houses on both sides were dark, only one light in a kitchen window making a yellow rectangle on a driveway. As they passed it, they smelled bacon frying, heard a fragment of music.

The light at 38th St. was red. They stopped, toes on the ground, waiting. A raccoon scuttled from under a hedge, hump-backed and quick, disappearing behind a parked car. In the hush, Corry heard the metallic *tick* from the light box before she saw it change from red to green.

Three blocks up Ralston Hill. The sky looked magic now, the edges wiped with pastels, peach and lavender and a blush of orange. Corry pedaled as hard as she could, felt her breath ragged in her throat, a trickle of sweat between her shoulder blades. Under the arched entrance to the park, into the broad, grassy picnic area that sloped down to the creek.

They abandoned their bikes to the grass, and walked to a low stone wall. Corry sat, cross-legged, her best friend beside her, and waited for the sun to rise for the last time.

She knew it didn't actually rise, that *it* wasn't moving. They were, rotating a quarter mile every second, coming all the way around once every twenty-four hours, exposing themselves once again to the star they called the sun, and naming that moment *morning*. But it was the last time she'd get to watch.

"There it is," Anna said. Golden light pierced the spaces between the trunks of the trees, casting long thin shadows across the grass. They leaned against each other and watched as the sky brightened to its familiar blue, and color returned: green leaves, pink bicycles, yellow shorts. Behind them lights began to come on in houses and a dog barked.

By the time the sun touched the tops of the distant trees, the backs of their legs were pebbled with the pattern of the wall, and it was daytime.

Corry sat, listening to the world waking up and going about its ordinary business: cars starting, birds chirping, a mother calling out, "Jimmy! Breakfast!" She felt as if her whole body was aware, making all of this a part of her.

Over by the playground, geese waddled on the grass, pecking for bugs. One goose climbed onto the end of the teeter-totter and sat, as if waiting for a playmate. Corry laughed out loud. She would never have thought to put *that* on her list.

"What's next?" Anna asked.

"The creek, before anyone else is there."

They walked single file down the steep railroad-tie steps, flanked by tall oaks and thick undergrowth dotted with wildflowers. "Wild," Corry said softly.

When they reached the bank they took off their shoes and climbed over boulders until they were surrounded by rushing water. The air smelled fresh, full of minerals, the sound of the water both constant and never-the-same as it poured over rocks and rills, eddied around logs.

They sat down on the biggest, flattest rock and eased their bare feet into the creek, watching goosebumps rise up their legs. Corry felt the current swirl around her. She watched the speckles of light dance on the water, the deep shade under the bank, ten thousand shades of green and brown everywhere she looked. Sun on her face, wind in her hair, water at her feet, rock beneath her.

"How much of your list did you get to do?" asked Anna.

"A lot of it. It kept getting longer. I'd check one thing off, and it'd remind me of something else. I got to most of the everyday ones, 'cause I could walk, or ride my bike. Mom was too busy packing and giving stuff away and checking off her own lists to take me to the aquarium, or to the zoo, so I didn't see the jellies or the elephants and the bears."

Anna nodded. "My mom was like that too, when we were moving here from Indianapolis."

"At least you knew where you were going. We're heading off into the great unknown, my dad says. Boldly going where nobody's gone before."

"Like that old TV show."

"Yeah, except we're not going to *get* anywhere. At least not me, or my mom or my dad. The *Goddard* is a generation ship. The planet it's heading for is five light years away, and even with solar sails and stuff, the trip's going to take a couple hundred years."

"Wow."

"Yeah. It won't land until my great-great—I don't know, add about five more greats to that—grandchildren are around. I'll be old—like thirty—before we even get out of the solar system. Dad keeps saying that it's the adventure of a lifetime, and we're achieving humankind's greatest dream, and blah, blah, blah. But it's *his* dream." She picked at a piece of lichen on the rock.

"Does your mom want to go?"

"Uh-huh. She's all excited about the experiments she can do in zero-g. She says it's an honor that we were chosen and I should be proud to be a pioneer."

"Will you be in history books?"

Corry shrugged. "Maybe. There are around four thousand people going, from all over the world, so I'd be in tiny, tiny print. But maybe."

"Four *thousand*?" Anna whistled. "How big a rocket is it?"

"Big. Bigger than big." Corry pulled her feet up, hugging her arms around her knees. "Remember that humongous cruise ship we saw when we went to Miami?"

"Sure. It looked like a skyscraper, lying on its side."

"That's what this ship is like, only bigger. And rounder. My mom keeps saying it'll be *just* like a cruise—any food anytime I want, games to play, all the movies and books and music ever made—after school, of course. Except people on cruise ships stop at ports and get off and explore. Once we board tonight, we're *never* getting off. I'm going to spend the rest of my whole entire life in a big tin can."

"That sucks."

"Tell me about it." Corry reached into her pocket and pulled out a crumpled sheet of paper, scribbles covering both sides. She smoothed it out on her knee. "I've got another list." She cleared her throat and began to read:

Twenty Reasons Why Being on a Generation Ship Sucks,
by Corrine Garcia-Kelly

1. I will never go away to college.
2. I will never see blue sky again, except in pictures.
3. There will never be a new kid in my class.
4. I will never meet anyone my parents don't already know.
5. I will never have anything new that isn't ~~man~~ human-made. Manufactured or processed or grown in a lab.
6. Once I get my ID chip, my parents will always know exactly where I am.
7. I will never get to drive my Aunt Frieda's convertible, even though she promised I could when I turned sixteen.
8. I will never see the ocean again.
9. I will never go to Paris.
10. I will never meet a tall, dark stranger, dangerous or not.
11. I will never move away from home.
12. I will never get to make the rules for my own life.
13. I will never ride my bike to a new neighborhood and find a store I haven't seen before.
14. I will never ride my bike again.
15. I will never go <u>outside</u> again.
16. I will never take a walk to anywhere that isn't planned and mapped and numbered.
17. I will never see another thunderstorm. Or lightning bugs. Or fireworks.
18. I will never buy an old house and fix it up.
19. I will never eat another Whopper.
20. I will never go to the state fair and win a stuffed animal.

She stopped. "I was getting kind of sleepy toward the end."
"I could tell." Anna slipped her arm around Corry's waist. "What will you miss most?"

"You." Corry pulled Anna closer.

"Me, too." Anna settled her head on her friend's shoulder. "I can't believe I'll never see you again."

"I know." Corry sighed. "I *like* Earth. I like that there are parts that no one made, and that there are always surprises." She shifted her arm a little. "Maybe I don't want to be a pioneer. I mean, I don't know *what* I want to be when I grow up. Mom's always said I could be anything I wanted to be, but now? The Peace Corps is out. So is being a coal miner or a deep-sea diver or a park ranger. Or an antique dealer."

"You like old things."

"I do. They're from the past, so everything has a story."

"I thought so." Anna reached into her pocket with her free hand. "I used the metals kit from my dad's printer, and made you something." She pulled out a tissue paper–wrapped lump and put it in Corry's lap.

Corry tore off the paper. Inside was a silver disk, about five centimeters across. In raised letters around the edge it said SPUNK-CORRY-ANNA-SPORK-2065. Etched in the center was a photo of the two of them, arm in arm, wearing tall pointed hats with stars, taken at Anna's last birthday party. Corry turned it over. The back said: *Optimae amicae aeternum.* "What does that mean?"

"'Best friends forever.' At least that's what Translator said."

"It's great. Thanks. I'll keep it with me, all the time."

"You'd better. It's an artifact."

"It is really nice."

"I'm serious. Isn't your spaceship going off to another planet with a whole library of Earth's art and culture and all?"

"Yeah. . . ?"

"But by the time it lands, that'll be ancient history and tales. No one alive will ever have been on Earth, right?"

"Yeah . . ."

"So your mission—if you choose to accept it—is to preserve this artifact from your home planet." Anna shrugged. "It isn't old now, but it will be. You can tell your kids stories about it—about us. It'll be an heirloom. Then they'll tell their kids, and—"

"—and their kids, and on down for umpity generations." Corry nodded, turning the disk over in her hands. "By then it'll be a relic. There'll be legends about it." She rolled it across her palm, silver winking in the sun. "How'd you think of that?"

"Well, you said you're only allowed to take ten kilos of personal stuff with you, and that's all you'll ever have from Earth. Which is why you made your list and have been going around saying goodbye to squirrels and stop signs and Snickers bars and all."

"Ten kilos isn't much. My mom said the ship is so well-stocked, I won't need much, but it's hard. I had to pick between my bear and my jewelry box."

"I know. And in twenty years, I'll probably have a house full of clothes and furniture and junk. But the thing is, when I'm old and I die, my kids'll get rid of most of it, like we did with my Gramma. Maybe they'll keep some pictures. But then their kids will do the same thing. So in a couple hundred years, there won't be any trace of me *here*—"

"—but you'll be part of the legend."

"Yep."

"Okay, then. I accept the mission." Corry turned and kissed Anna on the cheek.

"You'll take us to the stars?"

"You bet." She slipped the disk into her pocket and looked at the sky. "It's getting late."

She stood up and helped Anna to her feet. "C'mon. Let's ride."

MRS. ZENO'S PARADOX

Annabel meets Midge for a treat.

She enters a small café in the Mission District in San Francisco, bold graffiti-covered walls and baristas with multiple piercings and attitude. Sometimes it is the Schrafft's at 57th and Madison, just after the war, the waitresses in black uniforms with starched white cuffs. Once it is a patisserie on the rue Montorgueil; the din from the Prussian artillery makes it difficult to converse.

On entering the restaurant, she scans the tables for Midge, who is not yet there.

Annabel sits and requests an espresso. She asks for tea with milk. She waits until Midge comes before she orders, to be polite.

Midge arrives. She is young and cheaply dressed, in a cashmere coat, her stiletto heels clip-clip-clopping on the marble floor. Her hair is the color of faded daffodils, sleek and dark, perfectly coiffed. Her sneakers shuffle on the worn wood.

She kisses the air near Annabel's cheek. "Am I late?" she asks. She puts her handbag down on an empty chair. Its contents clank and tinkle, thump and squeak.

"I'm not certain," Annabel says. It is a small lie, a kindness to a dear friend.

The server materializes. "What will it be?"

Annabel answers and Midge says, "The same, please."

"You know," Annabel says, "I think I'd like a little something sweet."

"Oh, I shouldn't."

"Nothing gooey, nothing *too* decadent. A brownie?"

"Whatever you want. I'll only have a bite."

"Are you sure?"

"Absolutely." Midge pats her waist. "Just the tiniest bite possible."

The brownie appears on Fiestaware, a folded napkin, a lovely seventeenth-century porcelain platter. They gaze at it, fudge-dark, its top glossy, crackled like Arizona in July, sprinkled with powdered sugar.

Annabel cuts the brownie in half.

She eats it with obvious pleasure, flecks of chocolate limning the corners of her mouth. She blots her lips with a tissue, leaving an abstract smudge of chocolate and Revlon's Rosy Future.

"This is *too* good," Midge says, moistening her forefinger to pick up an indeterminate number of small crumbs.

"Stairmaster tomorrow," Annabel agrees. "Probably." She sips from her cup.

They talk about their jobs, the men they are dating, the men they have married. They have been friends since the beginning of time, Midge jokes.

"That's your half." Annabel points to the brownie.

"Oh, I couldn't. Not the whole thing."

Midge cuts the brownie in half.

They glance at the clock. Time is irrelevant. Annabel gets a refill. "Are you going to eat the rest of that?"

Midge shakes her head.

Annabel cuts the brownie in half.

After the twentieth division, the brownie is the size of a grain of sand. Midge extracts a single-edged razor blade from her large purse and divides the speck.

They discuss the weather. A chance of rain, they agree. Their conversation loops around itself, an infinite number of things to talk about.

Annabel puts a jeweler's loupe into her right eye and produces a slim obsidian knife from a leather case, its blade a single molecule thick. A gift from an ophthalmic surgeon she dated some time ago. She neatly bisects the dark mote and pops half into her mouth.

"Oh, go ahead. Take the last piece," Midge urges.

"No. Common sense says it's *yours*."

"I assumed as much." The smooth surface of Midge's handbag warps as she reaches into one of its dimensions to reveal an electron microscope.

Midge cuts the brownie—now an angstrom wide—in half.

"A sheet of paper is a million angstroms thick," Midge says, as if Annabel hasn't always known that. Annabel is a nuclear physicist. She is Stephen Hawking's bastard daughter. She is a receptionist at Fermilab.

Midge is quite fond of them.

Five cuts later, the room shimmers and shudders a bit. Annabel and Midge smile at each other.

"You *must* finish it off," Midge says, pointing to the apparently empty space between them. "It's just a smidge."

Annabel follows her finger and looks down, which is a mistake. The photons of visible light play air-hockey with the particle of brownie.

"I'm not sure where it is," she says.

Midge puts on her reading glasses and punches numbers into a graphing calculator with nimble fingers. She reaches through her handbag with a sigh. It will take ENIAC decades to process all that data.

"Ninety-nine percent probability that it's *here*," she says after an eternity. She closes her eyes. "Or in a teahouse on the outskirts of Kathmandu."

"Hard to tell in this phase," Annabel agrees.

The linear accelerator in the seventh dimension of Midge's handbag splits the now-theoretical brownie in half.

"The Planck length," Annabel notes. "Indivisible."

The server disappears into a worm hole. The vinyl booth, the check, and the known universe dissolve into an uncertain froth.

"That was lovely." Midge's voice is distant, indefinite. "We must do it again sometime."

"We have," says Annabel.

SINGING ON A STAR

I'm spending the night with my friend Jamie, my first sleepover. She lives two doors down in a house that looks just like mine, except for the color. I'm almost six.

My father walks me down the block after dinner, carrying my mother's brown Samsonite travel case. Inside are my toothbrush, my bear, a clean pair of panties (just in case), and my PJs with feet. I am carrying my Uncle Wiggly game, my favorite. I can't wait until she sees it.

Jamie answers the door. She has no front teeth and her thick dark hair is held back by two bright red barrettes. My hair is too short to do any tricks. Her mother, Mrs. Galloway, comes out from the kitchen wearing an apron with big daisies. The air smells like chocolate. She says there are cookies in the oven, and we can have some later, and my doesn't that look like a fun game! My father pats me on the shoulder and goes into Mr. Galloway's den to have a Blatz beer and talk about baseball and taxes.

There is only a downstairs, like our house. Jamie's room is at the end of the hall. It has pale pink walls and two beds with green nubbily spreads. Mrs. Galloway puts my suitcase on the bed next to the window, where Jamie doesn't sleep, and says she'll bring us some cookies in a jiffy.

I know Jamie from kindergarten. We are both in Miss Flanagan's afternoon class. We share a cubby in the cloakroom, play outside with chalk and jump ropes, and are in the same reading circle. This is the first time we've been alone together. It's her room, and I don't know what to do now. I put Uncle Wiggly down on the bed and look out the window.

It's not quite dark. The sky is TV blue, and if I scrinch my neck a little, I can see the edge of the swing set in my own backyard. I feel a little less lost.

"It's time to listen to my special record now," Jamie says. She holds up a bright yellow record, the color of lemon Jell-O. I can see the shadows of her hands through it.

She opens the lid of the red-and-white portable record player on her bookshelf. I'm jealous; I'm not allowed to play records by myself yet, because of the needle. Jamie plunks it down on the spinning disk and the room fills with the smooth crooning of a man's voice:

You can sing your song on a star,
Take my hand, it's not very far.
You'll be fine dressed just as you are . . .

"We have to go before the song ends," Jamie says. "So we can see Hollis."

Jamie is not this bossy at school. I nod, even though I don't know who Hollis is. Maybe it's her bear. My bear's name is Charles.

Jamie points to a door in the pale pink wall, next to my bed. "We have to go in there."

"Into the closet? Why?"

"It's only a closet sometimes," Jamie says, as if I should know this. She opens the door.

Inside is an elevator, closed off by a brass cage made of interlocking Xs.

"Wow." I have never been in a house with an elevator before.

"I know," says Jamie.

She pushes the cage open, the Xs squeezing into narrow diamonds with a creaking groan. "C'mon."

My stomach feels funny, like I have already eaten too many cookies. "Where are we—?"

"Come *on*," says Jamie. "The song's not very long." She grabs the sleeve of my striped shirt and tugs me through, pulling the brass cage closed again behind us. To the right of the door is a line of lighted buttons, taller than I can reach. Jamie presses the bottom button, L.

A solid panel slides in front of the brass cage, shutting us off from the room with the pink walls. There is a clank, and a whirr of a motor. I close my eyes. The elevator moves.

In a minute, it stops with another clank and the rattle of the brass cage squeezing open.

"Hi, Hollis," says Jamie.

"Why, hello Miss Jamie," a voice answers. "What a delightful surprise." It is an odd voice, soft and raspy, a bit squeaky, like a not-quite grown-up boy. I open my eyes.

I don't know where we are. Not in Jamie's house. Not anywhere in our neighborhood. Outside the elevator is a tall room with a speckled linoleum floor and a staircase with a wooden railing, curving up and out of sight. A rectangle of sunlight slants across the tiles.

I remember my swing set in the almost-dark. I feel dizzy.

"C'mon," says Jamie. She tugs at my sleeve again. "Come meet Hollis."

I step out of the elevator. The room smells old and dusty,

with a sharp tang, like they forgot to change the cat box. At first I don't see anyone. Then I notice a little room under the stairs. The floor inside is bare wood, and a man is sitting on a folding chair, reading a magazine with a flashy lady on the cover.

"Two surprises!" says the man. "What a great day this is turning out to be." He smiles as he closes his magazine, but his voice sounds sad, as if he's about to apologize.

"This is my friend Becka," Jamie says. "She's very good at jacks."

"A fine skill, indeed," Hollis says. "I'm pleased to make your acquaintance."

"Me too," I say.

I'm not sure I mean it.

Hollis looks as odd as his voice sounds. He is not young, and is very thin. The skin under his eyes droops like a bloodhound. His hair sticks out in tufts around his head, like cotton candy, but the color of ginger ale. He's wearing gray pants and a red jacket with a bowtie. On the pocket of his jacket is a black plastic bar that says HOLLIS in white capital letters.

"I want to go up to the roof today," says Jamie. "Will there be trains?"

"A most excellent question," Hollis says. "Let me check the schedule." He pulls back his cuff and looks at his wristwatch. The face is square and so yellowed I can't see any numbers. "Yes, just as I thought. Plenty of time before the next arrivals. And a good thing, too. I'm feeling a bit peckish."

I don't know that word, but Jamie laughs and claps her hands. "I was hoping you were," she says. "But—" She shakes her head. "But you can't leave your post."

"No," he says, even more sad than before. He looks around the empty lobby like he expects someone to appear. "No, I can't leave my post."

"I could go," Jamie says. She sounds as if she just thought of it. But I think they are telling each other an old joke, one I don't know.

Hollis snaps his fingers. "Why, yes you could. You're a big girl." He turns to me. "Are you a big girl too?"

I don't feel very big at all. Too much is happening. But I hear my own voice, telling my mother, "I'm a big girl now," when she didn't think I was old enough for a sleepover. "Yes," I say, louder than I mean to. "I'm a big girl."

"So you are," says Hollis. "So you are." He pulls a green leather disk out of his pocket, about the size of a cookie, with the top all folded over itself, and pinches the bottom. The folded parts open like a flower. When he holds it out to Jamie, I see that it's a coin purse. Jamie takes out two nickels.

"And one for your friend," Hollis says. He holds the purse out to me, and I take a coin. The leather petals refold around themselves.

"The usual?" asks Jamie. She sounds much older here.

"But of course," he says. "Farlingten's best."

Jamie leads the way. The front door of this building is glass and wood, with a transom tilting in at the top. I've never seen one before, but I hear the word in my head. *Transom.* I say it under my breath, and I can taste it in the back of my throat. I've never tasted a word before. I like that.

Out on the sidewalk, a white-on-black neon sign buzzes above our heads and stretches halfway up the tall brownstone building. HOTEL MIZPAH. WEEKLY RATES. This is a noisy place. Cars and trucks honk their horns under the viaduct, and men are yelling about money at a bar next door. I hear a clang and turn to see a green streetcar clattering down tracks in the middle of the street, sparks snapping from the wires overhead. The lighted front of the car says FARLINGTEN.

"What's Farlingten?" I ask Jamie.

"It's where we are, silly."

"Where are we, though?"

She huffs a sigh and puts her hands on her hips. "In *Far*lingten." She seems to think this is enough of an answer and skips a step ahead of me.

I want to go home. I don't know how to get there from this street.

My neighborhood has trees and front yards and driveways and grass. Here all I can see is dirty bricks and stone buildings, black wires criss-crossing everywhere. We come to the corner of the block. Above a wooden rack of magazines and paperback books is a faded green awning that says SID'S NEWS.

"This is Sid's," Jamie says. "It's my favoritest place."

Sid's isn't exactly a store, more like a cave scooped out of the corner, with shelves on both sides. On the left are a hundred different magazines, all bright colors and pictures. My parents only get *LIFE* and *TV Guide*. On the right are rows and rows of cigarettes in white and green and red packs, and boxes of cigars with foreign ladies on their lids. The slick paper and tobacco smell spicy, dry and a little sour. I almost sneeze.

In front of us, a woman in an orange cardigan, her glasses halfway down her nose, sits on a stool behind a counter full of more candy and gum than I've ever seen in one place in my whole life. Hersheys and Sky Bars, Jujubes and Paydays, twenty flavors of Life Savers in a rolled-log metal display—and dozens I've never seen before. I think about pirate gold and jewels, and Ali Baba, every treasure story I've ever heard. This is better.

"Wow," I say.

"See," says Jamie.

The woman behind the counter looks up. "Hey, kid. It's been a while."

"Hi, Mrs. Sid. How's business?"

"Can't complain," she says. "Whad'll it be today?"

"The usual." Jamie drops her two nickels onto the rubber OLD GOLDs mat that is the only clear space on the counter.

"Raxar it is. Can't say that I blame you. Two?"

"Three. This is my friend Becka. She's never had one."

Mrs. Sid raises an eyebrow.

"It's her first time here," says Jamie.

"Ah."

I shake my head. "No thanks, I want a Three Musket—"

"You can get those anywhere," says Mrs. Sid. "Try this." She reaches over the counter and picks up a candy bar with a pale, steel-blue wrapper, thicker than a Hershey, not as thick as a Three Musketeer. On the front, in shining silver letters, it says RAXAR. The X is two crossed lightning bolts. "Trust me. You've never had anything like it."

I take the bar and hold out the nickel in my hand.

Mrs. Sid shakes her head. "Keep it, kid. The first one is free." She rings open the cash register and rattles Jamie's nickels into the wooden drawer.

Back on the sunny sidewalk, the silver X winks bright and dull, bright and dull as I walk. *Farlingten Confectionary Company*, it says on the side. I start to pull open the paper wrapper.

"Not now," Jamie says. "Hollis doesn't have his yet."

I stop. I'm her guest, so I have to be polite.

When we get back to the door below HOTEL MIZPAH, Jamie puts her hands behind her back. Hollis is waiting by the elevator.

"What did you bring me?" he asks.

"Raxar!" Jamie says, and holds her hands out in front of her, a blue-gray bar flat on each palm.

"Hoorah," says Hollis. "It's the same, forwards and backwards." His voice sounds like he's very disappointed, but he's smiling and his droopy eyes are bright. "Now on to the penthouse."

Hollis hangs an OUT OF SERVICE sign on a nail by the elevator door and holds the brass cage open for us. He presses the very top button, and the elevator clanks and whirrs for more than a minute. I don't know *what* to expect when the doors open, but it's just a hallway, with the same dingy linoleum and stairs as the lobby.

We climb eight steps. At the top is a metal door that Hollis opens with a key. "Watch your feet," he says.

I step over the raised sill out onto a roof of gravel-embedded tar. A stone wall about a foot wide runs along all four sides. My sneakers make crunching sounds as I walk over to the nearest corner. Standing on tiptoe, I can rest my arms on the gritty top, and look out almost forever. It is the highest up I have ever been, and I feel like I'm flying, standing still.

From here, the world is made of boxes—straight-sided rectangles of brown and gray. Walls and streets, windows and doorways, rows of brick and stone ledges on buildings that look so small I could hold one in my hand. Below me are other rooftops with chimneys and water tanks and laundry flapping, and the flat black top of the buzzing MIZPAH sign.

I don't know how long I stand there, taking in all the lines and angles. When I look up, Jamie is waving at me from the opposite wall.

"It's almost time for the train!" she calls.

I crunch over to where she and Hollis stand. There are more boxes on this side, but also trees in the far distance, and the curve of a river. The light is golden, late-afternoon, as if the city has been dipped in butter.

Jamie points her Raxar bar at me. "When you hear the train, open yours and take a bite."

"Okay." I take it out of my pocket and, like the others, cock my head and listen.

After a minute, I hear the faint rumble of heavy wheels on invisible tracks, and the long, low notes of the train's whistle.

"Now," says Jamie.

I slide my finger under the glued flap. The steel-blue wrapper is heavy paper, lined with a thin foil, and crinkles as I unfold it. The bar inside is the same color as the afternoon light. I bite into one corner of it, and my mouth is flooded with magic. It tastes like toasted butter, malted milk, brown sugar, and flavors

I have no name for. The bar is solid at the first touch of my teeth, then crumbles and melts onto my tongue.

I look at the glittering lightning X, then at Jamie.

"Well?" she says. There are golden crumbs at the corner of her mouth, and her bar is already half gone.

"It's, it's—it's great," is all I can manage.

"I told you," says Jamie. She takes a huge bite of hers, most of what remains.

The train whistle sounds again, a little closer now, louder.

"What does the train say to you?" Hollis asks me.

"Let's have an adventure," I answer after a moment. I nibble at my Raxar bar. Tiny bites, making it last.

"Ah," he says. It is a long *ah*.

"What?"

"That means the people inside are going to the right place. They'll have a fine, merry time there."

"Where are they going?"

"It's different for everyone."

I nod. Another minute and there is only one bite of candy left. I put it in my mouth and hold it in my cheek, like a hamster, letting my new favorite flavor melt away until it is only a memory. Hollis holds his hand out for the empty wrapper.

"What does it sound like to you?" I ask.

He tilts his head, considering. "Like a saxophone," he says. "Mournful. A little tarnished."

"So what does *that* mean?" I lick my lips and find one more golden crumb.

"It means those people are going into the wrong future," he says, shaking his head. "They're all coming to Farlingten, and none of their dreams will ever come true."

My arm gets all goosebumps. "Does Jamie know that?"

"No," he says. "I don't think she does." He reaches over and touches the red barrette in her hair, sliding his hand down to stroke her cheek, the way my mother pets the cat. Jamie is looking out at the trees and doesn't seem to care.

"I'd like to go home, please," I say. My voice sounds very small.

"The light *is* fading," says Hollis. "I suppose it's time."

"Can we stay just a few—" Jamie starts.

"No," he says. "You're not safe here at night." He moves his hand to her shoulder and gives it a little squeeze. "Not yet."

He follows us across the gravel and inside, pausing to lock the metal door behind him. The stairwell is dark after the sunlit roof.

The elevator is waiting for us. Hollis opens the brass gate and pushes a button I hadn't noticed before, a squiggle between the 6 and the 7. Then he steps back out into the hall.

"Goodbye, Miss Jamie," he says, as he closes the gate. "I'll see you again soon." He looks at me. "It was nice to meet you, Miss Becka."

I nod, but I don't look up until the metal panel slides shut, and Hollis is gone.

The elevator clanks and whirrs. I cross my fingers—both hands.

When the door opens, the voice is crooning the last lines of the song:

> . . . *you can stay put, right where you are,*
> *Or sing your song up on a star.*

But that's not possib—

My legs shaking, I step out of the elevator into the room with the pale pink walls and my game lying on top of the green nubbily bedspread. I am so glad to see Uncle Wiggly. Jamie closes the gate and then the closet door.

She walks over to the record player, where the yellow disk is now going around and around, hissing like static, and lifts the needle.

"Isn't that the *best* place?" She slips the record into its cardboard sleeve. "We can play your game now, if you—" We hear footsteps in the hall, and Jamie turns to me, her eyes fierce.

"You *can't* tell. Not ever."

"But what if—?"

She grabs my arm, hard. "Promise. Or I can never go back."

"Okay." I pull my arm away. "Okay. I promise." I sit down next to Uncle Wiggly and look out the window.

Mrs. Galloway opens the door and comes in, carrying a plate of cookies so warm I can smell them. A cleaner's bag is folded over one arm. "Who's ready for chocolate chips?"

"I am," says Jamie. She takes two cookies and bites into one.

"How about you, Becka?" Mrs. Galloway holds the plate out to me.

I shake my head slowly. "My stomach feels funny."

"Oh?" Mrs. Galloway sets the plate down on the bed and puts the back of her hand on my forehead. "You don't have a fever," she says. "Do you want some Pepto?"

"I don't think so."

"Hmm. Would you like to go home, dear?"

I nod.

"Well, I'm not really surprised. Five *is* a little young for a big adventure like this." She pats my shoulder. "Let me hang up Jamie's good dress, and I'll walk you back."

She reaches for the knob of the closet door.

No! I want to shout. But when she opens it, nothing's inside except clothes on hangers and three pairs of shoes on the floor.

"The record's over," Jamie says. "And it's dark now." Her voice is cool, matter-of-fact.

"I'll see you in school," I say.

Jamie turns and closes the lid of the record player. "Maybe."

Mrs. Galloway walks me home through the last moments of twilight, and my mother fusses over me and puts me to bed. When she folds my pants over the back of my chair, a nickel falls out of the pocket.

"Where'd this come from?" she asks.

I don't know how to answer that. "Um, Mrs. Galloway. In case the ice cream truck came. But it didn't." I've never lied before. My stomach squirms. Nothing else happens.

"That was nice of her." She puts the nickel down on the bed-side table and tucks me and my bear under the covers. "Big day, honey. You'll feel better in the morning." She kisses my forehead.

When she's gone, I pick up the coin. It is smooth and round and nickel-sized, but the man on it is not Jefferson. On the back, F-A-R-L-I-N-G-T-E-N curves around a picture of an animal that's not a buffalo. I feel picky sweat and goosebumps again and I want to throw it away. But I don't. I think of pirate gold and Ali Baba and butter-light on tall, square stone. I can almost taste a Raxar bar. I get up and put the coin in the box on my dresser, under the felt lining.

Just in case.

In the darkness, lying in bed, even my own room seems strange now. A car drives by. A slanting square of light plays across my ceiling, corner to corner, glass and chrome reflecting the streetlight outside. My closet door leaps into the light for just a moment. I turn my head the other way. But when I close my eyes, I see the Xs of an impossible elevator and taste *transom* in the back of my throat.

Monday starts the last week of kindergarten. Every day Jamie puts her things in our cubby and sits on my right in reading circle. She watches me, but I don't want to talk to her. At recess I play Red Rover with other kids.

On Tuesday, we return our library books after Snack. I wait until Jamie is over by the biographies, and ask Mrs. Gascoyne if she knows where Farlingten is.

"Far-ling-ten? No, dear, not right offhand. But if you want, I can look it up."

Except she can't. There's no Farlingten in the phone book, or on the state map, or even in the big atlas of the whole world. No Farlingten anywhere.

Thursday night, the air is hot and thick. Thunder rumbles far away, but rain hasn't come to our house yet. I toss and turn, sweaty under just a sheet. Through my open window, I can hear the murmur of my parents' voices from the back porch, smell the sweet, acrid waft of smoke from my father's pipe.

Then I hear the music. Not from the hi-fi in our living room, but from outside, a few houses down. I jump, like I've been pinched, and the smooth crooning glides faintly over the distant thunder.

You can sing your song on a star . . .

It seems to go on forever. I look out my window and wonder about Jamie. I shudder when a train whistles somewhere in the distant darkness, all grays and browns. It does not sound like an adventure.

Jamie is not in school Friday afternoon.

My mother picks me up at three o'clock, because I have a box with my rest rug and paintings and papers to bring home for the summer. We are at the front door when Miss Flanagan calls from my classroom.

"Becka! You left this in your cubby." She hurries down the hall. "I'm glad I caught you," she says, handing me a stiff cardboard sleeve.

It's a record. On the TV-blue cover is a cartoon of a little girl with dark hair. She is sitting with her legs dangling over one arm of a bright yellow star. Across the top, in magic marker, it says BECKA.

I stare at it. That's not how I write my Ks.

"I've never seen that one before," my mother says. I can hear the question in her voice. She buys all my things.

I can't explain. I don't even know how it got into the cubby. "It was sort of a present," I say after a minute. I'm not sure I want it.

"Who—? Well, never mind. I hope you thanked them." My mother slips it under my rest rug, then puts the box into the back of the station wagon. I can feel it through the back of my neck as we drive.

She pulls into the parking lot of Ackerman's Drugs, six blocks from our house. "I need to pick up a few things," she says. "So I thought we might celebrate with a sundae, Miss First Grader."

Ackerman's smells like perfume and ice cream mixed with bitter medicine dust. The candy counter is next to the red-and-chrome soda fountain. While my mother buys aspirin and Prell shampoo, I look at every candy bar in the display. No lightning bolts. "Do you have a Raxar?" I ask the counter man, when he is done making a milkshake.

"Raxar?" He wrinkles his forehead. "Never heard of it."

I'm not really surprised.

When we pull into the driveway, there are police cars parked two doors down. My mother frowns, and carries my box to my room before she walks to the Galloways to see what's happened.

I put the record on my dresser, next to the box with the nickel.

That night my mother checks the lock on the front door twice after dinner. At bedtime, she tucks me in tight and kisses me more than usual.

"Can I have a record player for my birthday?" I ask.

She smiles. "I suppose so. You're a big girl now."

So you are, echoes Hollis in his odd, sad voice. *So you are.*

"I am," I say. "First grade."

"I know, honey." My mother sits down on the edge of my covers. "But even big girls can—" Her hand smooths the unwrinkled sheet, over and over. "When you were out playing, did you ever see your friend Jamie talking to a man you didn't know?"

I think, for just a second, then shake my head and keep my promise.

"Well, you be careful." She strokes my cheek. "Don't go anywhere with a stranger, even if they give you candy, okay?"

"I won't," I say. I don't look at the record on my dresser, and I wonder if I'm lying.

HEY, PRESTO!

On a grey Thursday afternoon, the fourth-form lounge was crowded with girls studying for exams. "I can't make heads or tails of this," one said with a sigh. She tossed her chemistry text onto the couch. "I'm just not the school type." She looked down at her Giles Hall uniform with a grimace.

"Have you thought about running away with the circus?" another girl asked.

"Oh, wouldn't that be a dream? Spangles and spotlights and applause. That's the life for me."

Several girls nodded in agreement. Polly Wardlow bit her tongue and kept her head down, her short brown hair falling over her eyes. None of the others noticed her look of disagreement. She concentrated on her own chemistry book, happy to lose herself in the refuge of equations and numbers—reliable, constant, and utterly practical.

Unlike her father, the magician. That was the family business, arcane secrets passed down from the men of one generation to the next. Even now Hugh Wardlow—Vardo! on his posters—

was performing somewhere on the continent, astounding the gullible with his illusions and legerdemain.

Perhaps just a bit of that had rubbed off, because Polly had a trick of her own. She knew how to make herself invisible. She kept quiet, sat at the back of each class, and sometimes wore a pair of window-glass spectacles, nicked from the props room after a pantomime in her second term. They hid her face and made her look more serious. With the exception of the cricket pitch—she was an athletic girl and quite a skilled bowler—Polly preferred her own company, and spent her time reading and preparing herself for university, where she would study science, not trickery.

"The post is here!" called a girl from the doorway. There was a mad scramble as girls leapt from couches and chairs and clustered around the table in the corner of the room. Polly waited until the crowd had dispersed before checking for a letter of her own. She was hoping to hear from her Aunt Emma, her late mother's only sister; Emma and her husband David taught at a small college in Sussex. Because her father was always traveling, Polly spent the summers with them and their three sons, exploring the woods and ponds by day, reading in their library each night.

But the only letter was from London, on Vardo! stationery.

She returned to her chair and opened it. Just a few lines, in bold blue ink, and they changed everything.

Your uncle has been offered a research position in America for the summer, a marvelous opportunity, and the boys have never been abroad, so they sail the end of May. Naturally, you will summer in London. Will meet your train on 7th June.
—Father

Polly read it once more, then gathered her books and retreated to her room. She lay on her narrow bed, gazing out the window at the sports field, but seeing in her mind the rolling Sussex pastures. She willed herself not to cry. She was fifteen, hardly a baby. And London did have the British Museum, and the Library. Besides, it was only for a few months.

She knew that if she told any of the other girls, they would swoon with envy. Their fathers were in shipping or insurance, barristers and judges, from all accounts stuffy, dull men, not dashing international celebrities. Who would understand that she viewed this summer with as much anticipation as a trip to the dentist?

Polly did not dislike her father, nor fear him. It was just that they were, for all intents and purposes, strangers. His face was familiar, but his habits and interests were mysteries. And he knew just as little about her.

Her visits during Christmas week were a mix of parties with his fashionable friends—from which she was dispatched early— and the occasional awkward supper. He was at the theatre until late, rose at noon, and spent the day at his club or at his workshop, tinkering with whatever it was that he did between performances.

It had not always been that way. When she was very young, he had delighted her with tricks—pulling shillings from her ears, making her stuffed rabbit appear and disappear, cracking open her supper egg and releasing a butterfly that hopped up onto the window sill.

Then her parents had gone on a tour of the Antipodes. Her mother contracted a fever and died on the ship home. Polly was seven. Her father locked himself away with photographs and grief, and a few months later, Polly was packed off to Giles Hall.

Hugh Wardlow was on the platform when Polly alighted from the train at St. Pancras. As always, his dark hair was slicked back with brilliantine, and his moustache was trimmed to a stiff brush, but he was not in his performer's top hat and tails, just a business suit.

"Hello, my dear," he said, leaning down to pick up her valise. She could smell the bay rum on his cheeks. "Hope I'm not late. There was a meeting at the admiralty, and it ran long."

"Have you joined the service?" War was brewing. It was all Mr. Patterson, the history master, had talked about for the last month of the term, but surely they would not be drafting men as old as her father?

"In a manner of speaking. They're forming a rather specialized unit—Stars in Battledress, catchy name—and they've offered to make me a captain."

"Will you be fighting? If there's a war?"

"Hardly. We'd be charged with maintaining morale and entertaining the troops, that sort of thing."

"Oh," Polly said. "I'm certain they'll appreciate it." They walked toward the station entrance. After a moment, she said, trying to keep her tone neutral, "You'll be traveling, then?"

"Not right away. In September, perhaps. Ah, here's a taxi." He held the door open as she got in, then settled himself beside her. "Alfred Place, Bloomsbury," he told the driver.

Polly sat quietly, watching the city stream by.

"But in the meantime," her father said when they stopped at a light, "I'm putting together another show." He pulled out his briar pipe. "The premiere is in a month."

"How very nice for you."

"Yes, quite." He lit his pipe and leaned back against the seat. "We're developing a new illusion for it. I've had to put a man on the door to keep prying eyes away until we open."

"So the public won't know?"

"And so other magicians can't—borrow. It's a rather cut-throat business." He sighed. "Once we're finished, it should play well, but there are more than a few kinks to work out before we get it on stage."

"You're in rehearsals now?"

"Day and night. I'm afraid your old dad may not be home for supper much, but duty calls." He tapped the driver. "This is it. Number twenty-three."

"They also serve who only stand and wait," Polly said, hiding a smile. "I'm sure I'll get along somehow."

For three days, Polly reacquainted herself with the house and the neighborhood, settling into a pleasant routine. She decided on an overstuffed chair in a sunny corner of the parlor as her reading spot, found a shop that stocked her favorite brand of sweets, and secured a library card. She dressed in comfortable trousers and a jersey and was out by the time her father woke, supped alone on soup and good bread, and was in bed reading or asleep by the time he came home.

So she was quite startled when she came down the stairs at half past eight, her mouth watering in anticipation of cook's cinnamon scones, to see her father seated at the table in his bathrobe, the *Times* folded beside his plate.

"You're up early." She helped herself to tea and, after a moment's hesitation, sat down beside him. At close quarters, she could see that his eyes were a bit red, and he had not yet shaved.

"Yes, well—" He brushed a finger across his moustache, as if reassuring himself of its presence, and cleared his throat. "I have a bit of a problem, and thought I might ask your help."

Wariness and curiosity vied for Polly's attention. The tea slopped into its saucer as she set it down. "What is it?"

"How tall are you now?"

"Excuse me?" She had not expected that.

He looked at her, eyebrow raised, and she said, hesitantly, "Five—five feet four. And a half. I think."

"Excellent. Are you limber?"

"I suppose. I'm quite good at sports." Polly pinched off a bit of scone, but her stomach informed her that at the moment it was not inclined to receive, and she put it down. "Why do you ask?"

"Well, you see——" He paused, turning the handle of his teacup, and Polly realized, another surprise, that he was as nervous as she. "Fact of the matter is, one of my assistants gave notice last night. Valinda Banks. Says she's been accepted to the Women's Auxiliary Air Force, of all things."

"I see," Polly said, as if it were a point in a debate. "But what does that have to do with——" she let her words trail off, because she was not yet entirely clear *what* they were discussing.

"Valinda is about your size and, well, the illusion has a rather small trap, no one else fits, and we haven't the time to build another." He smoothed his hand across the unwrinkled newspaper. "What do you say?"

"Wait. You want me as your assistant?" Polly's voice squeaked. His few female performers were always vivacious, attractive blondes. She was none of the above.

"I suppose I could advertise for someone just like you—small, smart, and a quick study——" He smiled at her, his moustache turning up at the ends. "But here you are. And you're a Wardlow. It's in your blood."

She sat very still, her unswallowed tea acrid in her throat.

"Now, now. It's not *that* difficult."

You wouldn't know, Polly thought. *You love to perform.* But he looked so earnest that she could find no excuse to refuse him. Finally she gulped and managed a weak, "I don't have any experience."

"No one does, not with this one. We're all learning from the ground up."

She took a deep breath. "All right. I guess I——"

He stood. "Splendid. That's just splendid." He leaned down and gave her a peck on the cheek. "You know how proud your mother would've been, seeing you in the act?"

Polly felt herself blush. She could not remember the last time her mother had been mentioned. Or that her father had kissed her. It felt both comforting and utterly alien. "I don't know what to say." *That* was the absolute truth.

"Say you'll come with me today, if only to have a look around. I'll give you a tour, show you the basics, then later I'll take you to supper at the Criterion, just the two of us." He gave her shoulder a squeeze and stepped back. "Well?"

"That sounds like a perfect day," Polly said, lying as convincingly as any actress. "Thank you, Father."

The St. James Theatre was in the heart of the West End, just off Piccadilly Circus, the streets clogged with black taxis and red buses. Every building was bedizened with electric-light signs and billboards as tall as houses.

The taxi dropped them in front of the ornate lobby doors. On either side were alarmingly large posters of her father—of Vardo!—dramatically backlit, hair and teeth gleaming, his hands cupped around an object invisible to the viewer.

In the middle of the day, the theatre was closed. Her father steered her around the corner into an alley. A man sat outside the stage door on a stool, smoking a cigarette.

He stood. "Afternoon, sir."

"Hullo, Alf. My daughter's down from school for the summer. I'm hoping she'll be a regular face around here."

"Anything you need, miss." He touched the brim of his cap and held the door open for them.

It took a moment for Polly's eyes to adjust from the brightness of a summer day to the dim corridor. Backstage, the theatre had none of the glamour of its public spaces. It was a dark-walled warren of cramped passageways with worn wooden floors and exposed brick walls, hung with wiring and massive loops of rope. Ladders and stairs canted off at every angle. She tipped her head back until her neck creaked and still could not see the ceiling, obscured by forty vertical feet of catwalks, pulleys, lights, and hanging canvas.

"Down here," her father said, pointing to narrow wooden stairs. She followed him to a low-ceilinged basement. Wooden beams were strung with bare electric bulbs; painted flats and discarded props and scenery lined the unfinished walls.

Polly had seen a few of her father's shows from the audience, the flash and the dazzle, the polished lacquered tables with gleaming brass fittings, the silks and velvet drapes. This place bore no relation to that stage, as far as she could tell. Yet when he turned, she saw that his face was alight with excitement, like a lad with a new toy.

"My workshop." He opened an unvarnished wooden door and gestured her inside. "This is where the real magic happens."

The room was long and reasonably wide, lined on one side by workbenches covered with tools and pieces of metal and what looked like laboratory equipment. Large machines stood in the middle of the space—enormous saws and lathes and drills, the floor beneath them covered in sawdust.

Her father took off his jacket and hung it on a rack by the door. "It occurred to me that you know very little about my work," he said, rolling up his shirtsleeves. "I suspect that you'll find it rather interesting."

Polly had her doubts, but her father looked more casual and relaxed than she could remember, and it had already been a day of surprises. She recalled an adage from one of her textbooks: *The first job of a scientist is to keep an open mind.* "Lay on, MacDuff," she said.

They walked slowly around the room. He showed her boxes with hidden panels that opened and shut with levers and pulleys; pistons that raised and lowered vases and other props; mirror-lined boxes that, when turned at an angle, would appear to be empty. With each object, he gave a concise explanation of the mechanics, and how it affected what the audience saw—or didn't see.

Another table held tins of pigments and binders, liquid rubber, cans of turpentine and pungent solvents. He demonstrated paints that glowed in the dark, or were such a matte black they rendered an object almost invisible in dim light.

Next was a sort of chemistry lab, jars of powders and crystals, beakers and glass rods, Bunsen burners, all familiar friends to Polly. She picked up a jar marked KCIO₃. "Potassium chlorate," she said. "What do *you* do with it?" At school they used it to produce pure oxygen, but there wasn't much to see.

"I'll show you." He spooned a little bit of the white powder onto a square of paper, then ran a finger across the shelf of chemicals until he found the jar marked SULFUR. He carefully sifted some of that yellow powder onto the white and covered it all with a second square of paper. "Stand back," he said.

Polly took a step away from the table.

He picked up a hammer and gave the paper a sharp blow.

BANG!

Polly jumped several feet.

"Effective, isn't it?" He wiped his hands on a rag. "The least bit of impact sets it off. I can dust an ordinary object with one, my wand with the other, tap once and—Hey, Presto!" he said in his booming, on-stage voice.

He leaned back against the table. "I don't suppose they've gotten to that part in your chemistry course."

Polly shook her head. "I have blown up a few beakers, though."

"Collateral damage. Part of many experiments." He replaced the two jars. "One of these days, I'd like to try and create an explosive paint. I have all the texts, I just haven't found the time." He pointed to a bookshelf in a corner. "Perhaps you could help with that. Your aunt says you're quite the scientist."

"You and Aunt Emma correspond?" This was news to Polly.

"Of course." He took out his pipe and lit it. "After your mother died, I'm afraid I just threw myself into my work, and distance became a habit." He smiled sadly through the smoke. "But never for a moment think that I don't care about you."

Polly felt her eyes prickle, and was at a loss for words.

"You're my daughter, Polly. More like me than you might imagine."

"How do you mean?"

"Well, you probably think that magicians create illusions," he said, crossing his arms. "But we don't. We study the same scientific principles you do, and use them to create a reality that supports a *belief* in illusions. Like this."

He picked up a piece of mirrored glass and began to show her how the angles and lines of sight changed what she saw. Polly was so fascinated that she did not hear the outer door open.

"Hey, boss," a red-haired man in coveralls said. "We got another one of those crank letters." He held up an envelope. "No return—" He stopped. "Who's the young chap? New hand?"

"In a manner of speaking. This *chap* is my daughter, Polly. Polly, meet Archie Mason, my right-hand man and chief engineer. I stole him away from the eggheads when he graduated from Oxford."

"You went to *Oxford?*" Polly stared. "And you're working here?"

"Didn't take much persuasion. This is loads more interesting than calculating bridge capacities." He pointed to a table with a metal base. "I invented *that*, by way of illustration."

Polly didn't think it was particularly impressive, but the man sounded awfully proud of it. The table's top was a wooden disc about half a meter in diameter and as thick as a manhole cover. It was mounted on a center post affixed to the floor. She smiled politely. "It looks quite—sturdy."

"It held Valinda," Archie said.

"That was the idea." The magician saw the puzzled look on his daughter's face. "Would you like a demonstration?"

"All right." Not much to demonstrate about a table, was there?

"Splendid. Climb aboard." He pointed to a step stool next to it.

"Aboard the table?"

"The table? Ah, I see. No, my dear. It's a piston-driven platform."

Polly shrugged and climbed up onto the disc. "Now what?"

"Look up."

She did, and saw a neat circle cut in the workroom ceiling. "Is that the stage?"

"It is indeed. Now stand very straight, hold your arms tight to your sides, and tuck in your elbows." He turned to Archie. "I'll run up top. Usual signal."

"Two raps. Right-o."

"See you in a moment my dear," her father said, giving her hand a squeeze, and dashed out the door. She heard his footsteps clatter on the wooden stairs, then silence.

"Is this—?"

"Safe as houses." Archie stepped over to a square metal box mounted on a support pillar a foot from the platform. He looked over at Polly, winked, and rested his hand on the lever protruding from its front.

A moment later, from right above her head, Polly heard two sharp knocks.

"That's the cue," Archie said. "Arms in tight, now." He pushed the lever up.

Beneath her feet, Polly felt the "table" begin to rise, as if she were in an elevator with no walls or surrounding cage. Her stomach churned as it did on carnival rides, as the disc went up, rapidly and smoothly and without a sound.

She counted under her breath and before she had reached *three* her head was going *through* the ceiling. Suddenly, the theatre was spread out in front of her, a vast bowl of gilt and velvet, rows of empty chairs stretching back and back into the dim reaches of the farthest balcony. In another second, the top of the disc reached the level of the stage floor and she felt it click into place, again without a sound.

"Bravo!" her father said from the wings. He began to clap. "Well done!" He gazed at her as if she were a rare treasure.

Polly stepped off onto the boards, her body a-tingle with the excitement of the ride, her cheeks flushed with the unaccustomed praise. She glanced down at the disc, its wooden top now nearly invisible amid the floorboards. "Is that what you wanted my help rehearsing?" she asked.

"Yes. What did you think? You looked like a natural."

Polly wasn't sure what she felt. This was not her world. But standing there in his shirtsleeves, a smear of dust across one cheek, hair hanging over one eye, her father looked happier than she had seen him in years. She wanted the chance to know that man better.

"I'll do it," she said.

Polly had the mornings to herself. She breakfasted with tea and scones and a book, so content in her solitude that for the first few days, rehearsals seemed like an interruption and she doubted her decision. Then she got caught up in the rhythm of the workroom, the flow of ideas, the easy conversations peppered with jargon that soon became second nature, like learning another language.

Each day she found herself more eager to get to the theatre and work alongside her father—Hugh—and Archie. She was pleased to find that, although they had vastly more experience than she did, in every facet of the work, they treated her as an equal when it came to solving the myriad small problems that came up in the creation of the show.

"*The Lady Vanishes* is a superb title for Polly's bit," Hugh said.

"It is," Archie agreed. "That's why Mr. Hitchcock used it for his latest film. And why *we* can't. The audience will think it's a publicity stunt."

"I suppose you have something better?"

"Not yet," Archie shrugged. "But we have a week to decide before—"

"*La Femme Perdu*," Polly said from atop the props trunk.

Both men turned.

"Huh?" Archie said.

"Didn't they teach French at Oxford?"

"I'm an engineer. Latin and German. What's it mean?"

"The Lost Woman."

"*La Femme Perdu*," Hugh repeated, rolling the words out. "It's good. It's better. *Lost* has such a melancholy mystery to it." He snapped his fingers. "We'll use it. Good work, my dear."

Polly nodded, pleased. "Thanks."

They began to rehearse the illusion on stage the next week. The set-up was simple: A woman in a gown and a man in a smoking jacket and fez are in a drawing room with flowered wallpaper, having cocktails. On stage is a drinks cabinet with six-inch wheels. Off-stage a shot rings out. "It is your husband!" the man shouts. "Hide in here." He opens the cabinet doors, she curls inside, he closes them, leaving one slightly ajar. The husband rushes in. The men argue loudly. The husband shoots. There is a puff of smoke—the other man disappears! The husband looks around, sees the cabinet, flings it open. The woman is gone! All that remains inside is the man's red fez.

At school, Polly had diligently attended cricket practice, and memorized logarithm tables and irregular French verbs, but nothing had prepared her for the repetition and endless detail of building an illusion. Everything was timed to the second. A single misstep would spoil it all.

The drinks cart had to be positioned precisely on the stage— over the lift and at an exact angle.

"I understand why it's over the lift," Polly said at the first rehearsal. "But that's a circle, so why is the angle so important?"

"Sit down in the audience," her father said. Polly went and sat in the second row. "What do you see?"

"The drinks cart."

"Anything between it and the floor?"

"No."

"Are you certain?"

"Yes. I can look between the wheels at the wallpaper behind it."

"So no one could possibly get out through the bottom of the cabinet without being seen?"

"No." Polly frowned. "But isn't that how I—?" She stared at the drinks cart.

"It is." Her father turned the cart at an angle. "Now what do you see?"

"The wallpaper behind it has gone all wonky."

He laughed. "Come back up and take a close look."

Polly did. Kneeling in front of the drinks cart, she could see a false front between the two wheels, painted so that it matched the wallpaper, but only at a particular distance and perspective. Hidden behind the frontpiece, the bottom of the cabinet extended down, flush with the floor. Inside was a sliding panel that opened over the disc of the lift.

"What about the fez?"

"Collapsible. It folds up and hooks into the roof of the chamber, invisible from the audience."

"That's ingenious," she said with real admiration.

"It's what I do." He smiled. "And why I want no one sneaking in to take a closer look."

Polly learned by trial and error. She had to wait to give Archie the pre-arranged signal—two sharp raps—until the men's shouts masked the sound of her knuckles. She lay curled on her side in the cabinet for an hour at a time, practicing and practicing her exit, a five-part ballet: slide the panel; climb onto the lift; unhook the fez; place it on the panel; and slide that shut again from below as she descended into the basement. Every single movement was choreographed.

Fortunately, *La Femme Perdu* was her only role. The other illusions were performed solo by her father, or with the help of Chaz Manning, his stage assistant, who also played the part of the jealous husband. After a week of rehearsal, she began to feel more comfortable with her part, although she doubted that performing would ever be her first choice. Upstairs required presence and flamboyance; downstairs, preparation and ingenuity.

When she had rehearsed to the point of exhaustion, she was excused to the workroom, curling up in a battered armchair with a text from the bookshelf, an eclectic mix of technical manuals and histories of magic. Archie often fetched them supper—meat pies and ale, a lemon squash for her—and she spent her evenings eating, reading, and making notes when interesting bits caught her eye.

Some afternoons, when the men were working on other parts of the show, Polly had quiet time to try out some of her ideas. She discovered that it was a very well-stocked workshop, more comprehensive than any of the school labs, and soon her table was covered with experiments-in-progress. Two weeks in, she abandoned her morning reading in order to get to the theatre early, to work before rehearsals.

The day before the show opened, she thought she had solved one of her conundrums. After many failed attempts—and two blistered fingers—she had finally calculated the correct proportions to make a dark sludge, the consistency of thin pudding, of potassium chlorate, sulfur, and a binding agent called British gum, mixed with a bit of water and some lampblack. She painted it onto a dinged-up wooden ball, one of several she'd found in a parts box of discarded props from previous shows. She gingerly set it on a square of oiled paper to dry.

"La Femme, you're needed up top," Archie said, coming in the doorway. He peered over her shoulder. "What's that? Looks like a little cannonball."

"Close enough. I *think* I've created an exploding paint. I'll know once it's dry."

"Hugh will be dead chuffed. If it works, you should get him to take it to the Magic Circle next month. Ought to be a big hit."

"If it works, I'll take it myself."

"Not unless you go in disguise. It's blokes only."

"Figures," Polly huffed, then grabbed the silky dress that was her costume.

"Fly, *mein fräulein*. Last rehearsal. Mustn't keep Himself waiting."

The lift was in its up position so she took the stairs to the dressing room. Once she'd changed, Polly observed her father from the wings. He was running through his patter for the first act, speaking to an imaginary audience. It was a full dress rehearsal—top hat, tailcoat, white tie—and the man on stage was no longer Hugh, but Vardo! His rich voice was so well-modulated that even his whispers carried to the back rows. He moved across the stage, waving his wand, his movements fluid but precise.

A few minutes later he stepped off for a glass of water.

"Why do you bother with a wand?" she asked. "Isn't that a bit of a cliché these days?" The tailcoat and hat, she now knew, were not just a costume, but were tools themselves, full of extra pockets and secret compartments that he used for his sleights.

"It's tradition. And it's useful."

"How?"

"With it, every move I make is dramatic. From the opening curtain, the audience sees grand gestures." He swept his arm out. "They get used to them, and don't notice when I whisk a card off the table, or drop it into a pocket."

"Aren't they watching the wand?"

"Yes, and that's it exactly. They watch the wand—not my *other* hand."

"Oh." Polly thought about that for a moment. "You use it to direct their attention."

"Precisely. *That* is my job, to distract them from what I'm really—" He paused, turned, and stared into the wings.

"What is it?" Polly followed his glance, but didn't see anything out of the ordinary.

He chuckled. "Nothing. Just another demonstration. I looked, so you looked. Human nature. And while you were looking—and listening to me prattle on—" He opened his hand. "Hey, Presto!"

"That's my watch."

"And that's my skill. It took me *years* in front of a mirror, learning how to look at one thing and manipulate another." He gave the watch back. "I've had to sack a few hands who thought this would be a cakewalk, and didn't like the discipline."

Polly gulped, wondering if she was about to be scolded.

He smiled. "Not you, my dear. You're a trouper. Now, if you're ready, we'll take it from the top again."

The morning of the show, Polly was nervous. More nervous than she'd expected. She could walk through her part in her sleep, had actually dreamed about it twice in the last week, and felt confident that she would get through it without mishap. And everything had gone well at the last rehearsal, with Archie and Chaz and the theatre crew as an audience. But performing for a packed house? Perhaps that accounted for the butterflies in her stomach.

She managed a piece of toast and some tea before closing herself into the parlor for a few hours with an Enid Blyton novel to keep her amused and distracted. Or so she hoped. But the fourth time she put the book down to check her watch, she gave in. If she was going to pace, she'd rather do it in the workroom.

Her father had not yet come down. She left him a note on the hall table, inside his hat, where he'd be sure to see it, and set off for the theatre. On rainy days she took the tube from Goodge Street to Leicester Square, but this particular morning was warm and sunny, not a cloud in the sky, and a walk might burn off some of the fidgets.

Polly strolled past the British Museum, threading her way through the throngs of tourists, then down Shaftesbury Avenue, stopping to look in shop windows along the way. With the fresh air, her appetite returned, and she bought a cream bun at a bakery, wiping the last crumbs off her blouse when she reached the stage door. As usual, Alf tipped his cup when he saw her.

"Will you be leaving again, miss?"

"I don't think so. Archie's bringing supper. Why?"

"I need to pop over to the chemists and pick up a tincture for the wife. Won't be gone long, but—"

"It's all right, Alf. I'll hold down the fort."

"Thanks, miss." He held the door open for her.

As she expected, the theatre was dark, just the ghost light that was always left on, center stage. She flipped the switch next to the basement stairs and went to the workroom.

The black-painted ball sat on her table. She turned on a lamp that illuminated the surface, but left the rest of the room in shadow, and touched a finger to the paint. Dry. She grinned to herself. Time for a test. She looked around for a suitable object, one that would allow her to strike a blow but not be *too* close, just in case. A brass rod the diameter of a cigarette and nearly a meter long fit the bill perfectly. Polly hoped her experiment wouldn't render it useless for its actual purpose, whatever that was.

She settled the ball into a toweling nest so that it wouldn't bounce or roll, and stepped back until the edge of the rod was just above the sphere. "One. Two." She took a deep breath and raised the rod a foot in the air. "Three!"

BANG!

She jumped, her ears ringing, as the rod jerked and clattered to the floor.

It worked! Polly shook out her stinging hand, all of the morning's nerves gone. She had done it! She could hardly wait to show her father.

When her adrenaline had settled to a more normal level, Polly picked up her log book and recorded the results. She retrieved the rod, inspecting it for damage: just a small black smudge where contact had been made. And the ball? She tilted the lamp and looked closely. Except for one star-shaped grayish spot, it also appeared unchanged. She jotted down these findings, returned the rod to Archie's workbench, then, thirsty from her exertions, polished off the last of a rather flat lemon squash from the night before.

Her watch showed a little after noon. It would be hours before Archie or her father arrived. She pulled a book from the shelf and settled into the armchair to wait. She was deep into an account of Robert-Houdin using magic to avert a war when she heard a man shouting upstairs.

What was going on—?

Her thoughts were interrupted by the sound of running feet overhead and her father's loud stage voice: "Get away from that!"

Bits of dust fell from the ceiling as two men pounded across the stage.

Polly leapt from her chair.

"Sack *me*, will you?" The unknown man shouted. "Now you'll pay, Wardlow!"

"You're mad, Jim." Her father. "I'm going to—"

In a terrifying echo of the act, she heard a shot, and her father cried out.

Polly stood motionless, in shock. But a moment later, from the stage floor, she heard their signal: two sharp raps.

After a month of rehearsals, her response was swift and automatic. The lift. Draw attention. Misdirection. She looked around for a suitable prop, or a weapon. Nothing.

Except the black ball.

She scooped it up, thought for a fraction of a second, then grabbed another, unpainted ball as back-up. She slid them into the pockets of her trousers, then climbed onto the disc-topped lift. She knelt, stretching an arm out to the control lever, and flipped it with her fingertips.

The disc began to rise silently. Polly straightened up, tucked her arms against her sides, and counted. One . . . two . . .

At *three* she reached up to slide the panel of the drinks cabinet open, and tucked herself into its interior. One of the doors was ajar. Across the stage she could see her father lying on the floor, holding his arm. A bearded man with a gun stood over him.

So Polly Wardlow took the stage.

She eased the black ball out of her pocket, cradling it in her right hand, and took a deep breath.

"Hey, Presto!"

She sidearmed the ball toward the back of the theatre.

It bounced over the boards, and with each impact, a sound like a shot rang out: BANG! BANG! BANG! BANG!

The man jumped away, looking about wildly.

Polly rolled out of the cabinet and onto her feet. With the speed and skill she'd learned at Giles Hall, she threw the second wooden ball, aiming at his knee as if it were the stumps on the cricket pitch.

The ball hit with a resounding *crack* and the man fell with a thin scream.

Her father reacted swiftly, reaching out with his good arm to retrieve the gun, and got to his feet. He stood over the other man, the barrel pointed at his chest.

Without taking his eyes off the man, he said, "Are you all right?"

"I'm fine." Polly saw that her hands were shaking and put them in her pockets. "How badly are you hurt?"

"My left arm—could use some—attention," he said, his words coming out in small gasps.

"I'll call for a doctor." She pointed to the man. "Who is he?"

"Jim Finney. He used to work for me." He shifted his arm and grimaced. "You might telephone the police as well."

"Right-o." She turned toward the hallway, but stopped when he called her name. "Yes?"

"That was a brilliant entrance, darling. Right on cue."

Archie arrived just after the police. He and Polly stood outside the stage door with Alf. They watched as the bearded man was loaded onto a stretcher and handcuffed to the rails.

"It's all my fault," Alf said, wringing his cap in his hands.

"Not entirely," Archie said. "Finney's been hounding Hugh for the last month, threatening to shut down the show. If he hadn't gotten in, he would have tried again tonight and who knows how many might have been hurt."

"With a full house, it could have been much worse," Polly nodded. She turned to Archie. "What did he do, when he worked here?"

"Nothing well. Thought he was the gods' own gift to magic, but he couldn't even manage a proper sleight. Bumbled any number of set-ups before he was sacked. I thought we'd seen the back end of him."

"Sounds like a nutter."

"Through and through." He shook his head. "But he was no match for you, I hear. I gather your magic paint worked?"

"Like a charm." She grinned. "More like a whizz-bang, actually."

"You're a right wizard, Polly. And I want the whole story,

soup to nuts. But now I have shows to cancel and meetings with the press—and you need to go and see how Himself is getting along."

Polly found her father sitting on a cot backstage, his left arm in a sling, bandaged from elbow to shoulder, his eyes closed. The doctor beside him looked up when he heard her footsteps.

"So you're the young heroine," he said. "Quick thinking." He handed her a bottle of pills. "I gave him a shot for the pain, but he'll be wanting two of these before bedtime."

"Is he going to be all right?"

"In a few weeks. It went through muscle, not bone, nothing broken."

"Will he still be able to—?" She gestured at the stage.

"I expect a full recovery. He'll be a little stiff for a while, but there's no need to worry." He patted her on the arm. "No need at all." He shut his black bag. "Do you want me to call a taxi for you?"

"No, thank you. I can manage."

When the doctor had gone, Polly sat beside the cot. She leaned over and kissed her father's cheek. His eyes fluttered open. "Polly."

"I'm here, Dad."

"You were very brave."

She looked away for a moment, her face reddening. "I mightn't have moved if I hadn't heard my cue."

"But you did. Although I must say I was expecting a diversion, not a cavalry charge." He took a breath and stood, swaying only slightly. "Let's go home, shall we?"

She took his good arm and they walked slowly across the stage. "Hold up a tick," Polly said. She leaned over and retrieved the black ball, its surface now mottled with gray stars. She slipped it into her pocket.

"You're going to tell me all about that?"

"Yes," she said. "I suspect you'll find it rather interesting."

"Exploding paint?"

She nodded.

"Genius!"

Polly smiled. "I'm a Wardlow. It's what we do."

ECHOES OF AURORA

Cedar River was a summer town.

You've seen it, or one just like it. Off a state highway, on the edge of a lake—a thousand souls, more or less, until Memorial Day. Then the tourists come, for swimming and fudge and miniature golf. They laugh, their sunburns redden and peel, and when the first cool autumn breezes ripple the water, they leave. The carnival is over.

Jo Norwood grew up in the flat above her family's penny arcade. When she was eleven, her mother ran off to Milwaukee; after that Jo helped with repairs and opened in the mornings, filling the change machine and rolling the wooden clown out to the entrance before she could escape to her tree house. There she nested, hidden behind the screen of green leaves, cotton in her ears muffling the hurly-burly and the melancholy cheer of the carousel. The day after high school graduation, she ran away too, and did not return until her father's funeral.

In those thirty-five years, Disneyland and the interstate had lured the tourists away to brighter lights, and Cedar River had become ordinary. Norwood's Amusements sat shuttered at the end of Beach Street, garish paint faded beyond pastel.

The mortgage was paid off; Jo's father had sold the carousel horses, one by one, to collectors, for property taxes. But when she screeched open the big wooden doors, she was not quite prepared for the emptiness.

The air was cool and almost sweet with mildew and the first blooms of rust. A score of pale rectangles on the concrete floor were memorials to Norwood's former glory. Only the fortune-teller, the Magic Ray, the nickelodeon, and half a dozen brass-cranked Mutoscopes remained, each of them coated with a film of gray dust.

Jo was single and newly retired, unsettled and unencumbered. Her time was her own, but she had no desire to linger. She would sort and sift through her inheritance and sell anything of value, find a realtor, put a few things in storage. Two weeks. A month at the most.

She awoke in her old bedroom, the oak outside the window fractal against the colorless April sky. A few tiny green buds, like match heads, dotted the filigree of bare, dark twigs. No coffee in the cupboard. She walked two blocks to Lake Street and had breakfast at the café, dawdling over the crossword and a second cup until there was nothing to do but begin dismantling.

Bert Norwood had been a tinkerer, his workshop a narrow room at the back of the arcade. A wall of cubbyholes and cabinets held gilded fittings, ancient light bulbs, half-toned sepia postcards of cowboy stars no one remembered, all smiling teeth and gabardine. Jo made lists and teetering piles, temporarily creating chaos out of order. As she laid unmourned bits of her past out on the counter, she began to tap her foot and sing along with the nickelodeon.

"Be kind to your web-footed friends—"

Jo stopped, holding a Lash LaRue card in mid-air.

Whose nickel had turned that on?

The arcade floor was dim, the only illumination a row of whitewashed windows high along one wall. The paint had flaked away in places, and in a finger of afternoon light, sparkling with dust motes, a copper-haired woman was dancing. She wore a loose green sweater that floated out from her body as she turned and spun, like a leaf before a hard spring rain. The melody echoed, a brass band in a tin box; the piano keys clicked under invisible fingers.

John Philip Sousa ended with a flourish. A floorboard squeaked under Jo's shoe. The dancing woman looked up and waved, as if they were old friends, reunited after a long absence.

"Do I know you?" Jo called. Possible. It was a small town.

"I'm Aurora." She smiled. "Rory."

The voice was soft, but strong; the name was unfamiliar, but its timbre fluttered the short hairs on the back of Jo's neck.

"Uh, sorry. I think you've got the wrong—"

"You grew up here. You had a tree house."

Such a small town. Jo took a step closer, puzzled. The woman's face was smooth, unlined cream. She'd have been a baby when Jo left.

"Yeah, I did. So?"

"Your tree is dying."

"What, are you from the county?"

"No. Come and see."

"Not now. I'm kind of busy and—"

"Come and *see*." Rory stepped into another bit of sunlight. Her eyes were green too, flecked with bits of gold. They tickled a fragment of memory with no context to anchor it, and Jo felt herself nod.

Standing in the gravel driveway, she could see half a dozen sawed-off stubs of branches spiraling the oak's trunk. One long silvered limb hung overhead at a precarious angle. The cluster of buds on the side nearest the building was the only sign of life.

"I hadn't even noticed," Jo said, staring at the wide-ringed stub that had once held her tree house. A gust of wind came up off the lake, skittering trash across the gravel, and she hugged her arms to her chest. "Thanks. I'll—I'll call someone to take care of it."

"Not yet." Rory shook her head and shouldered a knapsack, worn leather the color of walnuts. "You're shivering. Come upstairs," she said, as if it were her house. "I'll make tea." She held out her hand.

For no reason that she could ever explain, Jo followed, slipping her palm into Rory's, like a child about to cross a busy street. Her fingers tingled with the contact.

The summer that her mother left, Jo's favorite toy was a potato. An odd choice for the daughter of a machinist. No moving parts. But with a penny and a nail and a bit of wire, it became a battery, strong enough to elicit a faint incandescent glow from one of the tiniest bulbs.

Jo climbed the back stairs, holding Rory's hand. For the first time in decades she felt that same flicker of connection from an unexpected source.

Rory made a face at the box of Lipton's. She produced a tin of lapsang souchong from her knapsack and put the battered kettle on to boil. The leather pack, she said, was everything she owned— notebooks and pens, a change of clothes, a toothbrush, and a small, lumpy drawstring sack. She held it up. "The rest of my trousseau."

"What do you do?" Jo asked.

"I'm a poet, a storyteller—fairy tales and fables, mostly. I've always liked this one."

That made no sense. But nothing had, since Jo'd come back. Everything was as familiar as it was alien, and in that setting, in the early spring twilight, logic and Rory could not co-exist.

Rory smiled, and logic lost.

By the time they switched from tea to wine, rainy darkness had turned the kitchen windows to funhouse mirrors, reflecting the florid walls, wavy and indistinct.

"Where do you live?" Jo asked an hour later. "I'll give you a ride home. It's pouring out there."

"Hmm." Rory cocked her head, then held out her hands, palms up. "I don't know. I haven't gotten that far yet. I suppose I should stay with you." She stood to pour the last of the Merlot into Jo's glass.

"I guess," Jo said. She wasn't sure if she was still sober enough to drive on slick country roads. "I'll see if I can find clean sheets, and make up my father's bed."

"Oh, we can make up something better than that." Rory finished the last inch of wine in her glass. "I know how it starts," she said.

"How?"

"Once upon a time, you kissed me."

Jo woke up the next morning curled around a still-warm pillow. Through the doorway she could see Rory at the kitchen table, her head bent and intent, silent but for the soft scritch of pen on paper. A flurry of motion, pen sweeping wide, crossing out unruly words. A small sigh. Rory bit the top of her pen and stared into space, as if an elusive phrase were etched into the wallpaper, hidden among the tea roses. Jo pulled on a pair of sweats and a t-shirt and padded out in her bare feet.

She had been a quiet, solitary child, and in middle age considered herself a private person, practical and self-sufficient. Not a prude—she'd had some lovers—but not accustomed to awkward good-mornings after unlikely evenings. She cleared her throat as an introduction.

Rory looked up. "Hi. There's coffee on the stove."

What? "How? There wasn't any."

"I made some." She waved a hand at her knapsack and the open bag of Starbucks French Roast on the counter.

"Oh. Thanks." There wasn't a Starbucks within a hundred

miles. And last night the knapsack hadn't had—But damn, it smelled good.

Jo filled a mug and leaned against the table. "What are you working on?"

"A new story." Rory turned and kissed Jo's fingers, curled around the handle of the mug. "So many possibilities."

The second time Jo got up that morning, she took a shower. When she came out of the bathroom, combing her fingers through her short, salt-and-pepper hair, Rory was back at the table, staring at a blank page.

"I have to go to the Walmart, out by the highway." Jo rested her hands on Rory's shoulders. "Boxes and tape and labels. Do you want to come along?"

"I need to stay here. Be back for lunch," she answered, and picked up her pen.

Jo left the packing supplies downstairs and walked into the kitchen expecting sandwiches. The table was covered with a bright, Indian-print bedspread identical to the one she'd had in her first apartment. Small bowls and plates held strawberries, a wedge of crumbly cheese, half a baguette, slices of avocado, green olives, pink curls of prosciutto—*where had she gotten that?*—a fan of shortbread wedges.

"What's all this?"

"Magpie lunch." Rory opened the fridge. "Sit. There's more coffee if you need to work this afternoon but—" She grinned and put a pitcher on the counter. "I made sangria, too."

A thin orange slice floated in ruby liquid, colors that shouldn't work together. But they did, and Jo accepted the invitation. She feasted on a panoply of nibbles and let the edges of responsibility soften into a long, languid afternoon.

April became May. The buds on the oak unfurled to celadon flags, and color crept back into the world. In the mornings, while Rory hummed and scribbled, Jo opened cupboards, filled boxes, made lists and phone calls. She emptied the workbench drawers into neatly labeled Ziploc bags, made two solo runs to the town dump. Lunch was sometimes a sandwich, but sometimes a magpie, and Jo grew quite fond of the way the afternoon light played through the bedroom window.

They didn't talk about where they were from or what had come before. Their days were filled with laughter and small touches, like a cat bumping against a leg to reassure itself that the world was as it should be. Rory skipped and sang and made up holidays for them to celebrate.

"It's the ninth. No work today."

Jo raised an eyebrow.

"The nines are for joy," Rory said. "For feasts and blue flowers and the connecting of hearts." She didn't always talk that way. If she ever *went* to the grocery, Jo doubted that she'd stand in the checkout line answering "Paper or plastic?" in iambic pentameter. But arm-in-arm or spooned around each other, Rory's words wove her into a place she could never have imagined—and never wanted to leave.

The weather grew warmer. Jo opened the double doors downstairs to the endless blue sky, and Rory sat with her back against the wood, her hair like flame in the sunlight.

The man from the circus museum in Baraboo was coming after the Fourth of July to make an offer on some of the machines. Jo had her father's toolbox open on a stool next to a cast-iron peepshow called *Through the Keyhole*. Its risqué images skipped and stuttered, and she had opened the side, exposing the gears and wheels. Her father, a methodical packrat, had saved the tattered schematic, but she hadn't made much progress.

"What's it supposed to do?" Rory asked.

"It's a dirty movie—at least it was seventy years ago." Jo laughed. "The woman does the hootchy-cootchy and takes off some of her clothes. But right now she dances worse than I do."

"You dance."

"No, I don't."

"Not *ever?*"

"Nope, 'fraid not."

"Liar. You dance with me in bed."

Jo felt her face redden. "Not the same."

Rory just smiled and shook her head. She peered into the machine. "Where's the film?"

"There isn't any. It's like a big, round flipbook. Hundreds of photos. But when you see one after another after another, you get the illusion of motion. Persistence of vision." She dug a handful of nickels out of a small canvas bag in the toolbox. "Here. Go take a look at *When the Lights Are Low.*"

Rory spent an hour peering, fascinated, into the brass eye-pieces of the other machines. Jo discovered the problem—a gear worn almost smooth, connecting only once every dozen turns of the wheel—and found a spare part that fit.

She hadn't expected to come across anything of her own in the apartment—she'd been gone most of her life, and her father was not a sentimental man. But the next morning, on a shelf at the back of his closet, behind his Sunday hat and a framed medal from the war, she did: a manila folder with a handful of crayon drawings, leaf prints, and fat-lined kindergarten papers. She climbed down from the stepstool and took the folder into the kitchen, where the light was better.

A flat black tin of watercolor lozenges and a sketchbook lay open on the table. Rory swirled a brush in a tumbler of pale orange water.

"I didn't know you painted." Jo opened the folder.

"This story needs color," Rory replied. She reached for one of the stiff pieces of construction paper, spatters of red and yellow tempera outlining the spiky contours of a maple leaf. "You made this?"

"Every fall until fourth grade. Then we just pressed leaves in the encyclopedia. There was a prize for collecting the most different kinds."

"Have you ever seen the cave paintings in France?"

It was a non sequitur, but Jo had gotten used to them. "Lascaux," she nodded. "Not in person, but I had a textbook, in college. Hunters' drawings: bison and spotted horses."

"And hands. Your picture reminds me of the hands." Rory laid her left one flat on the table, its back spotted with freckles. "Ten thousand years ago, an artist put his hand on the cave wall and held the pigment in his mouth, then spit it through a hollow reed." She was silent for a minute, then asked, "Are there any blank peepshow cards downstairs?"

"No, but the reel for *Seeing Is Believing* only has a handful left. The backs are blank."

"That'll work. And I need one of your father's pipes."

"Okay. Why?"

"I want to paint your hand."

When Jo returned, Rory removed the bowl of the pipe, then reached into her wonder-filled knapsack and produced a jar of rust-colored powder. "Red ochre," she said. "Put your hand on the card and hold very still."

Rory tipped half the jar of powder into her mouth, and held the pipe stem in her teeth. She leaned over Jo's hand and puffed damp russet clouds around each splayed finger. Jo closed her eyes; Rory's breath defined the edges of her senses.

"Done. Lift straight up. Don't smear it."

Jo did, and looked down at a red card with a perfect white hand shape at its center.

"See. Lascaux. They knew." Rory nodded. "When we're gone,

we leave a void where we used to be." She leaned over and began to lick away the specks of pigment from Jo's knuckles.

August arrived with humidity that made sweat drip off Jo's nose when she filled the last Goodwill box with her father's shirts and work boots. Too hot to be upstairs, even with all the windows open. There wasn't much left to do in the arcade—the man from Baraboo had written a nice check and taken everything but the nickelodeon and the broken peep show. But the space was cool and dim, and most afternoons a thunderstorm massed over the lake, and rain roared down from a pewter sky, making small rivers that snaked across the gravel.

One evening, after, they sat out on the small balcony at the top of the back stairs with cold bottles of cider, two middle-aged women listening to the drips off the eaves, the world golden in the setting sun.

"I used to love the woods this time of year," Jo said. "Everything's that deep, lush green."

Rory laughed. "What do you mean, everything? There's a rainbow out there. Hickory leaves aren't the same green as a chestnut's, or a poplar's, or—" She took a long, slow swallow of her cider and scooched closer, leaning against Jo's shoulder. "Doesn't matter. In a couple of weeks, even someone as chlorophyll-challenged as you will be able to see the difference."

"I know. Summer's almost over." Jo shook her head. "I never thought I'd still be *here*." She put her cider down on the weathered wood. "But it's all done. The Grange is going to store the nickelodeon for me, and the realtor said she can come by Monday to pick up the keys. We can hit the road any time you're ready."

She felt Rory shift, tense, and grow still.

"One more month," she said after a long time. "I need to finish the story."

"If you've got your notebook, can't you do that anywhere?"

"Not this one," Rory said.

So they stayed. One after another, the supple green leaves of the oak were veined with yellow, and the view from the balcony turned calico, a patchwork of rusts and reds and browns among the green. Rory wrote while Jo ran errands, swept the arcade floor, thought about where they might go, tried not to be impatient.

Every morning, she woke and watched another oak leaf glide past the window, drifting slowly down onto the gravel.

"I've got a task for you," Rory said, her head on Jo's chest, her voice muffled.

"What?"

"There are only a few leaves left on the oak. Catch one for me today and make a spatter print?"

"How come?"

"An illustration for the end of this chapter." She unfolded herself and leaned over the side of the bed for her knapsack. "Here. Yellow ochre." She handed Jo the jar. "Use the back of a peepshow card, and spit it."

Jo made a face. "Can't I just use a toothbrush and a popsicle stick to make the spatter, the way we did in school?"

"No. Then there'd be none of *you* in it."

"But—" Jo stared at the jar.

"Don't worry. It's just ground-up clay. And after," Rory grinned, "I'll think of some way to cleanse your palate."

Later that night, Jo came in from the bathroom to find Rory sitting in bed, a pair of glasses perched on the end of her nose. Jo had never seen her wear them before.

"Cuddle up with me," Rory said. "I need to read this to you. It's time."

The carnival comes to every town
for a month or two
before cold winds strike the set.
Autumn is the festival of death.
The chorus prepares for the season's curtain;
only the most elaborate shrouds will do
for the grand finale.
Leaves don't fall—
they just let go.
One by one they pirouette,
a curtsy so deep it touches the ground,
no applause but silence.

The carnival comes every year;
not all the cast returns.
If you look, you can see
the orphaned dryads
passing among the humans.
They are the old women,
withering and flamboyant,
sparse hair the color of persimmons,
going out in a blaze of glory—
too-bright scarves
and spots of rouge that shout:
Attention, please!
Dance with me while you can;
it's not that long a run.
If you blink, you'll miss my closing number—
and it's your loss, dearie.

Silence filled the small bedroom. Jo sat stiff, unmoving against the headboard. "Tell me that's only a poem."

Rory laid the pages on the bedside table and put her glasses on top of them. She slid under the covers and snuggled close. "I can't."

Jo looked at her in the lamplight, the fine lines around her eyes; white and silver twined amid the copper curls. "The tree is dying." Her voice sounded hollow. "That's the first thing you said to me."

"You loved her. No one else ever cared."

"I felt safe there."

"I know. I remember." Rory tucked her arm through Jo's. "I was so afraid you wouldn't come back. The wheel turned and turned, then I only had one summer left."

"What's going to—?" Jo asked.

"Just love me tonight." Rory kissed her, both gentle and fierce. "Then love me again tomorrow."

Rory glowed as she shrank into herself, veins prominent under tissue-thin flesh. They stayed cuddled under the blanket for two days, touching more than talking. The last morning, Jo was awake before dawn. She lay facing the window, her head on Rory's chest, rising and falling with each shallow breath. A breeze whispered against the side of the house and, with no sound at all, the oak tree gave up its final leaf. As the yellow scrap drifted down, Jo felt a faint tremble under her cheek, then stillness.

The sun was high above the trees across the lake before Jo moved, and then only because nature called, a force too strong to ignore. When she returned, two minutes later, the bed was impossibly empty. Rory's knapsack sat on the pillow, an envelope propped against it.

Jo stared. Jo sat on the edge of the bed. After a minute or an hour or a week—what did it matter?—Jo opened the envelope. A folded page from Rory's notebook held the spatter prints they had each made: the red, Jo's hand; the yellow, a void where an oak leaf had been.

She unfolded the paper and read:

The next chapter is yours again.
It cannot happen here.
Take some acorns from my tree.
Find somewhere safe to hibernate, and wait for spring.
Then begin a new carnival.
But before you go,
Put these in your peep show—
    one on each side of the wheel.
And don't blink.

Jo moved slowly, mechanically. After some time, she dressed and went downstairs. A nickel lay on the bare workbench beside the gilt-rimmed Mutoscope. The title card, in angular 1920s script, now read: *Echoes of Aurora.* She tried to smile, but that touched a hurt too big. She mounted the spattered cards onto the empty wheel, three hundred gaps between them. Jo closed the cast-iron door.

She dropped the nickel in the slot. The light came on, revealing a red card, a white hand. She turned the brass handle.

Red. Yellow. Hand. Leaf.

She cranked faster. Nothing but an orange blur, and her eyes stung with the first real tears.

Then behind her, out on the darkened floor, the nickelodeon began to play itself. *Lonesome Woman Blues.*

The orange began to shimmer. The images flickered, re-formed, focused. Through the eyepiece, Jo watched as Rory curtsied and held out her hand, saw herself bow and accept.

And in the last finger of afternoon light, in an empty penny arcade, they danced.

FRIDAY NIGHT AT ST. CECILIA'S

Rachel Sweeney came into the Student Lounge and threw her book bag on the couch. She smiled when she saw the backgammon board, already set up on the table by the window. She loved games, and life at St. Cecilia's would be intolerable without these Friday nights with her friend Addie.

A chittering flock of girls passed on their way to the stairs, duffels and satchels over their shoulders. Two peered in, but saw that it was only Rachel and continued on. Sara had a car and they were all off for a weekend's adventure. Rachel was grounded. Again. They wouldn't have invited her anyway.

She sat down and fiddled with the backgammon stones, black and white, making neat and ordered rows. She liked the round heft of them, liked the soft clicks as they slid together. The late afternoon light through the window blinds striped the worn wooden table, highlighting initials engraved in the varnish by decades of ballpoint pens. Rachel rolled the white dice, over and over, and watched the clock.

It wasn't like Addie to be late. But she *was* bringing the pizza, since she'd lost last week. Antonio's must be really crowded. Rachel glanced over at her book bag. If Addie didn't come soon, they wouldn't be able to sneak a smoke before the sisters returned from vespers.

Forty-five minutes later, the room was all shadows, and Rachel was still alone. She looked at the light switch across the room, but didn't bother turning it on. She ran a hand through her short dark hair, making up excuses for Addie. None of them lifted her disappointment.

"What's this?" asked a voice from the doorway. "Sitting in the dark all by your lonesome?" The light came on.

Rachel blinked at the sudden brightness. It was the new housekeeper. "Oh. Mrs. Llewelyn. Hi."

The older woman leaned her mop against the battered couch next to the door. "Backgammon is it? I learned it as a girl. *Bach cammaun*, in the old tongue. The wee battle." She shook her head. "But as I recall, it's not much sport for one."

"Tell me about it," said Rachel. "I've been waiting for Addie, but she hasn't shown up."

"Addie. That tall girl with the glasses?" Mrs. Llewelyn frowned. "Oh dear. Did she not tell you she was going off with the others, then? She's been gone nearly an hour."

"No way. *Addie* wouldn't go with—" Rachel bit her lip, her eyes surprised with tears. When she trusted her voice again, she said, "Well, her choice, I guess. I'll go to my room. I've got a test Monday." She plunked the dice into their leather cup and reached for the first line of stones.

"Now, now, dearie. It's not as bad as all that. I'd thought to take a bit of a break about now, so if you'd fancy a game with an old woman—"

Rachel really wasn't in the mood anymore. But it would be worse, all alone in the silent dorm. And it seemed a little rude to say no. "Sure, I'll play you."

"I accept the challenge with pleasure." Mrs. Llewelyn made a small curtsy and sat down across the table. Rachel smiled despite herself.

Mrs. Llewelyn was a dumpling of a woman, with a bun of chestnut hair going gray at the temples. She wore a white smock with ST. CECILIA'S stitched over one ample breast, and *Maeve* in red script across the other. She beamed at Rachel, her cheeks filling her face, her eyes twinkling.

Rachel picked up the dice. She rolled a nine and moved two of the black stones. Mrs. Llewelyn rolled, moved a white stone, and began chattering about her neighbors and their children and other people Rachel didn't know. Rachel nodded now and then, but didn't feel the need to say anything. The click of the stones and the periodic clatter of the dice were familiar and soothing, and she was soon lost in the game.

With the first of her stones only two spaces away from her inner table, Rachel grinned. She was going to win. Mrs. Llewelyn rolled a three—not a good roll at all—and tossed the dice over to Rachel's side of the board.

They clipped the edge of the wooden tray and skittered across the table. Rachel grabbed for them, but wasn't quick enough. They fell to the floor and rolled to the edge of the hot air register. Rachel watched in dismay as first one, then the other disappeared through the brass grating.

"Oh, look what I've gone and done." Mrs. Llewelyn put a hand to each cheek. "Clumsy old fool, that's what I am."

"It's okay," Rachel said after a few seconds. She looked at the backgammon board, then picked up the black stone in front of her. "It was nice playing with you, while it lasted." She sighed. "I should go study. Church History's not my best class."

"Now, now. Hold up just a tick." Mrs. Llewelyn rummaged in the pocket of her white smock. She pulled out some crumpled tissues, the stub of a pencil, half a roll of Life Savers, and a tube of lip balm, piling them on the tabletop. "Ah, I thought as much. Here we go. They're a bit unusual, but they'll do." She handed Rachel a pair of iridescent blue-green cubes and stuffed the other items back into her pocket.

"You carry *dice* with you?" Rachel asked.

"Oh, I pick things up here and there whilst I'm cleaning. And I like a little gamble now and then." She winked at Rachel. "Don't tell the sisters."

"Not likely."

The dice were heavier than she expected, with an odd, cold feel. Rachel rolled them across her palm, her skin tingling, and threw them onto the board. They came up double twos. Good, but not quite enough. She moved, and on the next turn, Mrs. Llewelyn set her white stone atop Rachel's black one, knocking it out of play. Rachel needed to roll a five to get back on the board, but couldn't. Three tries. She watched in frustration as Mrs. Llewelyn rolled double fours twice, then a double six to win the game. What rotten luck.

"Dear, dear. And you were so close. But that's gammon for me—double the stakes."

"Triple, actually," said Rachel. "That was *back*gammon, not gammon." She was still staring at the board, rolling the dice back and forth in her palm, reviewing the last few moves. How could she have lost? She glanced at the clock. Only seven-thirty. "Two out of three?"

Mrs. Llewelyn looked toward her bucket and mop, still propped against the couch. "Oh, well, all right, I accept. I shouldn't, really. What if one of the sisters came by, saw me playing games—on their Lord's nickel? But I'm quite enjoying this."

"Yeah, me too," said Rachel. "Let me just take five and go to the girls' room." She walked down the hall, still fiddling with the dice in her hand. She slipped them into the pocket of her green blazer when she entered the toilet stall. A few minutes later, she was back.

"I was having myself a think, while you were gone," Mrs. Llewelyn said. "This is such a dreary room. What say we move to my lodgings down below for the next game? No one will bother us, and we can have a nice pot of Earl Grey." She cocked her head at Rachel and smiled. "Would you play on those terms?"

"Sure," Rachel shrugged. The Lounge *wasn't* particularly comfortable.

"Excellent." Mrs. Llewelyn laughed and clapped her hands. Rachel was startled by the smell of a sweet, pungent smoke, like burning cloves, as the linoleum beside the door shimmered with the same blue-green iridescence as the dice, then opened up into a large black hole.

"I can't remember if this goes to the Study or the Conservatory," Mrs. Llewelyn said. "But that hardly matters, now, does it?" A wrench appeared in her hand. She raised an arm and clipped Rachel neatly above the ear. She laughed again, the laugh turning into a cackle. Through half-closed eyes, Rachel watched as the woman's body shimmered, then folded in on itself. A huge raven hovered in the air. It tugged at the hem of Rachel's green plaid skirt and dragged her down into the impossible hole.

Rachel sneezed and opened her eyes. She was curled on her side, one cheek resting on the floral border of a wine-red Oriental rug. It smelled of tobacco. She sat up very slowly and touched the tender, walnut-sized lump on her temple. Ouch. She looked around. Not in the dorm anymore, that was for sure. But the room seemed oddly familiar.

The rug lay on a floor of polished white tiles. A statue of a woman in flowing robes, a sheaf of wheat in her arms, anchored one corner. A dozen potted palms in ornate urns flanked a wall of French windows that opened onto terraced gardens—clipped precise lawns and beds of white flowers. Geometric blocks of sunshine overlaid the pattern of the rug, the light warm on her arms.

Wait. It was nighttime. What the—?

"I'm afraid you've had a nasty tumble," said a deep, British voice.

"Huh?" Rachel startled and turned to her left. In a corner filled with more potted palms sat a bald man in a brocade armchair. He had a thick gray bristle mustache and wore a tweed jacket that seemed to have snips of twigs and moss woven into the fabric. He laid a slim leather volume on the arm of the chair.

"It was rather abrupt," he continued. "None of the usual warnings. I was immersed in one of Kipling's lesser works—not up to his usual form, really, but a compelling tale, nonetheless—quite enjoying myself, when the secret passageway opened, and down you came, knocking yourself senseless on the base of that lovely Ceres."

Rachel stared at him, her mouth open. Where *was* she? "How long have I been here?" she asked out loud.

"Not long. Not long at all. Less than five minutes, I'd imagine. I've rung for a spot of tea. I suppose smelling salts might be in order, but I'm afraid we haven't any. I say, do you like Kipling?" He held up his book.

"I don't know. I've never kippled." It came automatically, and she regretted it. This was not the time to be a smart-ass.

But the man in the chair chuckled. "Bit of a wit, eh? I shall endeavor to recall that one for the others, at supper."

"Where *am* I?" asked Rachel.

"How extraordinary! Don't you know?"

She shook her head, which hurt. "I haven't got a clue."

For some reason, this made him roar with laughter. "Oh, excellent. Excellent. What a wit you have, young lady." He wiped his eyes with a white handkerchief. "What a delightful wit."

Rachel eyed the man warily. He must be crazy. She was funny, but hardly ever made jokes that went over her own head. She stood up and moved toward the doors. Once she was outside, she'd have a better idea how to get back to the dorm.

"Look, it's been nice chatting with you, but I've gotta go. I've got a test—" She stopped in mid-sentence and stared at a pair of red wire-rimmed glasses lying at the base of one potted palm.

Addie's glasses.

Rachel's hand shook as she picked them up. "Where did you get these?" she asked. Her voice came out in a frightened squeak.

"I have no idea," he said calmly. "I suppose the other girl dropped them on her way out."

"What. Other. Girl?"

"Why the one who tumbled down the passage last. An hour ago, at least. Tall girl, in a skirt like yours."

St. Cecilia's plaid. Rachel's stomach felt like ice. "Where *is* she, Mr.—" She let his unfinished name hang in the air.

"Plum," he said. "Professor, to be exact. Cambridge. Magdalene don, retired."

"Yeah, right," Rachel said. "Professor Plum. And I'm—" She stopped and stared at him. He *was* Professor Plum. He looked exactly like the picture on the Clue card. Impossible. Except here she was. Rachel looked around the room again, and pieces slowly fell into place. They were absurd, surreal pieces, but had a certain logic to their arrangement.

"Don't tell me," she said. "This is the Conservatory."

"Naturally," replied the professor. "You took the secret passage from the Lounge, didn't you?"

Rachel shut her eyes and tried to imagine the layout of the Clue board. The passage, if she could find it, would take her back to the Lounge. Or at least *a* lounge. The chances of it being the Trinity House lounge at St. Cecilia's seemed slim. From this room she could go to the Billiard Room or the Ballroom. But which way was *out?*

"Where's Addie now?" she asked again.

"She left."

"Through the passage or the door?"

"Why, neither one. She simply disappeared. Not at all uncommon here."

"Really?"

"Yes, well, you see, Mrs. Peacock and I, Colonel Mustard and the rest, we never leave. Can't, you know. The rooms are all connected by doors, but there's no door to the outside." He sounded a little sad. "On the other hand, your kind comes and goes. You appear suddenly, traipse about until you come to a conclusion, and then *poof!* Off you go. As if you had never been."

"Conclusion?" Rachel thought for a moment. "Oh. Duh. Who did it, and with what."

He waved his hand impatiently. "Yes, yes, of course. I favor the knife, myself. Simple classic lines. I can't abide blunt instruments."

Like a wrench. Rachel rubbed the bump on her head and got an unpleasant image of Mrs. Llewelyn's smock-covered arm descending. The final piece fell into place. "Mrs. White. In the Lounge. With the wrench."

When she said the word *wrench,* a flash of blue-green lightning and that pungent clove smell filled the air. Professor Plum shimmered, his features becoming as translucent as sautéed onions. Then he was gone. The solid lines of walls and furniture dissolved into pointillist colors that swirled slowly around her, wrapping her in a thick, warm cocoon that spun her away.

The garden was sunny. Alternating squares of grass and white clover stretched off as far as a city block. Rachel stood up, a little dizzy, and looked around for the French doors to the Conservatory. No building in sight. A wooden ladder stood a few yards to her right, leaning against an earthen terrace a little taller than she was. Maybe she could see better from up there?

She took a step toward the ladder, but ran *smack!* into an invisible barrier at the border of the green grass square.

Weird.

The air shimmered and a flat cardboard disk appeared, floating waist high. It looked like the base for a pizza, painted with six colored wedges. Pinned to its center was a white plastic arrow.

Weirder by the minute.

"S-s-s-spin," hissed a tiny voice.

Rachel looked down. Next to her left heel was a thin brown snake. Great, she thought. If there's one thing Catholic school teaches you, it's never, ever listen to a talking snake in a garden.

"Go away," she said. "Shoo."

"S-spin," the snake said again. "Across squares. Slide chutes. Scale ladders-s-s."

Chutes and Ladders? The kid's game? Rachel had played it at her cousin Debbie's, years and years ago. She must have said some of that out loud, because the snake started talking again.

"She says *Snakes* and Ladders-s-s."

She? Goosebumps rose on Rachel's arms and the side of her head throbbed. The same *she* that had turned into a black bird and dragged her down a non-existent hole in the Lounge floor? "Who is she?" Not just the housekeeper, that was obvious.

The snake tried to answer. Rachel watched it writhe and move its mouth, but no sound came out.

"Maeve?" she said, taking a guess. "Maeve Llewelyn?"

"Yes-s-s-s!" the snake hissed in relief. "It's sound snakes can't say easy."

"But what *is* she?"

"Shape shifts," said the snake.

That wasn't very useful, Rachel thought. Maybe a more practical question. "What do I have to do?" she asked the snake. She felt like Eve.

"Spin. Finish is success-s-s," it said enigmatically. "Sadly, snake stuck. Save snake?"

"Why can't you—? Oh, you can't climb ladders."

The snake shook its head slowly from side to side.

Rachel was not the sort of girl who was afraid of reptiles. "Okay, you can wrap around my arm," she said, bending down. "Don't bite."

The snake wrapped itself around the sleeve of her green

cotton blazer, just under her elbow. "Thanks-s-s," it said. Its tiny red tongue flickered once, tickling a bit. Then it settled down and lay its head flat on the outside of her arm. "S-s-spin," it said.

Rachel spun the white arrow. It landed on a yellow wedge with a large 3, and she walked across into the next square easily. White, green, white. She climbed the ladder up to the top of the wall and whistled in surprise. Two hundred feet of steep hillside was terraced with stepped-back earthen walls topped with plots of green and white squares. The air was warm and fragrant with the spice of clover and newly mown grass.

Spin, move. Spin, move. Rachel landed on a square with an enormously long ladder. Thirty-two rungs later, she crawled off and flopped down in a patch of white clover.

"Exit," hissed the snake. "S-s-see?"

She looked up. On the top of the last terrace, and a few squares to the left, a brick wall surrounded a portal of soft, overlapping petals, like a rose or a sea anemone. Its center shimmered that iridescent blue-green.

"Jeez. Finally," Rachel said. "Let's get out of here." She flicked the spinner with her hand. The yellow wedge with the 3. One. Two. Threeeeeeeeeeeeeeeee—

Rachel's feet went out from under her as she slid into a shiny red culvert, arms flailing. The metal tube twisted right, left, and right again. She banged her elbow on the first turn, then tucked her arms in. That protected her and the snake, but physics—as usual—was not her friend. Her more streamlined body went faster and faster until the ride ended with a butt-jarring thump in a patch of green grass.

"Shit," said Rachel. She rubbed her back and her elbow and reflexively looked around for a scowling nun.

"Chutes-s-s," said the snake, sadly.

They were almost down to the bottom of the garden again. Rachel heard a faint laugh, a far-off cackle, and the spinner floated down the hillside, cresting each terrace as if it were carried on an invisible wave. It hovered next to her. She spun.

They were near the top for the fifth time when their current ladder ended in a patch of grass where Mrs. Llewelyn—or whoever she was—sat on a small sofa. She wore a long white dress embroidered with flowers and jewels. On her lap, she balanced a bone china saucer in a delicate rosebud pattern.

"Ah, there you are. And not a moment too soon. Earl Gray gets a bit cloying when it sits too long, if you ask me." She took a small sip.

"Where's Addie?" Rachel demanded as she stepped off the ladder. The snake quickly slithered into the breast pocket of her blazer, disappearing behind the St. Cecilia's crest.

"Now, now. Don't you use that tone with me." Mrs. Llewelyn waggled a finger. "Remember, you're in my lodgings now, dearie."

Rachel took a deep breath. "Yes, ma'am," she said politely. She'd been dealing with nuns for three years. She knew the routine. "Where can I find Addie, ma'am?"

"Oh, she's in a safe place, never you mind. Pity she couldn't stay for tea. But you'll see her soon enough." Mrs. Llewelyn took another sip. "Care for a cup?"

"No, thank you. I'd like to go back to my room now, if I may." Rachel was laying it on as thick as she knew how.

"You would, would you? Just like that? Not how a wager works, dearie. You have to win your way home. Two out of three, you said." She chuckled as her teacup shimmered. The raven flew off with a cackle.

When the bird was just a tiny speck in the blue sky, the snake emerged from Rachel's pocket and coiled around her arm again.

"I won Clue," said Rachel, talking to herself as much as to the snake. "I only have to win this, and I can go home, right?"

"Slight chance," the snake agreed.

"Well, how long have *you* been here?" she asked.

"Since sixty-six."

"What!?" Rachel didn't like the sound of that at all. "How come?"

"Dice hers."

"But this game doesn't use dice."

"Dice once," the snake said. "Snake eyes so easy." It looked up at her and blinked.

"Let me get this straight. Now the game has a spinner because you can roll snake eyes any time you want?" Rachel was getting pretty good at interpreting.

"Yes-s-s."

"That's not fair. It's like loading the di— Oh." The end of the backgammon game. Double fours, double sixes. She reached into the side pocket of her blazer. "These are her dice," she said.

"Excellent." The snake's tongue flicked in and out. "Let's see."

Rachel held the blue-green cubes out on her palm. The snake undulated down her arm.

"Snake eyes," it said.

"What?"

"Show snake eyes."

"Oh, sorry." Rachel turned the two dice so that a single dot faced up on each cube. The snake butted them with its head until they were side by side. Then it opened its mouth and delicately placed one fang in the center of each dot. When it moved away, a single drop of milky venom lay pooled on each die.

"Suck," it said.

Rachel was not particularly squeamish, but poison was another matter. "Is there any other way to—"

"S-s-s-suck!" the snake commanded.

Rachel shuddered, considered her options, then lowered her head and sucked the venom off the dice. It burned her tongue, like Tabasco with an aftertaste of cloves.

"Soon, set stakes. Snake eyes," the snake said.

She had no idea what that meant. After a minute, the snake

nudged her hand with its blunt head, and she put the dice back in her pocket.

"S-s-spin," it said.

She spun. Again and again and again. The muscles in her thighs felt like jelly from climbing the ladders. Worse than gym class. Her body was bruised and sore from the chutes, and she had no idea how much time had passed. Hours? Days?

Eventually she got lucky. The spinner landed on the orange 5, and Rachel stepped across the squares. One. Two. Three. Four. Five. She stood at the bottom of the short ladder that ended in the center of the anemone-like portal.

"Success-s-s-s-s," announced the snake.

"About friggin' time," said Rachel, wearily. She climbed to the top of the ladder. For the first time ever, she would be happy to return to St. Cecilia's.

"Yes-s-s. Snake sentence served. Assistance so nice." The snake uncoiled itself from her arm and slithered through the portal. As the last bit of its tail disappeared, Rachel saw a boy in flannel slacks and a school blazer, as fleeting as an after-image. He tipped his cap to her, then he was gone.

In the far distance she thought she heard an angry cry.

Rachel stepped off the ladder and everything began to whirl.

She opened her eyes, expecting to see the nubby beige couch in the Lounge. But no. She was sitting on a sidewalk, her back to a telephone pole, downtown. Nowhere near St. Cecilia's. And it was morning. She'd been out all night, off-campus. That wasn't good.

Across the street was a seedy brick hotel—ROOMS $2, WEEKLY RATES—with a fly-specked purple sign that said MEDITERRANEAN CAFÉ. Next to it was a storefront, windows covered with plywood and graffiti. The pink neon of a corner bar buzzed on and off overhead.

Bad neighborhood. At least it wasn't another game. Maybe the bar had a pay phone? She was under-age, but she could say it was an emergency. Sister Margareta would come and get her in the van. There'd be lectures, and she'd be grounded again, for the rest of the year, probably. Under the circumstances, she could live with that.

Rachel walked down to the corner, but one look inside the bar convinced her not to go inside, not even in broad daylight. She waited for the light to change. The stores looked a little more prosperous—and a lot less threatening—a few blocks down.

Not a busy street. Just one parked car, and it really didn't fit the neighborhood—a little silver sportster, an old two-seater Bugatti. A miracle it hadn't been totally stripped. Rachel waited another two minutes for the light to turn green, then gave up and stepped off the curb to jaywalk. Halfway across the intersection she ran face first into—nothing. She rubbed her nose and looked up at the street sign.

BALTIC AVENUE.

Baltic? Mediterranean? Not again.

Rachel beat her fists on the invisible wall. They bounced off without a sound. "I want to go home, damn it," she shouted. "I don't have to play again. I won your stupid games! Two out of three."

Her voice echoed off the grimy brick walls. The silver sports car shimmered. Mrs. Llewelyn climbed out, wearing a white silk jumpsuit with *Mab* stitched across the left breast.

"Temper, temper," she said in a scold. "You're the one set the terms. 'Twas backgammon, you said. Triple the stakes."

"So, what? I have to win—" Rachel counted on her fingers "—six out of nine? That'll take forever."

"Or so it will seem," said Mab, the Queen of the Faeries. "But I have time. All the time in the world." Her smile was warm; her eyes weren't. The shadows of the derelict buildings deepened and somewhere in the distance, thunder rumbled. Rachel shivered.

"Now what?" she asked, trying not to sound as scared as she felt.

The queen pointed to the gutter. In a litter of broken glass and cigarette butts was a pair of white dice. "I believe it's your turn."

Yuck. Rachel picked up the dice with her fingertips and wiped them off on a dark line in the plaid of her skirt. She found a clean patch of asphalt, knelt, and rolled a four.

The queen scooped up the dice and they crossed the street, passing an H&R Block office, closed. They stepped across a set of railroad tracks into another neighborhood, a row of rundown clapboard houses, most of them painted a pale, faded blue. On the far side of Oriental Avenue, Rachel felt the invisible wall again

"Take a chance," the queen said, pointing.

It looked like a mailbox, except for the pale green paint and the giant pink question mark on its side. Rachel pulled the lid open and took one of the small orange cards from the bin.

"Take a ride on the Reading," she said. "If you pass GO, collect $200."

In an instant they were moving down the sidewalk. Or the sidewalk was moving them. Hard to tell. They turned right past a forbidding stone building, sped by a long row of brownstone apartments, and turned again at an enormous corner lot that said FREE PARKING. The sidewalk widened, the houses grew larger. The lawns on Ventnor Avenue were green and lush; they turned a third time and glided by the huge, gated mansions on Pacific and the posh condos of Park Place. Around the fourth corner, passing the fly-specked hotel again, they came to an abrupt halt on the railroad tracks next to the closed tax office.

"Do you want to buy it?" The queen handed Rachel two pale gold hundred-dollar bills.

"What?" The ride had made her a little nauseous.

"The railroad. Do you want to buy the Reading Railroad?"

Of course. The railroad. Always buy the railroads. Best properties on the board. "Sure," she said.

The queen snatched back the two bills and handed Rachel a black-and-white cardboard deed and the dice.

Rachel sighed. She was doomed. No one ever *wins* Monopoly. You just play until it's time for dinner, or your friends have to go home. It never actually ends. She sighed again and rolled the dice—a three and a two.

Queen Mab picked them up and started down the now-familiar block. "Well, well," she said as they strolled past the clapboard houses and garish mailbox, "now you can play against your little friend." She stopped in front of the stone structure. Thick, rusty iron bars covered the single chest-high opening. JUST VISITING was stenciled in faded letters on the cracked concrete sidewalk.

"I want to go home," said a voice from inside the Jail. Freckled hands wrapped around the bars. Myopic eyes squinted at Rachel.

Addie.

Rachel started to yell, but one look at the queen's face convinced her that was not a good idea. "What have you done to her?" she said in her most polite, talking-to-nuns voice.

"Oh, she's in a bit of a pickle, truly. But she's done it all to herself, I'm afraid. Backgammon's not *her* game either. Wagered and lost. And now? Three turns and no doubles. She doesn't have the fifty dollars for the fine, and it seems she's hasn't a Get Out of Jail Free card to her name." The queen shook her head in disappointment. "And we were having such a lovely game 'til then, weren't we, dearie?"

"Not exactly," Addie said. "I had to mortgage Boardwalk, but I still own St. James Place. If you land on it, the rent will be enough to get me out of here."

"I'll try," said Rachel. "But I'm not sure—"

"Yeah, I know. We've really done it this time, haven't we, Rache?"

"Yep. Deep shit." Unless—? Rachel took a deep breath. "You let her go, right this minute," she demanded, as loud as she could.

"You're not very bright, are you?" The queen scowled. "I've warned you about using that tone with me. You Catholic girls have no respect for the old ways."

"Well, if I'm so disrespectful, shouldn't *I* be the one in jail? Addie's a good girl. Not a troublemaker like me." Rachel glared, as if she deserved to be punished. It wasn't hard.

The queen arched one chestnut brow. "You're offering to take her place?"

Rachel crossed her fingers. "I am."

"All right, dearie, suit yourself, then."

Rachel saw the blue-green flash, and in an instant she was on the other side of the iron bars. The stone wall was damp and cold against her body, and the inside of the Jail smelled like piss.

Addie stared at her from the sidewalk. "What are you doing?" she asked.

"I'm a *lot* more used to detention than you are," Rachel said. "Trust me." She pulled Addie's glasses out of her pocket and handed them through the bars.

"Nice to see you," Addie said, putting them on.

"You too." Rachel smiled, then turned to the queen. "I've learned a lot about keeping my word, ma'am," she said. "I suppose I'll be grateful some day."

"Not all lessons are easy," Mab agreed.

"But a wager is a wager. Rules are rules," Rachel continued.

The queen nodded. "That they are."

Rachel waited two seconds, then asked, "So, ma'am, now that I'm the one in jail, shouldn't *I* get three turns with the dice to try and roll doubles? That's only fair."

The queen considered this. "I suppose it is. You may have your three chances." She put the white dice on the window ledge.

Rachel looked at them, then back at the queen. "Want to up the stakes?"

115

"What now, you foolish child?" The queen sounded impatient.

"If I can roll doubles on the first try, you let Addie go home."

Mab tapped her lip thoughtfully. "Unlikely, but possible. A sporting chance. All right, I accept."

"Great." Rachel paused, counted to three in her head, and made a move to pick up the dice. She stopped, her hand in midair. "Wait a sec. Want to go double or nothing?"

The queen narrowed her eyes. "Are you daft?"

"No. I mean, what if I can roll double—oh, I don't know, how 'bout ones—on the very first roll, you let *both* of us go?"

"And if you fail?"

Rachel shrugged. "I guess we stay here forever. No two out of three, no six out of nine. We're yours."

"Rachel! Are you nuts?" Addie cried. "The odds are thirty-six to one. Against you."

The Queen of the Faeries laughed. "She's correct. Seems you have no idea what you've just done. But I accept. Roll. Your fate is in your own hands."

"Here goes." Rachel blew on her hands, shook them out, and reached for the dice again. Then she snapped her fingers. "On second thought, I think I'll use these." She pulled the blue-green cubes out of her pocket, and watched the queen's eyes widen.

"Where did you get those?" she snarled.

"You handed them to me," Rachel said. "In the Lounge."

The queen clenched her fists and Rachel could see that she was angry. She held her breath.

"'Twas a faerie gift, and freely given," said the queen with a sigh. "Roll."

The cubes were cold and heavy in Rachel's hand. She hoped the snake had known what he was doing. She wished as hard as she had ever wished for anything. Then she opened her hand and let the dice tumble onto the stone ledge.

Snake eyes.

The wall of the jail began to shimmer. Rachel stepped through the translucent stones and blinked in the sunlight. A flash of blue-green vaporized the Jail behind her, obliterating the dice as well. A few wisps of smoke hung in the air and slowly dissipated.

Rachel put her arm around Addie and looked over at the Faerie Queen, standing a few feet away, her chestnut hair now streaked with white.

"You tricked me," she said, her voice thinning to a whisper. They watched her hair turn completely white, and her skin grow pale. The bird-shape became visible beneath her clothes. As she changed, the buildings and streets lost definition as well. Bricks evaporated into smoke, signs and shops misted and blurred, the horizon flickered.

"Shut your eyes," Rachel said when she smelled the first strong whiff of cloves. The air crackled like sizzling rice. She felt a breeze and the sound of flapping wings an instant before the blue-green flash so bright she could see it through closed eyelids.

Then everything was still.

Rachel sat on the linoleum floor of the Student Lounge, her back against the ugly beige couch, her arm still around Addie. The windows were dark, and the clock on the wall said 7:45. Impossible. She'd only been gone fifteen minutes?

The Lounge smelled like burning cloves.

Addie leaned over and kissed her on the cheek. "You were amazing."

"I missed you," Rachel said. She stroked Addie's brown curls for a moment, then stood up. "And now I'm starving. Let's go to Antonio's and get a pizza. Have a smoke. I *really* need a smoke."

"I thought you were grounded."

"I am." Rachel pulled a pack of Marlboros out of her book bag. "But there are worse punishments." She thought about the snake and shuddered. "Besides," she said, reaching down for Addie, "the nuns are going to be a little busy for the next few days."

"Yeah. How come?"

Rachel grinned. "They'll need to find a new housekeeper." She turned off the light and they walked arm in arm into the silent hallway.

CALIGO LANE

Even with the Golden Gate newly bridged and the ugly hulks of battleships lining the bay, San Francisco is well-suited to magic. It is not a geometric city, but full of hidden alleys and twisted lanes. Formed by hills and surrounded by water, its weather transforms its geography, a fog that erases landmarks, cloaking and enclosing as the rest of the world disappears.

That may be an illusion; most magic is. Maps of the city are replete with misdirection. Streets drawn as straight lines may in fact be stairs or a crumbling brick path, or they may dead end for a block or two, then reappear under another name.

Caligo Lane is one such street, most often reached by an accident that cannot be repeated.

In Barbary Coast bars, sailors awaiting orders to the Pacific hear rumors. Late at night, drunk on cheap gin and bravado, they try walking up Jones Street, so steep that shallow steps are cut into the middle of the concrete sidewalk. Near the crest of the hill, the lane may be on their right. Others stumble over to Taylor until they reach the wooden staircase that zigzags up a sheer wall. Caligo Lane is sometimes at the top—unless the stairs have wound around to end at the foot of Jones Street again. A lovely view of the bay is a consolation.

When it does welcome visitors, Caligo Lane is a single block, near the crest of the Bohemian enclave known as Russian Hill. Houses crowd one edge of a mossy cobblestone path; they face a rock-walled tangle of ferns and eucalyptus, vines as thick as a man's arm, moist earth overlaid with a pale scent of flowers.

Number 67 is in the middle, a tall, narrow house, built when the rest of the town was still brawling in the mud. It has bay windows and a copper-domed cupola, although the overhanging branches of a gnarled banyan tree make that difficult to see. The knocker on the heavy oak door is a Romani symbol, a small wheel wrought in polished brass.

Franny has lived here since the Great Fire. She is a cartographer by trade, a geometer of irregular surfaces. Her house is full of maps.

A small woman who favors dark slacks and loose tunics, she is the last of her line, a magus of exceptional abilities. Her hair is jet-black, cut in a blunt bob, bangs straight as rulers, a style that has not been in vogue for decades. She smokes odiferous cigarettes in a long jade-green holder. They are usually tobacco.

The ground floor of number 67 is unremarkable. A small entryway, a hall leading to bedrooms and a bath. But on the right, stairs lead up to a single, large room, not as narrow as below. A comfortable couch and armchairs with their attendant tables surround intricate ancient rugs. A vast library table is strewn with open books, pens and calipers, and scrap paper covered in a jumble of numbers and notations.

Facing north, a wall of atelier windows, reminiscent of Paris, angles in to the ceiling. Seven wide panes span the width of the room, thin dividers painted the green of young spinach. Beyond the glass, ziggurats of stone walls and white houses cascade vertically down to the bay and Alcatraz and the blue-distant hills.

Visitors from more conventional places may feel dizzy and need to sit; it is unsettling to stand *above* a neighbor's roof.

Bookshelves line two walls, floor-to-ceiling. Many titles are in unfamiliar alphabets. Tall art books, dense buckram treatises, mathematical apocrypha: swaths of cracked, crumbling leather spines with gilt letters too worn to decipher. Four flat cases hold maps, both ancient and modern, in a semblance of order.

Other maps are piled and folded, indexed or spread about willy-nilly. They are inked on scraps of parchment, cut from old textbooks, acquired at service stations with a fill-up of gas. They show Cape Abolesco and Dychmygol Bay and the edges of the Salajene Desert, none of which have ever been explored. On a cork wall, round-headed pins stud a large map of Europe. Franny moves them daily as the radio brings news of the unrelenting malignance of the war.

At the far end of the room, a circular staircase helixes up. Piles of books block easy access, less a barricade than an unrealized intent to reshelve and reorganize.

There will be much to do before the fog rolls in.

The stairs lead to the center of the cupola, an octagonal room with a hinged window at each windrose point. Beneath them is a sill wide enough to hold an open newspaper or atlas, a torus of horizontal surface that circles the room, the polished wood stained with ink, scarred in places by pins and tacks and straight-edged steel, scattered with treasured paperweights: worn stones from the banks of the Vistula, prisms, millefiori hemispheres of heavy Czech glass.

Even in a city of hills, the room has unobstructed views that allow Franny to work in any direction. A canvas chair on casters sits, for the moment, facing southwest. On the sill in front of it, a large square of Portuguese cork lies waiting.

Downstairs, on this clear, sunny afternoon, Franny sits at the library table, a postcard from her homeland resting beside her teacup. She recognizes the handwriting; the postmark is obscured by the ink of stamps and redirections. Not even the mailman can reliably find her house.

She glances at the card one more time. The delayed delivery makes her work even more urgent. She opens a ledger, leafing past pages with notes on scale and symbol, diagrams and patterns, and arcane jottings, turning to a blank sheet. She looks again at the postcard, blue-inked numbers its only message:

$$50°\text{-}02'\text{-}09''\ N\ 19°\text{-}10'\text{-}42''\ E$$

Plotting this single journey will take weeks of her time, years from her life. But she must. She glances at the pin-studded map. When geography or politics makes travel or escape impossible, she is the last resort. Every life saved is a mitzvah.

Franny flexes her fingers, and begins. Each phase has its own timing and order; the calculations alone are byzantine. Using her largest atlas, she locates the general vicinity of the coordinates, near the small village of Oświęcim. It takes her all night to uncover a chart detailed enough to show the topography with precision. She walks her calipers from point to point like a two-legged spider as she computes the progressions that will lead to the final map.

For days she smokes and mutters as she measures, plotting points and rhumb lines that expand and shrink with the proportions of the landscape. The map must be drawn to the scale of the journey. She feels the weight of time passing, but cannot allow haste, sleeping only when her hands begin to shake, the figures illegible. Again and again she manipulates her slide rule, scribbles numbers on a pad, and traces shapes onto translucent vellum, transferring the necessary information until at last she has a draft that accurately depicts both entrance and egress.

She grinds her inks and pigments—lampblack and rare earths

mixed with a few drops of her own blood—and trims a sheet of white linen paper to a large square. For a week, the house is silent save for the whisper of tiny sable brushes and the scritch of pens with thin steel nibs.

When she has finished and the colors are dry, she carries the map upstairs and lays it on the cork. Using a round-headed steel pin, she breaches the paper's integrity twice: a single, precise hole at the village, another at Caligo Lane. She transfers the positions onto gridded tissue, and pulls the map free, weighting its corners so that it lies flat on the varnished sill.

She has done what she can. She allows herself a full night's rest.

In the morning she makes a pot of tea and toast with jam, then clears the library table, moving her map-making tools to one side, and opens a black leather case that contains a flat, pale knife made of bone, and a portfolio with dozens of squares of bright paper. She looks around the room. What form must this one take?

Scattered among the dark-spined tomes are small angular paper figurines. Some are geometric shapes; others resemble birds and animals, basilisks and chimeras. Decades before he was exiled to Manzanar, a Japanese calligrapher and amateur conjuror taught her the ancient art of *ori-kami*, yet unknown in this country.

The secret of ori-kami is that a single sheet of paper can be folded in a nearly infinite variety of patterns, each resulting in a different transformation of the available space. Given any two points, it is possible to fold a line that connects them. A map is a menu of possible paths. When Franny folds one of her own making, instead of plain paper, she creates a new alignment of the world, opening improbable passages from one place to another.

Once, when she was young and in a temper, she crumpled one into a ball and threw it across the room, muttering curses. A man in Norway found himself in an unnamed desert, confused and overdressed. His journey did not end well.

The Japanese army might call this art *ori-chizu*, "map folding," but fortunately they are unaware of its power.

Franny knows a thousand ori-kami patterns. Finding the correct orientation for the task requires a skilled eye and geometric precision. She chalks the position of the map's two holes onto smaller squares, folding and creasing sharply with her bone knife, turning flat paper into a cup, a box, a many-winged figure. She notes the alignment, discards one pattern, begins again. A map is a visual narrative; it is not only the folds but their sequence that will define its purpose.

The form this one wishes to take is a fortune teller. American children call it a snapdragon, or a cootie-catcher. It is a simple pattern: the square folded in half vertically, then horizontally, and again on the diagonals. The corners fold into the center, the piece is flipped, the corners folded in again. The paper's two surfaces become many, no longer a flat plane, nor a solid object. A dimension in between.

When she creases the last fold, Franny inserts the index finger and thumb of each hand into the pockets she has created, pushes inward, then moves her fingers apart, as if opening and closing the mouth of an angular bird. Her hands rock outward; the bird's mouth opens now to the right and left. She rocks again, revealing and concealing each tiny hole in turn.

Franny nods and sets it aside. The second phase is finished. Now the waiting begins. She reads and smokes and paces and tidies. The weather is one element she cannot control.

Four days. Five. She moves the pins on the map, crosses off squares on her calendar, bites her nails to the quick until finally one afternoon she feels the fog coming in. The air cools and grows moist as it is saturated with the sea. The light softens, the world stills and quiets. She calms herself for the ritual ahead, sitting on the couch with a cup of smoky tea, listening to the muffled clang of the Hyde Street cable car a few blocks away, watching as the distant hills dissolve into watercolors, fade into hazy outlines, disappear.

The horizon lowers, then approaches, blurring, then slowly obliterating the view outside her window. The edge of the world grows closer. When the nearest neighbors' house is no more than an indistinct fuzz of muted color, she climbs the spiral stairs.

She stands before each window, starting in the east. Everything outside the cupola is gone; there are no distances. Where there had once been landmarks—hillsides and buildings and signs—there is only a soft wall, as if she stands inside a great gray pearl.

San Francisco is a different city when the clouds come to earth. Shapes swirl in the diffused cones of street lamps, creating shadows inside the fog itself. They are not flat, but three-dimensional, both solid and insubstantial.

When all the space in the world is contained within the tangible white darkness of the fog, Franny cranks open the northeast window and gently hangs the newly painted map on the wall of the sky. She murmurs archaic syllables no longer understood outside that room, and the paper clings to the damp blankness.

The map is a tabula rasa, ready for instruction.

The fog enters through the disruption of the pinholes.

The paper's fibers swell as they draw in its moisture.

They draw in the distance it has replaced.

They draw in the dimensions of its shadows.

She paces. Transferring the world to a map is both magic and art, and like any science, the timing must be precise. She has pulled a paper away too soon, before its fibers are fully saturated, rendering it useless. She has let another hang so long that the fog began to retreat again; that one fell to earth as the neighbors reappeared.

She watches and listens, her face to the open window. At the first whisper of drier air, she peels this map off the sky, gently easing one damp corner away with a light, deft touch. There can be no rips or tears, only the two perfect holes.

Paper fibers swell when they are wet, making room for the fog and all it has enveloped. When the fibers dry, they shrink back, locking that in. Now the map itself contains space. She murmurs again, ancient sounds that bind with intent, and lays the map onto the sill to dry. The varnish is her own recipe; it neither absorbs nor contaminates.

Franny closes the window and sleeps until dawn. When she wakes, she is still weary, but busies herself with ordinary chores, reads a magazine, listens to Roosevelt on the radio. The map must dry completely. By late afternoon she is ravenous. She walks down the hill into North Beach, the Italian section, and dines at Lupo's, where she drinks raw red wine and devours one of their flat tomato pies. Late on the third night, when at last the foghorn lows out over the water, she climbs the spiral stairs.

She stands over the map, murmuring now in a language not used for conversation, and takes a deep breath. When she is as calm as a still pond, she lights a candle and sits in her canvas chair. She begins the final sequence, folding the map in half, aligning the edges, precise as a surgeon, burnishing the sharp creases with her pale bone knife. The first fold is the most important. If it is off, even by the tiniest of fractions, all is lost.

Franny uses the knife to move the flow of her breath through her fingers, into the paper. Kinesis. The action of a fold can never be unmade. It fractures the fibers of the paper, leaving a scar the paper cannot forget, a line traversing three dimensions. She folds the map again on the diagonal, aligning and creasing, turning and folding until she holds a larger version of the angular bird's beak.

When the fog has dissolved the world and the cupola is

cocooned, Franny inserts her fingers into the folded map. She flexes her hands, revealing one of the tiny holes, and opens the portal.

Now she stands, hands and body rigid, watching from the open window high above Caligo Lane. She sees nothing; soon sounds echo beneath the banyan tree. Shuffling footsteps, a whispered voice.

Motionless, Franny holds her hands open. She looks down. Beneath the street lamp stands an emaciated woman, head shorn, clad in a shapeless mattress-ticking smock, frightened and bewildered.

"Elzbieta?" Franny calls down.

The woman looks up, shakes her head.

Three more women step into view.

Beyond them, through a shimmer that pierces the fog, Franny sees other faces. More than she anticipated. Half a dozen women appear, and Franny feels the paper begin to soften, grow limp. There are too many. She hears distant shots, a scream, and watches as a mass of panicked women surge against the portal. She struggles to maintain the shape; the linen fibers disintegrate around the holes. Three more women tumble through, and Franny can hold it open no longer. She flexes her trembling hands and reveals the other hole, closing the gate.

After a moment, she calls down in their language. "*Jestes teraz bezpieczna.*" *You are safe now.* She reverses the ori-kami pattern, unfolding and flattening. This work goes quickly. A fold has two possibilities, an unfolding only one.

The women stand and shiver. A few clutch hands.

Franny stares at the place where the shimmer had been. She sees her reflection in the darkened glass, sees tears streak down a face now lined with the topography of age.

"*Znasz moją siostrę?*" she asks, her voice breaking. *Have you seen my sister?* She touches the corner of the depleted map to the candle's flame. "Elzbieta?"

A woman shrugs. *"Tak wiele."* She holds out her hands. *So many.* The others shrug, shake their heads.

Franny sags against the window and blows the ash into the night air. *"Idź,"* she whispers. *Go.*

The women watch the ash fall through the cone of street light. Finally one nods and links her arm with another. They begin to walk now, their thin cardboard shoes shuffling across the cobbles.

Slowly, the others follow. One by one they turn the corner onto Jones Street, step down the shallow concrete steps, and vanish into the fog.

GOODNIGHT MOONS

I'd always dreamed of living on Mars. From the first time I went to the library in Omaha and found the books with rocket ships on their spines, discovered Bradbury and Heinlein and Robinson. Later, I heard real scientists on the news saying it could happen—would happen—in my lifetime.

I didn't want to stay behind and watch.

A big dream, but I was disciplined, focused. I took physics and chemistry, ran track after school, spent my evenings stargazing from the garage roof—and my nights reading science fiction under the covers. I graduated valedictorian, with a full scholarship to MIT, and got a doctorate in mechanical engineering, then stayed on for a second degree in astrobotany. We'd need to grow food, once we arrived.

My husband was an electronics genius, but a small flaw in Pete Morrison's left eardrum grounded him early in the NASA program. We lived outside of Houston while I trained: endurance, microgravity, EVA simulations. I even survived the "vomit comet" with flying colors.

When they announced the team for the Mars mission, I made

the list. Four men and two women: Archie, Paolo, Rajuk, Tom, Chandra, and I were overnight celebrities. Interviews, photos, talk shows—everyone wanted to know how it felt to be the first humans to go to another planet.

Our last public appearance was at the launch of the *Sacagawea* with her payload of hydrogen and the gas extractor that would fuel our trip back. She would be waiting for us when we landed, in another thirty months. Once she was up, we disappeared for two years of training and maneuvers in Antarctica and the Gobi Desert, the most extreme conditions Earth could offer.

Pete and I said our farewells the night before the launch team was sequestered for the final countdown week. Champagne (for him), filet mignon, red roses, and a king-size bed. Then I was isolated with the others at the base, given so many last-minute shots, tests, and dry runs that I felt like a check mark on an endless to-do list.

But I made it. On a sunny Tuesday morning, the *Conestoga* roared up into a bright blue sky. Billions of people watched us set out for a new world.

Free fall was a relief after the crush of the launch. We'd be floating in zero-g for seven months. Archie and Paolo were a little green around the gills at first, but they got their sea legs soon enough. For me, it was as easy as swimming.

The tedium of a long voyage set in once we established our routine. Cramped quarters, precious little privacy, and not much to do once we were past the moon. I checked my instruments, sent data packets back to Mission Control, took my turn in the galley. Then on day 37, I tossed my cookies so suddenly there wasn't even time to grab a barf bag. Everyone laughed, no one harder than Paolo and Archie.

For three days, nothing wanted to stay down. Didn't feel like zero-g effects. More like a bug. Chandra, the medical officer, took my vitals. No fever, blood pressure normal—for these conditions. When she took an EPT stick from the supply closet, I laughed. "No way. Brand-new implant when we got back from the desert."

"Just a precaution," she said. "By the book. Anything abdominal I can rule out is a plus."

The only plus was the symbol on the stick. The second one as well.

"Jeez." Chandra whistled through her teeth. "Protocol says—"

"I know." Pregnant personnel are restricted to ground duty. Pregnant personnel assigned to flight missions are immediately reassigned. That was why we both had the implants. A one-in-a-million chance, but mine was defective.

Human error? Technical glitch? For two years, we'd gone over every phase of the mission, tens of thousands of parts, maneuvers, systems—anything could go wrong at any time. We had reams of contingency plans. Every snafu had some kind of backup. Except this.

I zipped up my flight suit. "You have to tell Tom," I said. Another protocol. Information that might affect the crew or the mission had to be relayed to the captain.

"Yeah."

"Wait til tomorrow? I need to tell Pete first."

She put her hand on my arm. "Okay." She hesitated. "There's only one option. You know that."

I nodded. If one crew member becomes unfit to serve, the mission is aborted. It had happened once on the space station. Appendicitis. The whole crew had to evacuate back to Earth. And that wasn't possible for us, not in an orbital transit. Earth wouldn't be in the same position as when we'd left, and we didn't have enough fuel to realign. I *had* to be fit for duty.

"Tomorrow," I said.

My bunk was the only private place. I pulled the curtain across and leaned against the bulkhead, my hand on my still-flat belly. Chandra was right. And, in theory, that was a choice

I'd always supported. So why did I feel like I had to pick—my dreams or my future?

This was an exploration mission. Seventeen months on the surface. We didn't have the supplies or the technology or the infrastructure to start colonizing. That was decades down the road, and only if *we* succeeded.

When the communication window opened, I sent a message to my husband. I told him what had happened and what I had to do. The fourteen-minute delay for his reply seemed endless. And when it arrived, the words on the screen surprised me.

"Can't let you do that, Zoë," it said.

Before I could type my reply, the next message arrived. That one was from CNN, asking for confirmation.

Then all hell broke loose.

Tom and the rest of the crew stared at me as the queue backed up with message after message. Mission Control was furious. Two different generals sent conflicting orders from millions of miles away.

But the public response was instant and overwhelming. News sites headlined WELCOME FIRST MARTIAN BABY! Within an hour, I was the hot topic of blogs, newscasts, and water-cooler discussions all over the globe. A contest offered a million dollars for the person who named "The First Citizen of Space." It was a circus—and NASA had never been so popular.

The furor showed no signs of dying down, but at least Earth continued to rotate, and we lost the comm signal after a few hours. I went to my bunk, but didn't sleep much. When I got up, the screen held a terse communiqué from Mission Control: "Seventh crew member authorized."

I was relieved. I was scared. The rest of the crew did their best to hide their feelings. An order was an order.

The Surgeon General issued a statement. Barring any complications, the likelihood of transit-oriented problems in the next six months was low. The fetus was in a water-filled sac, exactly the sort of environment the crew had trained in for zero-g. As long as radiation levels were closely monitored, she believed a full-term pregnancy was entirely possible. Deceleration and landing, however, would require further consideration.

Would I still fit in my landing couch? What about my pressure suit—it wasn't designed to stretch. I'd never paid much attention in home economics, but the suit was just engineering, and I was able to make some alterations.

A few days shy of my eighth month, we began the descent to the surface. The baby kicked the whole way down. Fortunately, the landing was textbook: no system failures, no injuries, no unexpected terrain. And out the porthole, we could see the *Sacagawea* a hundred meters away, plumes of vapor wafting from its lower vents. Our ride home.

That first night, Rajuk broke out the bottle of whiskey he'd smuggled on board, and we toasted our places in history. I drank my share; all the medical texts said it wouldn't make much difference, not at that stage. No one knew what difference cosmic radiation and zero-g had already made.

The baby and the planet were both terrae incognitae.

I had studied Mars for more than twenty years. I wasn't prepared for how eerily beautiful and utterly alien it was. Everything was shades of reddish brown, no greens or blues. The horizon was too close, the sky too uniform, the lighting flat. Daylight was butterscotch, as if it were always afternoon, half an hour before dusk. At night, the two small, lumpy moons rose into the starry blackness, Phobos slowly in the west, tiny Deimos in the east.

I was, of course, restricted to the ship. For two weeks I had to watch as the others took turns out on the dusty metallic surface, kicking up puffs of iron oxide with every step. I could feel the floor vibrate as they opened the cargo bay, unloaded the rover, began to set up a base. It took a full day to anchor the *Conestoga*, turning her from a spaceship into a permanent habitat, for us, for future crews.

We had all cross-trained in each others' fields, so I was busy checking schematics, logging soil samples, monitoring pressure levels and hatch seals. I gave hand signals through the porthole as Tom and Paolo unrolled my inflatable greenhouse and moved the equipment in. As soon as they connected it to the Hab and its atmosphere, I started my own work.

The first seedlings were unfurling in the hydroponic tank when my water broke.

Chandra had set up the medical facility as soon as we landed; everything was ready. Like the Russians' rats, which gestated in zero-g, my labor was long and slow. The gravity of Mars— only one third Earth's—meant less strain, but less pull when I pushed. Finally, on day 266 of the mission, Mars day 52, I heard a loud, strong cry.

"It's a girl," Chandra said a moment later. I saw a red, wrinkled face, then she was on the counter, being weighed and measured and tested. "Only five pounds, a little underweight, but otherwise she seems remarkably healthy." Chandra laid her on my chest.

A few days later, a woman in Indiana would win a million dollars for naming my baby Virginia Dare Morrison—the first child born in the New World. But as she lay there, suckling for the first time, I murmured, "Podkayne of Mars," and we just called her Poddy.

The *Conestoga* had not been stocked with infant necessities, so we had to make do. T-shirts were diapers. Archie made a mobile from some color-coded spare parts and dental floss, dangling it above the hammock that hung in my bunk. A blanket became a snugglie; while I worked, I carried her like a papoose from another, older frontier.

I breast-fed her for the first eight months, not much extra draw on the closely measured rations. She got sponge baths, just like the rest of us. When she was teething, her cries filled the Hab—the bunks were only soundproofed enough to offer a bit of privacy—and the rest of the crew grumbled about lost sleep. But they watched her when it was my turn in the rotation to be outside, and she heard lullabies in four different languages.

Martian gravity is kind to toddlers. At thirteen months, Poddy massed eighteen pounds, but her chubby legs only had to support six as she pulled herself up and began to walk. It's impossible to childproof a spacecraft, but we blocked off the lab and the stairs to the upper level of the Hab, and strung tether cords across the hatchways. She could climb like a monkey.

She bounced and hopped the length of the greenhouse, laughing at the top of her lungs and bounding about in a way no Earth baby could. I sent vids to Pete, and they were replayed everywhere; a dance called the Poddy Hop was the new craze. Plans were made for a homecoming tour the next year: FIRST MARTIAN RETURNS.

But that *was* a problem, said the doctors.

Martian gravity *might* turn out to be sufficient for healthy growth. No one knew. Poddy's stats were being studied by scientists everywhere, and would provide the data for future missions. But travel in zero-g was not a possibility, not at her age. She was still developing—bones and muscles, neurons and connections. She would never recover from seven months in free fall.

Every member of the crew already had muscle-mass and bone loss from the trip out. I'd known from day one that once the mission was over, I'd spend the next two years in hospitals and gyms trying to get as much of it back as I could.

For Poddy, they said, the loss would be irreversible. Mission Control advised: Further study needed.

A month before takeoff, I got their final verdict.

Poddy could not return to Earth.

If she did, even as an adult, she would never walk again. She would be crippled by the physics of her home planet, always in excruciating pain, crushed by the mass of her own body. Her lungs might collapse, her heart might not take the strain.

"We had not planned for children," Mission Control's message ended. "We're sorry."

I read the message three times, then picked her up and kissed her hair. I'd always dreamed of living on Mars.

Future missions would bring supplies, they promised. Clothes, shoes, a helmet, a modified pressure suit with expandable sections and room to grow. From now on, they would carry extra milk and vitamins, educational materials, toys and games. Engineers had begun working on a small-scale rover. Whatever she needed.

The next ship *should* arrive in seven months.

Tom reassigned duties for a five-person crew. By the time the *Sacagawea* was ready for launch, Poddy was talking. Just simple words. *Mama, Hab, juice.* She waved her tiny fingers at the porthole as her aunt and uncles boarded: *Bye-bye Chanda, bye-bye Tom. Bye-bye.*

We would never see them again.

Like my great-grandmother, I was a pioneer woman, alone on the frontier. Isolated, self-sufficient by necessity. Did it matter, I wondered as I heated up our supper, whether it was a hundred miles of prairie, a thousand miles of ocean, or millions of miles of space that separated me from everything and everyone I had known?

I read to Poddy, after the meal. A picture book, uploaded a week before, drawings in primary colors of things she would never see: TREE, CAT, HOUSE, FATHER. For her Earth was make-believe, a fantasy world with funny green grass and the wrong-color sky.

GOODNIGHT MOONS

On the first of two hundred cold, black nights, Deimos and Phobos low in the sky, I sat by the porthole and cuddled my daughter, whispering as I rocked her to sleep.

Goodnight, Poddy.

Goodnight, moons.

GONE TO THE LIBRARY

The attic was hot on a late summer morning. Particles of dust swirled in the sunlight that shone through the west-facing window. Isabel Flanagan sat on the floor, her back against a heavy wooden trunk, a black marbled composition book in her lap.

She could hear the muffled roar of the vacuum as her mother cleaned the living room, two floors below. The house on Mercer Street had been in the family since the end of the Civil War; after her father's ship was sunk by a torpedo, late in 1944, her mother had supported them by taking in guests. Most were scientists who came to Princeton for conferences at the Institute for Advanced Studies.

Einstein lived a block away.

Izzy quietly turned the pages of the notebook. It had been her father's, when he was a boy, and was full of what looked like homework, with some doodles and games of tic-tac-toe. William Flanagan had died when she was just a baby, and other than a few pictures, the notebook was all she knew about him. She wasn't supposed to be up here—Mama frowned on rummaging and tracking dust through the house—but as long as the vacuum was running, she was safe. She turned another page just as the roaring stopped.

Izzy sat very still.

"Isabel?" Her mother called up the stairs. "We have errands to run, and you haven't finished your chores."

She sighed. Chores were *never* finished. Putting away dishes, folding pillowcases, setting the table. She put the notebook back into the trunk and stood up, tiptoeing to the attic door, her bare feet making no sound on the warm, worn wood. She was down the narrow stairs and in front of the bathroom before she answered.

"Just a second!"

She stepped across the pink tiles and flushed the toilet, giving herself an excuse, then went downstairs.

"There you are," said her mother. She had taken off her apron and was holding her pocketbook. She looked at the clock. "We have to get to the post office before it closes, and we need groceries. You know we have a guest coming tomorrow."

"Yes, Mama," Izzy said.

"Can I watch Howdy Doody when we get home?" Izzy pushed the cart down the canned foods aisle of the Shop-Rite. Her mother added creamed corn and green beans to the basket.

"*May* I. And what's the magic word?"

"May I watch Howdy Doody, *please?*"

"If there's time after we make the beds. We have a busy week ahead."

"I know, Mama."

Mrs. Flanagan wheeled the cart into a checkout line. "Now you can play the register game," she said, as if that were a treat. "It'll be good practice. School starts next week."

Izzy shrugged. She liked numbers, but adding up all the

groceries in her head as fast as the checkout girl could hit the keys wasn't exactly her idea of *fun*.

The cans of corn moved down the belt and the white tabs jumped up at the back of the machine with a soft *ka-ching*, like ducks in a shooting gallery. Twelve cents, four times, which was easy. Then the beans. The first one was thirteen cents, and she smiled, because there were four of them too, and that was fifty-two cents!

$$48 + 52 = 100$$

Inside her head, she could *see* the numbers, like puzzle pieces, slotting together perfectly to form a nice even dollar rectangle.

The checkout girl was fast. Izzy lost track, a little, when the roast went through—$2.37—because it was a big number and it ended with a seven. Those were hard because they almost never made nice shapes. But at the end, Izzy was only sixty-eight cents off. She looked up expectantly. Mama sometimes bought her a Tootsie Pop when her answer was close.

"Well, you've been out of school for a whole summer," her mother said, shaking her head. "Maybe you'll do better next week."

Izzy sighed and helped load the bags into the station wagon. By the time all the groceries had been put away and the last pillowcase had been fluffed and placed just-so, it was too late for *Howdy Doody*—again. She bit her lip. Once school started, there wouldn't be *any* afternoon TV.

It wasn't fair.

When her mother got out her mending box and sat down in the living room with a glass of iced tea, Izzy made her escape. Picking up her library book, she opened the back door without a sound and stepped out into the yard.

Newly cut grass clippings clung to her bare legs like jimmies on an ice cream cone, and her hair hung sweaty-damp on the back of her neck, but that was okay. For an hour or two, she was free to just sit and read.

She sat against the stone wall that separated their yard from the woods, grateful for the shade of the elm. She was near the end of a chapter in *Charlotte's Web* when she heard the solid *thwack* of a bat hitting a baseball. A second later a white missile whizzed over her head and landed in the underbrush beyond the wall with a swishing of leaves and a soft thud.

Silence, for a moment, then a babble of boys' voices. She stood up. In the yard on the other side of the Taylors' manicured lawn was a trio of crewcut boys. New kids, moved in last month. "Crap," one of them said. "It's in the woods."

He headed for the chain-link fence at the back of his own yard, and had one sneaker wedged a foot up before he looked through and swore again, "Shit. Blackberries. Big thorns." He pointed at Izzy. "There's no bushes under *your* wall. Get my ball?"

Izzy thought for a moment. The boy knew swear words, so she was kind of afraid to say no, but she wasn't allowed to go into the woods. Since she was little, her mother had warned her about thorn bushes and getting lost in the acres of trees. Besides, she'd heard older kids say parts were haunted, and if you walked in too far, you'd never get out again.

She looked at the wall. There *was* a gate, its hinges speckled with rust. Izzy didn't even know if it would open. She had tried the handle before; nothing budged. Last summer she'd poked around under the ivy with a stick and found a latch at the very top, but hadn't been tall enough to reach it.

Today she was.

"Okay," she yelled.

Izzy tugged on the bolt. Stuck. She tugged again and again. Finally, with a series of small squeaks, it slid open. She pulled the iron handle; the hinges made an ear-splitting screech. The gate opened about a foot, then stuck tight. She looked back at the house to see if her mother was watching, then squeezed through to the other side.

A soft verge of grass and dandelions grew at the base of the wall; the blackberries petered out at the edge of the Taylors' property. She pulled the gate not-quite-shut and looked for the ball, finding it quickly, too pale and perfectly round to be part of the natural chaos. It lay underneath a clump of damp leaves; she picked it up, disturbing a legion of rolly bugs and one fat salamander that slithered away into a pile of three flat stones. The top stone was painted with a faded red crosshatch.

That wasn't nature, either.

Curious, she squatted down. Beyond the stones was what looked like a narrow path leading deeper into the woods. She wanted to see where it led. Probably just more blackberries, but she'd been doing chores all day. Everything had to be tidied up, "neat as a pin," when guests were coming. After that, even blackberries sounded like an adventure.

Izzy walked to the verge of grass and threw the baseball as hard as she could, shouting, "Ball!" Through the chain-link she saw it land next to a birdbath and knock over a garden gnome. She headed away from the sudden clamor.

No one had used *this* path in a long time, that was for sure. Saplings sprang back, hard, against her bare arms when she pushed through. Twigs snagged at her ankles, and her white socks were soon covered with a carpet of tiny green burrs that would take forever to pick out. But it *was* a path, marked by more piles of rocks topped with the same red-painted crosshatch.

The woods were cool and quiet on a hot August afternoon. Izzy could smell the earth, almost sweet from decomposing logs, with a bitter undertaste from layers of fallen leaves. Except for the sound of her feet crunching along, all she heard were birdcalls and the occasional rhythmic *knock-knock-knock* of an unseen woodpecker.

The path ended at a falling-down wooden fence with a narrow stile, its boards warped and moss-covered. Izzy put one careful foot on the bottom step. It creaked, but held her weight.

She climbed up and sat at the top, her mouth open in surprise at the ruins of what had once been a large and elaborate garden, not just a backyard.

Spindly rosebushes arced their thorns over stone benches and a sundial. The edges of a gravel walkway were blurred with weeds; wildflowers grew waist-high. Dozens of bees droned lazily in midair. A huge maple tree, still thick-leafed with summer, blocked her view of the house. All she could see was a bay window, its top half a beautiful stained-glass peacock.

She sat on the stile for a few minutes, savoring the discovery, wondering if she should keep exploring. Going into someone's garden was different than walking in the woods. It was trespassing. If anyone still lived in the house, she'd get caught. They'd call her mother and *then* she'd really be in trouble.

And if this was a haunted house—

Izzy whispered a prayer and crossed herself, then climbed down into the garden. Gravel skittered under her sneakers and the bees flew off to a safer distance. Nothing else happened.

She stepped around a bush and barely stopped an out-loud gasp. The house was *huge*, with a tower and lots of old-fashioned windows, every inch covered in fancy Victorian gingerbread; all of it needed painting.

Now she was *sure* nobody still lived here.

Oops. In the driveway was a round-fendered Buick with a Princeton sticker and 1952 New Jersey plates, just like her mother's car, all legal and up-to-date.

Uh-oh.

Izzy stepped into the shadows and scrunched down. She listened for voices, but heard only bees. She eased along one side of the house, stepping carefully, her Keds almost silent. A wide porch held a line of peeling Adirondack chairs and wrapped all the way around the front of the house. *That* was even grander— stone pillars and more stained glass, greenish copper letters over the entrance that said THE BRAMBLES.

It was a mansion, the biggest house she'd ever seen in real life. But except for the Buick, it looked like no one had been here for years, like it really *might* be haunted.

She hesitated, then stepped up onto the porch, a board creaking underfoot.

"Hullo," said a boy's voice. "Have you seen a giant turtle?"

Izzy gave a little yelp and jumped back, whacking her elbow on a drainpipe. Cradling her arm, she looked around to see who'd said that.

It took her a moment to notice that the massive front door was open, just a crack, a foot in a brown leather oxford wedged into the gap.

"How giant?" she asked. Her brain was full of other questions, but that was the first one that came out of her mouth.

The shoe moved and the door opened to reveal a boy a year or two older than her, sitting cross-legged on the floor. He made a circle with his arms, wider than his body. "Bigger than this."

"Wow. Is he missing?"

"No. Just hiding. He's very old. Grandaddy sent him for my daddy's birthday. He's magic."

Izzy tried not to laugh, because that would be rude. She liked to *read* about magic—*Mrs. Piggle-Wiggle* and *Mary Poppins*, even if Mama and the nuns thought those books were nonsense— but she knew it was never true in real life. "Sure he is."

"Not my Daddy. Lotion."

"*Lotion?*"

"My turtle."

"That's a funny name." Even for an imaginary pet.

"He's Chinese," the boy said, as if that explained everything. He stood up and pushed the door open. He had short brown hair and was taller than her by a couple of inches, but she could tell there was something wrong with him. One side of his forehead looked like a dented can, and his eyes didn't look straight at her, just a little beyond.

Oh. Real. Imaginary. They were probably about the same to him.

"Who're you?" he asked.

"I'm Izzy. I live on Mercer Street, on the other side of the woods," she said, slowly, the way she talked to kindergarteners at school.

"I'm Bibber." He stopped and shook his head. "No. The man from the bank says I'm too old. Now I have to be Robert." He looked from side to side, as if someone might be hiding on the porch, then whispered, "*You* can call me Bibber."

"How old *are* you?"

"Twelve. Last month."

"Oh." Older than she'd thought. "I'm going to be nine. In December." She leaned against one of the pillars. "Do you live here?"

Bibber nodded.

"Must be a really big family."

"No. Just Higgins and Cook and Mrs. Addison, the housekeeper. She's having a Day Off."

"How 'bout your mom and dad?"

"Mommy died having me and Daddy's in the war hospital. He's sleeping and he won't wake up."

"I'm sorry," Izzy said.

"I know. That's why the bank man makes the rules for me." Bibber pointed at the doorway. "You wanna come in?"

"I guess so." He didn't *look* dangerous. Izzy was curious, and she felt sorry for him. Not just because he was—slow, but because she knew how it felt to have a war steal your father.

Inside, the house was cool and dark. Heavy velvet curtains covered the windows and massive furniture loomed around her. The walls were covered with big, gilt-framed paintings of dead birds and fruit.

"I don't play in here," Bibber said. "Sometimes Lotion hides under the sofa."

They walked through three rooms with high ceilings and fireplaces tall enough to stand up in. A long table with twelve chairs around it was bigger than her whole dining room at home.

The next room was one she didn't know a name for, with high-backed leather armchairs, small side tables, and cabinets full of foreign-looking objects: curved knives, lacquered boxes, intricately carved figurines. Downstairs, her house only had a living room and a dining room, a kitchen and a utility porch.

"What did your grandfather *do?*" she asked.

"He went far away on boats and bought things." Bibber pointed to a cabinet. "He kept some of them."

"Yeah. I can see."

"This is *my* favorite room," Bibber said, opening the double doors.

It was a library, floor-to-ceiling bookcases with rails that held two wooden ladders. Beneath the stained glass was the bay window she had seen from the stile. It had a cushioned seat and its curtains were tied back; in the sunlight, the leather spines of the books—brown, tan, deep green—felt like an extension of the woods.

A table with two glass-shaded lamps sat in the center of the room, chairs on either side; a thick carpet with ornate dragons and flowers covered most of the parquet floor.

"Mine too," Izzy said. It was just the sort of room she'd read about and longed for, cozy and enclosing, a world of its own, the perfect place to sit for hours and hours, lost in a book. "Have you read all these?" she asked, her mouth open in wonder.

Bibber didn't answer. He looked down at the carpet, staring at the head of a curled green dragon.

"Bibber?"

"I can't read by myself," he mumbled. "I know all my letters—and my numbers—but—"

"Oh." That was the saddest thing Izzy could imagine. "Where do you go to school?"

"I don't. Nanny taught me lessons in here." Bibber sat down and wrapped his arms around his knees. "Then she went away."

Izzy hesitated, then sat down too. "Maybe the bank man will get you another Nanny."

"No." Bibber began to rock back and forth. "He says I am too old. Mr. Winkle has hair now, so I have to go to Vineland."

"He can't send you *there*!" she blurted. Vineland was the state school for the feeble-minded. It was terrible. It was so bad the nuns threatened to send kids there when they didn't do their homework, or failed a test.

"He is." Bibber looked like he might cry. "And I can't take Lotion."

How could they forbid an imaginary animal? Izzy traced a finger along the plush wool of a dragon's spiked tail. "When?"

"Next week," Bibber said. He wiped his eyes with the edge of his wrist. "I wanna stay here."

"I would too," said Izzy.

They sat in silence for a few minutes. Bibber stood up. "I'll show you my picture book."

"Okay."

He went over to a bookshelf, pulled out a pebbled black volume, opened it, shook his head, took out another. "There he is!" he said, sounding very happy.

Bibber laid the book on the long table and motioned for Izzy to come see. When she leaned over, she saw that it wasn't a real book, just a scrapbook, the pages filled with snapshots and postcards and ticket stubs. Someone had written names and dates and notes under each photo in black ink.

"That's my Daddy, on his birthday." Bibber pointed to a photo of a boy kneeling with his hand on the edge of what *could* be a large turtle shell. The rest was cut off by the camera. The caption underneath read:

10-year-old Bobby with a gift from Father,
all the way from Nanking China!

A birthday card pasted next to it said:

A puzzler for you, son. Can you find the secret?

"Wanna see another one?"

Izzy nodded.

Pinching the bottom corner between his fingers, Bibber carefully flipped the page. A larger photo showed two boys in knickers sitting cross-legged on either side of a huge tortoise, its shell painted with a complicated design of connected dots.

"See. Daddy and Lotion."

The caption read: *Bobby and friend Bill admire the new addition.*

Izzy gasped out loud.

The turtle was real.

And "Bobby's" friend was her father.

Izzy walked back through the woods, the light slanting low through the trees now, her mind full of questions. When she reached the gate in the stone wall, she felt like she'd been gone for hours and hours. But the boys were still playing ball, and when she went in the back door, her burr-covered socks hidden in the pocket of her shorts, her mother was just adding mayonnaise to a potato salad.

"Isabel, there you are," her mother said. "Where did you disappear to?"

"It was hot, so I took a walk." It was not a lie. She got a tumbler from the cupboard and drank a glass of water.

"Oh. All right. Supper's about ready. You can set the table now."

Izzy put the everyday plates and napkins on the Formica-topped table. The dining room was for guests. And Thanksgiving.

"Where did you go on your walk?" her mother asked, handing her a plate with cold chicken and salad.

"Um—down to the library." She crossed her fingers in her lap. That was *mostly* true.

"Good for you. It was too hot to bake anything, so I made an icebox cake for our guest tomorrow night. Don't touch."

"I won't." Izzy was used to FHB—family hold back. She had an Oreo for dessert.

Her after-dinner chores done—dishes washed and dried, table wiped down for crumbs—Izzy peeked around the corner into the living room. Mama was knitting and watching *Arthur Godfrey*. Good.

"I'm going to read for a while."

"Lights out at nine," her mother said, without looking up.

Izzy passed by her room and opened the door to the attic— slowly, so it wouldn't squeak. She climbed the narrow stairs in her bare feet and sat down next to the trunk and pulled out her father's composition book, hoping it would explain why *Bibber* had a picture of him.

The pages were full of what she thought was homework from the olden days: arithmetic problems, spelling words, and circled notes like "bring lunch Thurs!" Doodles and tic-tac-toe games lined the margins. She turned the pages, sweat dripping between her shoulders. Five more minutes and—

One of doodles caught her eye—it looked like a map, a wiggly line marked by circles—with a cross-hatch pattern! Below it, in capital letters, it said: SECRET PASSAGE OF THE LO-SHU CLUB.

Izzy felt a tingle of excitement flutter through her body; the attic was too hot to sit still. She slid the composition book into the back of her shorts and tiptoed down to her bedroom, snicking the door just shut behind her. A breeze fluttered the curtains at the open window. She lay down on her bed with relief.

The next two pages of the composition book were filled with tic-tac-toe games, a few with the usual Xs and Os, but more with *numbers* in the squares. Two people had played; the 4s and 8s were drawn different, in black and in blue ink. Around them were dozens of addition problems, like the drills Sister Lugori gave for practice, but all in batches of three:

$$4+9+2$$
$$3+5+7$$
$$8+1+6$$
$$4+5+6$$

She stared as the numbers started to make shapes in her head, then got up and sat at her desk with a clean sheet of paper, doodling and chewing on the end of a pencil, deep in thought.

"Lights out, Isabel," her mother called from the hall. "Big day tomorrow."

Rats. "'Night, Mama."

Izzy turned off her desk lamp and got into bed, counting to 100 five times before turning on her flashlight under the covers. She used her other hand to hold the notebook open and continued to study the sets of numbers.

Half an hour later, her neck had a crick, and she was fighting back yawns. Uncle. She was too tired to think any more. As she closed the book, a flash of bright red caught her eye. Izzy sat straight up, spilling the covers away.

Inside the back cover of the composition book, in red-ink capital letters, she read:

THE OATH OF THE LO-SHU CLUB.

ANY MEMBER IS MY BROTHER, AND I WILL RESCUE HIM

FROM DANGER, NO MATTER WHAT, NO MATTER WHERE.

I HEREBY SWEAR BY THE SIGN OF THE MAGIC TURTLE.

Underneath were two crosshatches and two signatures— William Flanagan. Robert Wilkins.

Bill and Bobby.

Izzy woke up with her arms wrapped around the composition book, the flashlight down by her feet. She stashed both under her mattress and went down to breakfast, racing through corn flakes and orange juice so that she could return to her quest. Then her mother got out the vacuum cleaner.

"I'll carry the Hoover upstairs. You can do the bedrooms while I tackle the linens. I want to be done ironing before the heat really hits." She patted Izzy on the arm.

After the carpets, it was dusting the dining room, setting three places with the nice china, mopping the kitchen floor. Izzy didn't have a free moment until after lunch—cold cheese sandwiches—when Mama went off to the cleaners and the bank and the drugstore. "I'll be back around three. Don't make a mess."

Izzy retrieved the notebook and sat at the empty end of the dining room table with a pile of scratch paper, adding up the mysterious numbers, until she suddenly smiled. There *was* a pattern. She was checking her work, one more time, when the doorbell rang.

She put down her pencil and went to the screen door. An older lady with blond hair and glasses stood on the front porch in a plain blue dress, a cardigan sweater folded over one arm. Probably from the Women's Club, raising money for the March of Dimes again.

"Can I help you?" Izzy asked.

"I'm Dr. Hopper. I believe I'm expected?"

Holey Moley. Their guests were usually scientists. Only big brains got invited to the Institute's conferences. But none of them had been a lady before.

"Oh. Sure. Please come in," Izzy said, in her most polite, talking-to-guests voice. "My mother will be home—pretty soon, I think." She held the door open, saw a suitcase, and remembered to ask, "Do you need help with that?" Dr. Hopper was on the skinny side.

"No, thank you. I can manage." She picked up the small Samsonite case and walked into the front hall. "What a lovely home."

"Thanks." Izzy thought hard. She'd watched her mother check guests in, lots of times, but—"Have a seat," she said, pointing to the dining room table. "Um—would you like some iced tea?"

"Thank you. It's rather warm today."

Izzy went into the kitchen and stood on a chair to get down one of the nice glasses. She had to tug, hard, at the frozen lever on the aluminum ice-cube tray, so the pieces came out broken; she crossed her fingers that wouldn't matter. She took the sweating glass and a napkin out to the table.

Dr. Hopper tapped a pencil on the pile of scrap paper. She looked up when Izzy came in. "I see you're working on the Lo-Shu problem."

Izzy *did* catch the glass before she dropped it all the way, but it still splashed enough to soak the napkin. She set them both on the table. "How do *you* know about that?"

"I'm a mathematician." Dr. Hopper took a sip. "Legend says it was first discovered by a Chinese emperor who noticed this pattern on the shell of a divine turtle, and thought it was an omen."

"A *turtle?*" Lo-Shu. *Lotion?*

"That's the story." She smiled at Izzy. "Mystical poppycock, of course. Although it *is* the most common variation of an order-three magic square."

"Magic? It isn't math?"

"In ancient times, it was both." She patted the papers on the table. "Why don't you sit down and show me what you know." She might be a guest, but she sure sounded like a teacher.

Izzy sat and thought for a moment. "Well, it's a square, three across, three up and down. And it has all the counting numbers with no repeats." She pointed to one of the diagrams.

$$
\begin{array}{ccc}
4 & 9 & 2 \\
3 & 5 & 7 \\
8 & 1 & 6
\end{array}
$$

"Do you see a pattern in the digits?" Dr. Hopper asked.

"I think so. The numbers going across add up to fifteen. So do the ones up and down. Every time."

"Very good. In this configuration, fifteen is the 'magic' number. It's the sum of every row, column, and diagonal."

"What can you do with it?" Sister Lugori sometimes gave extra credit for using math in real life.

"An interesting question." Dr. Hopper smiled. "Many of my colleagues believe that *pure* mathematics is about truth, unconnected to everyday life. It exists in a perfect world, where no—" She turned. "Oh, hello."

"Hello. Welcome." Mrs. Flanagan came in the front door and held out her hand. "I'm Eileen Flanagan. We spoke on the phone." She looked down at the stack of papers. "I see you've met my daughter, Isabel."

"Oh yes. We've been discussing higher mathematics."

"Really?" Mrs. Flanagan frowned. "I do hope she hasn't been a—"

"Not at all. I'm enjoying myself," Dr. Hopper said.

"Well, we do try to make our guests feel at home. Let me show you to your room." Mrs. Flanagan pointed toward the stairs. "You're at the back, on the right. A lovely view of the woods this time of year." She looked down at the suitcase. "May I take that for you?"

"No, thank you," said Dr. Hopper. "I can manage."

Sister Lugori had never told them that there was a perfect world where math could be magic. Maybe that was for older grades. Izzy had lots and lots of questions, but knew better than to bother a guest. So she helped toss the salad for dinner, and poured iced tea into the pitcher while her mother chatted with Dr. Hopper in the living room.

Dinner was almost fun. They had spaghetti, Izzy's favorite,

and Dr. Hopper wasn't boring, like most of their guests. She'd been in the Navy during the war, a WAVE, but in a laboratory, not a boat, working on something called a computer—a machine that could do arithmetic. Now she worked for some important company, building an even bigger one.

"They're the first machines man has created to serve his brains, not his brawn," Dr. Hopper said, buttering a roll. "One day children will use something like UNIVAC for their home-work, instead of memorizing multiplication tables."

Mrs. Flanagan frowned. "But how will they *learn* anything?"

"Rote learning is overrated, if you ask me. School time is better suited for teaching students to *use* numbers, to see the patterns and connections. That's what mathematics is really all about."

Izzy smiled. She had never told Mama about numbers making shapes in her head, but she thought maybe Dr. Hopper would understand. "I like story problems," said Izzy.

"Good for you. Why?"

"Because the answers make sense. I mean—" Izzy bit her lip, thinking. "Like if the question is about eggs, I'm pretty sure it's not going to be a fraction. Nobody takes a third of an egg to a picnic."

Dr. Hopper laughed and patted Izzy's hand. "You're a very practical thinker." She reached into the pocket of her sweater and took out a pack of Luckies. "Do you mind, Mrs. Flanagan?"

"Eileen, please. And not at all. Let me get you an ashtray." She went into the kitchen.

"What's your conference about?" Izzy asked.

"Let me see. Tomorrow's schedule has papers on combina-torics, twin primes, set theory, and imaginary numbers."

"Make-believe ones? Like, um—fifty blibbity-blips?"

Her mother thumped the ashtray and a book of matches down. "Isabel! That's no way to speak to—"

Dr. Hopper held up a hand. "It's quite a reasonable conjecture," she said, lighting her cigarette. "But no. It refers to numbers like this one." She took a mechanical pencil from the same pocket and wrote on the inside cover of the matchbook: $\sqrt{-1}$. "The square root of negative one."

Mrs. Flanagan shook her head. "I was an English major, and algebra was a long time ago, so forgive me if I'm mistaken, but when you multiply two negatives, isn't the answer always positive?"

"Yes," Dr. Hopper said. "Every time."

"So the square root of negative one is impossible."

"No, only imaginary." Dr. Hopper tapped the ash off her cigarette. "I know it sounds like mathematical fiction, but it's quite a useful concept in electromagnetics and quantum mechanics."

"Oh. I see," Mrs. Flanagan said with a tight smile.

Izzy could tell Mama was only being polite, but *she* had a bazillion questions about how numbers could be magic and how imaginary things could be useful.

"Are you lecturing about that at the conference?" Mrs. Flanagan asked. She began to stack the dishes.

"No, Dr. von Neumann and I are part of a symposium on recent developments in electronic data coding. Among other things, we're going to be discussing one of *your* favorite games." She turned to Izzy.

"Oh, yeah? Which one?"

"Tic-tac-toe. A bright young man at Cambridge—England— has programmed a computer called EDSAC to play. The Xs and Os are on a cathode ray display, like the picture tube in your TV."

"It's a pretty simple game," Izzy said. Why would the brains be talking about *that*?

"Exactly. It's a finite two-person game with perfect information."

"Huh?"

"Sorry." Dr. Hopper leaned back in her chair. "Let's see. First of all, it means there's no luck involved. No dice or spinner. A player—human or machine—can know every possible move, because there are only a limited number."

Izzy nodded. "I know. Nine."

"Not even close. Try 362,880."

"Uh-*uh*!"

"Truly." Dr. Hopper drew a tiny tic-tac-toe board on the matchbook. "So. On the first move you have nine choices where to put an **X**, right?"

"Sure. That's what I *said*."

"Yes. But what about the next move? One square is full, so the second player only has *eight* choices of where to put an **O**. Seven choices for the second **X**, and so on until someone wins. Or ties." She stubbed out her cigarette. "That big number—362,880—is nine times eight times seven times six—" She waved her hand in the air. "Etcetera, etcetera."

"Why on earth would anyone bother building a machine that plays games?" Mrs. Flanagan asked, setting the icebox cake in the center of the table.

"A game is a series of logical choices and decisions. Programming a computer to do *that* is the first step in replicating human intelligence. Tic-tac-toe will help us build a better future." Dr. Hopper stood up. "That cake looks scrumptious, but may I use your phone first? It's a local call. Dr. von Neumann."

Mama seemed to be in a bit of a daze. Guests usually talked about the weather, or how the Phillies were doing that season. "Of course," she said after a moment. "On the table, in the hall. Coffee?"

"Please. Black, two sugars. I'll only be a minute." Dr. Hopper put her napkin down beside her plate and left the room. Izzy heard her dial, then say, "Johnny? It's Grace. Are we still on for breakfast tomorrow?"

Izzy lay in her bed, looking out at the stars, and thinking about numbers. She knew they were useful, but hadn't known they could be *magic* until Dr. Hopper said so. And *she* was at the Institute, with Einstein, the smartest man in the world, so it must be true.

Numbers and Vineland—and her father—made her toss and turn, unable to sleep. The boy who wrote in the notebook had sworn to rescue his best friend, but Bill couldn't save Bobby from the war. He hadn't even saved himself.

What if *she* took the oath and kept their promise?

Izzy could rescue Bibber from Vineland.

The next morning, Dr. Hopper went off early in a taxi. While Mama packed up cookies for a Women's Club meeting, Izzy snuck upstairs and filled her pockets with chalk and pencils and a pen. She tucked some scrap paper into the composition book that held the secrets of the Lo-Shu Club, and waited until she heard the station wagon leave.

Izzy left a note—*Gone to the library*—and headed into the woods, pulling the gate almost shut behind her. When she reached the stile, she climbed over, chalking a mark onto the garden side, then crept along the edge until she could peer through the big bay window, one pane open to catch the summer breeze.

Bibber lay on his stomach, moving a line of toy soldiers around a fort made of blocks. Izzy tapped on the glass.

He looked up, his round face filled with a smile. She climbed over the sill and put her finger to her lips—*Shh*.

"Why are we being very quiet?" he whispered.

"So your housekeeper can't hear us."

"Oh. She won't," Bibber said. "She is in the kitchen with Cook. She leaves me alone until my lunch." He shrugged. "Unless I make a big noise."

"What time do you eat?" Izzy asked in her normal voice.

"Lunchtime."

That wasn't much help, but she guessed they had until noon, at least. Plenty of time. "Do you know how to play tic-tac-toe?"

"Uh-huh. I'm pretty good."

"Okay." As she drew the grid on a piece of scratch paper she said, under her breath, "I swear by the sign of the magic turtle." Out loud she said, "You go first."

Bibber clutched the pencil and drew a tiny X in the top right corner, and she followed with an O below it. She wanted to put her O in the center—that was always the best move—but she had to let Bibber win the first game. When he drew his third X in a row, he laughed. "I told you. I am good at this."

"Yep. So you get to draw the next one."

He did, his tongue in the corner of his mouth, concentrating on making the four lines straight as arrows.

There. They had both drawn the secret sign that made them members of the Lo-Shu Club. "Now you are my brother," Izzy whispered. "I will rescue you from danger." She made an O in a corner square, and let Bibber win again.

"Where do you keep Lotion?" she asked.

"He crawls all over the downstairs. Right now he's under the table."

"Here?" Izzy moved one of the chairs and squatted down. On the carpet was the biggest tortoise she had ever seen—even bigger than the one in the Bronx Zoo. At her movement, he turned his head and looked at her with a yellow, reptilian eye.

"How do you get him to come out?" They couldn't lift him, not even the two of them. He was the size of an ottoman.

"I wait until he's hungry," Bibber said. "Wanna feed him now?"

"What does he eat?" Lotion looked as prehistoric as a dinosaur, with scaly front feet the size of salad plates. He might eat *any*thing.

"Fruit and stuff. Leftover salad. Watch." Bibber pulled a handful of slightly squished blue-black grapes from his pocket. He piled them a few feet away from the edge of the table.

In real-life slow motion, Lotion rose up and lumbered forward, one leg at a time, until he stood over the grapes. He extended his surprisingly long neck, lowered his head, and mashed the grapes into his mouth in three pulpy bites.

"It's bad to feed him on the rug," Bibber said, pointing to a purple stain that was *almost* invisible against the elaborate floral design. "Mrs. Addison says."

"I see why." Izzy stared at Lotion's back. She'd planned to draw the Lo-Shu numbers on him with chalk, but the pattern was already carved into his shell. Nine squarish plates, the center one marked with five dots like Monopoly dice, faint traces of red dye still visible.

Lotion was already magic.

The rest was up to her. Izzy circled the room, chalking $\sqrt{-1}$ on the four walls, the window frame, the doors, the table, and the shelves of each bookcase.

"What are you doing?" Bibber asked.

"Making things imaginary." It was pure math, so it would exist in a world of its own, unconnected to the one where Vineland waited.

When she had marked everything important, she made one more circuit, checking her work, then turned to Bibber. "Can you sit on Lotion?" The tortoise had eased back down to the floor, and lay with his eyes shut. He *looked* sturdy enough.

"Sure. Sometimes I even ride him." Bibber straddled the carved shell and scratched the tortoise on the top of its leathery head.

Izzy circled the room again, taking a few books from the shelves: *The Adventures of Huckleberry Finn, Treasure Island, The Wind in the Willows, Peter Pan, The Jungle Book, The Wizard of Oz.* She added a dictionary and the scrapbook with the picture of their fathers to the stack.

Then, stepping around Bibber, she arranged the eight books in a square, three on a side, with Lotion at the center to make nine.

"What are those?"

"Books I think you'll like."

"I can't read." Bibber frowned. "I told you."

"You will. This kind of math makes a perfect world." She drew four crossed lines in ink on the soft skin on the back of Bibber's neck and filled the grid with numbers.

$$
\begin{array}{ccc}
4 & 9 & 2 \\
3 & 5 & 7 \\
8 & 1 & 6
\end{array}
$$

Magic turtle, magic boy.

"That tickles." Bibber laughed.

"Sorry." She patted his hair. "But we need tic-tac-toe to build a better future." She thought for a minute. When she blew out the candles on her birthday cake, she made a wish. "Keep Bibber out of Vineland," she said aloud, then added, *"Please."*

There. That was the last magic word she knew.

"Now you can climb off Lotion and live happily ever after," she said. She patted his head again and turned toward the door.

"Are you leaving?" Bibber frowned. "Don't you want to be happy ever after, too?"

"Oh. I—" Izzy looked around at the light-filled room of books and light and comfortable chairs, a room she'd always dreamed of. Plenty of time to sit and read, uninterrupted, no vacuuming, no dishes, no guests, no nuns. *Nobody* telling her what to do. She smiled. "Well, maybe just until lunch."

Bibber nodded. He settled back onto the rug and busied himself with his toy soldiers and his fort. Izzy walked to a bookshelf, tilting her head to look at the titles on the spines, and finally selected *The Lilac Fairy Book.* She carried it over to the window seat and sank into the cushions with a contented sigh, the book open on her lap.

A soft breeze from the window, fragrant with roses, riffled the pages. She leaned against the sill: the flowers were in full bloom, walkways crisply white, the grass neatly clipped. Beyond the sundial, where there had once been a mossy stile, an unbroken line of trees stretched endlessly in all directions, rising up and up to meet a cloudless blue sky.

Izzy smiled. All the time in the world. She bent her head to a fairy tale, and began to read.

HOUSEHOLD MANAGEMENT

In September, the autumnal gales beset London with exceptional violence. For a week, the wind has screamed and the rains have beaten against the windows like beasts in a cage.

In weather such as this, few people come calling. The streets are deserted, not just in Marylebone but throughout the city. Although an inconvenience for many, it is a respite for those like myself, a woman of a certain age whose pleasure it is to sit by the hearth with a cup of tea and a good book, safe and secure from the elements raging outside.

For others, however, it is an unbearable confinement. Such is the case with my upstairs lodger. For two days I have heard him pacing incessantly across his rooms, back and forth, up and down, muttering and cursing. He has lived in my house for a score of years, and I can tell from the dull sound of his tread that his usually keen spirit is chafing against the involuntary inaction occasioned by the storm.

After I took up his breakfast this morning, I was granted a brief reprieve, but within the hour his pacing ceased and he began to play his violin. Not a melody, merely the sound of a bow being swept across loosely tuned strings. The noise is dreadful. I try to ignore it and go about my chores, dusting the shelves and airing the linens, but the infernal, funereal wailing and screeching is worse than the howling of the wind.

He is, perhaps, the worst tenant in all of London. His malodorous chemical experiments have left stains on each rug in his rooms, he is prone to insomnia, and the drapes on every window reek of his strong tobacco. To his credit, his payments are princely, his rents promptly paid, and in his dealings with me he has always been unfailingly polite.

In return I provide him lodging, prepare his meals, accept packages, relay messages, greet visitors, and manage all the domestic details of his life. It is an arrangement that ordinarily suits us both.

But this noise is intolerable. With a sigh, I stopper my ears with cotton wool and go into the kitchen to do the washing up. The running water helps to cover the sound. When the last of the plates is dry, I pour a cup of Earl Grey and venture back into the parlor. Quiet? I remove the cotton wool. The screeching— oh bliss—has stopped. I settle into my favorite chair by the fire with one of Mrs. Southworth's novels and—

Bang!

I nearly jump out of my skin. On the mantel one of my little Staffordshire dogs teeters and threatens to tumble.

From above I hear faint ticks as bits of plaster—my plaster— fall from his sitting room wall to the floor. He is a man of keen intelligence, and when he is working on a case, when he has a focus, his considerable energies are channeled. But when he is idle, when he has naught to engage his nimble mind save foolery, bravado, and cocaine, he endeavors to relieve the tedium in any way he can. His weapon of choice, I know from past experience, is a revolver.

Bang! Bang!

I close my book, mutter a mild oath of my own, and go to

the kitchen to prepare his luncheon tray. Perhaps once I am upstairs, I can put a stop to this by distracting him. It will be the matter of a moment to notice something amiss—there is always something amiss in *his* rooms—and to feign the sort of hysteria he believes is so common to my sex. By the time I am "settled" on his sofa, he will have poured the tea himself, given me a tentative, almost avuncular pat on the hand, and be most attentive for a few minutes. Long enough, I hope, for me to slip the revolver into my knitting bag and spirit it away. He will notice its absence, of course, but in his current state will likely assume that he has mislaid it, and the ensuing search through his unholy mess of papers and apparatus will afford me a few moments of peace.

Bang! Bang! Bang! Bang! Bang!

Oh, dear lord. He has already reloaded. Tea and hysteria will not be enough to divert him today. I hesitate for a moment, aware that I am well-paid for his proximity, which *does* entitle him to a certain amount of privacy. I am loath to interfere, no matter how outrageous his actions. But his eccentricities have tried my patience to the breaking point. I am a reasonable landlady, and have more than a modicum of understanding. He has never known the gentle rule of a woman, and cannot help himself.

But I can.

And I shall.

For my own sanity, not to mention the furnishings, I have found that, on extremely rare occasions, it is in my best interests to see that he is kept occupied.

In a city such as this, it is a matter of no difficulty whatsoever to obtain any number of noisome items that might be required for the management of a proper household: ratsbane, flypaper, tablets for the complexion, even the Paris green wrapper from a box of sweets, the dye soaked off in a bowl of scented water. In a well-appointed kitchen, a practised hand such as my own can use the most common of ingredients to create a marvelous variety of unique teas and unusual recipes.

My late husband was fond of my cooking, and I made certain that he had a nice tea each afternoon. An almond cake, perhaps? With enough sugar, any residual bitterness was well-disguised. Or a savory biscuit—a strong curry powder masked any underlying flavor. He was especially fond of the pleasing and unusual tang of my clotted cream.

Alas, our marriage was brief. He had a temper, but my baking *could* coax him into the parlor at teatime. I would pour, then offer him a plate of cookies, often taking one myself. They do not affect me in the least. I began taking Dr. Mackenzie's arsenical complexion wafers after the first bout of our honeymoon, increasing the dosage gradually over time. When he was contrite, my husband so admired the roses in my cheeks and my bright eyes. To this day, I am the very picture of health, and quite immune to my own delicacies.

Bang! Bang!

It is time. I wrap myself in my heaviest shawl against the weather and leave the house with a covered basket of scones and cream for Vivian, a neighbor whom I began visiting when the storms began. She has been feeling more and more poorly with each passing day, and grows convinced that her husband, an apothecary and uncaring fellow, may be tiring of her. She is beginning to suspect foul play.

My visits seem to cheer her. Each afternoon I listen to her sad tale, and if she begins to weep, I proffer a linen handkerchief, laundered in a soap of my own formulation, dabbed with a bit of my special elderflower water. I have assured her that my clever—if vexing—lodger might be of assistance. Today I will insist that she accompany me back to the house.

It is the least I can do.

SPONDA THE SUET GIRL
AND THE SECRET OF THE FRENCH PEARL

Times were lean. The capital had been under siege for months and supplies were running low. In the provinces, drought and disease had decimated the herds and parched the fields at the height of the summer growth. Food prices had soared, and little was available, even on the clandestine market, which was bad news indeed for a scrawny thief called Natto.

He stood at the counter of a tavern by the wharves one afternoon, nursing a tankard of sour ale and hoping to glean a lead that might put some coins in his rattling purse. Natto was not overly particular about where his profits came from, as long as they came steady and often. They had not, recently.

"It's called the French Pearl," a man named Petin said from one of the tables. "The emperor has offered a prize of a thousand royals for the man who discovers its secret and delivers it to him. A thousand royals!" He slapped his hand onto the battered wood for emphasis.

Natto's mouth twitched. Petin was no friend of his, nor was his companion Masquiat. They would not speak if they noticed his attention. He brought out his little knife and began to dig at his filthy nails, feigning disinterest as he listened.

"All that for a pearl?" Masquiat asked.

"Not just any pearl. Some say it has the power of everlasting life." He looked over to the counter, smiled, then signaled for another cup of dark wine. "But its secret is hidden in a wizard's lair." He shook his head and drank.

"I see," said Masquiat. "And how do you come to know this?"

"Three nights ago I made the acquaintance of a man, a tax collector, who had been traveling for a fortnight. Twitchy fellow, always scratching at one part or another. He was forced by weather to spend the night in a wretched village at the back of beyond, and saw the wizard himself."

"He told *you?*"

"After a fashion. He was not used to strong drink. A small investment on my part loosened his tongue." Petin shrugged. "After he'd had a few, I relieved him of his purse, and was quickly repaid."

"Where is he now? Describing your ugly face to the authorities?"

"No. Sadly, late that evening, he lost his footing out on the docks. But not before he drew me a map." Petin opened his coat, allowing a glimpse of ragged paper.

"Then why are you not gone in search of this so-called treasure?"

"What, do battle with a wizard? I have a bad leg." Petin laughed. "And I like it here just fine. But wine does not come cheap. This map will bring a pretty penny when I find a fellow with a few pieces of silver who fancies himself an adventure."

"True," Masquiat said. "But where will you find such a man?"

"I have prospects. Tomorrow I'm meeting—"

"How much?" Natto said, standing.

Petin looked up. "I don't barter with scum like you."

Natto laid his hand on his knife. "How much?"

"More than your purse has seen in years."

"How much?"

There was silence, the sort that made a few men reach for their weapons. Finally Petin smiled. It was not a friendly smile. "Ten silver crowns. Take it or leave it."

Natto had the money, but only just. Still, ten crowns against a prize of a thousand royals? He would be a fool not to take *that* wager. "Done," he said. He dug the coins out and laid them, one by one, onto the wood.

Petin picked the first up and bit it to be sure, then reached into his coat and took out the map. "It is yours."

The paper was rough, the map crude, but Natto recognized the capital and its bay and the steep mountain ridges surrounding it. One road wound up and through them, a jagged line that ended at a labeled X. "Fossepuante?"

At the sound of that name, Masquiat quickly made the sign of warding. He stared at Petin, who laughed.

"Ah, now even *you* see why I was in no hurry to make the journey." Petin quickly scooped the coins from the table and jabbed his knife into the wood. "I would wish you good luck," he said, waving a hand, dismissing Natto, "but in times like these, one hates to waste a wish."

The whitewashed room of the outbuilding behind the inn was small and extremely tidy, two walls lined with shelves of jars and bottles containing powders and tinctures of a hundred hues and consistencies, all neatly labeled. A wide table ran the full length of a third wall. At one end stood a row of brown crocks filled with a pale opalescent substance. At the other, next to a stack of leather-bound books, paper flags sticking out from a dozen pages, a chemist's apparatus consisting of flame and stand and beaker bubbled with a smell faintly reminiscent of a Sunday roast.

Standing at the center of the table a trim, bespectacled young woman in a linen smock, her dark hair pulled back into a tail, took up a knife and a thick block of suet and minced the brittle beef fat into a small pile. She weighed the shreds, made a notation in a lined journal, and added the mass to the beaker, stirring it with a glass rod. She was reaching for a jar marked POTASH when a knock came at the door.

"Anna?"

"Who's there?" she called.

"Just me, Sponda."

"Oh. Come in, come in."

A red-haired girl entered the room.

"This is a nice surprise," the chemist said, kissing her on the cheek. "I didn't think I'd see you until supper."

"I wanted to bring this back, before it got mixed up with my kitchen spices." She set down a jar marked DRIED ROSEHIPS. "It worked like a charm. That so-called tax collector only stayed one night."

"A bed full of itching powder will do that." Anna replaced the jar on its proper shelf.

"Do you really think he was here to steal your—?" She glanced at the row of crocks.

"The emperor is offering a thousand royals as a prize, Sponda. That's temptation enough."

"I suppose. How's it coming?"

"I made a new batch this morning, and added both lime and potash. That helped the texture. It's creamy as butter, and spreads as smooth."

"But—?"

"But the flavor still isn't right. Nor the color. Too white. This morning I boiled some carrots. Once the paste dries, I'll grind it into powder. A pinch should make the spread yellow enough for a proper presentation."

Sponda stuck a finger into one of the crocks and licked off a bit of the creamy substance. "It doesn't taste *bad*," she said.

"Makes me think of a farm, wholesome and fresh. But I don't think I'd care for it on my morning toast."

"I know. And it's that last bit of caring that's going to get us the prize, if I can figure it out before anyone else does." She smiled. "The first man-made, edible fat. Cheap, plentiful, and will last for *weeks* without going rancid. Imagine what that will mean for the poor, not to mention the navy, which I think is the emperor's first concern."

Sponda licked her finger again. "It does need a little something."

"I know, and I've got a few ideas. We're getting close." Anna smiled. "But it won't get done if I stand here talking."

"I'll leave you to your experiments." Sponda went to the door, stopped, and blew a kiss. "Supper's at six. Raisin clootie for dessert."

Natto was uncertain of his purchase; Petin could not be trusted. But having spent the silver, he readied himself for a journey. He stole a full wineskin and a loaf of bread, and bedecked his coat with a handful of rude charms and amulets in case there *was* a wizard.

He made further enquiries about the village, Fossepuante, and was not reassured when, a number of times, the response was widened eyes and the sign of warding. But he had been able to discover that there was an inn. Not the finest lodgings, although one man said that his supper had been the most delicious suet pudding he had ever eaten.

This was the first good news Natto had gotten since he bought the map. He fancied himself a gourmet—although glutton would be closer—and nothing delighted him more than a good pudding.

Putting that thought ahead of any others, he set out from the capital on a crisp autumn morning. Once he passed the army checkpoints that ringed the city he had the road to himself. It narrowed as it climbed, the sound of his horse's hooves muffled by a carpet of fallen leaves, scarlet and golden and copper. The trail had not been much traveled; few had business in the region beyond the cliffs, which was populated by more cattle than people.

From the summit, the land spread out before him, vast grazing plains mottled by rocky outcrops. The once-green fields had been parched to pale straw, the streams mere trickles. Late in the afternoon on the second day of his travels, saddle-sore and weary, he was glad to see a thin plume of smoke on the horizon. Fossepuante.

He rode for another hour and was close enough to see the outlines of low stone buildings when the smell hit him. The putrid emanations made his eyes water and his gorge rise, filling his throat with the sour remnants of his midday meal.

What foul protection had the wizard devised to guard his treasure? Natto touched the amulet on the collar of his rough wool coat and muttered an oath under his breath. He yanked on the reins and forced his horse to advance in the direction of the village.

The stench grew stronger with every step. Natto pulled his neckerchief up over his nose, the odors of tobacco, wine, and sweat masking, for the moment, all other smells. That moment did not last long.

By the time he reached the first outbuilding, the horse was slogging and Natto imagined that his own face was the tint of a greenish putty. His stomach roiled, and for the first time he could remember, even the idea of ale was repellent.

Fossepuante consisted of a single muddy street bordered by a handful of stone buildings, half-timbered and thatched. The sign on the two-story inn said THE POND AND CLOOTIE in faded gold letters. Next to it was a stable. The horse whinnied at the oddly welcome odor of manure.

At a distance of some hundred yards was a large barn surrounded by wooden fencing. Scores of animals lay in heaps amid swarms of flies; above them hung a dreadful cloud of grayish vapor.

The wizard was clever, Natto thought. Unless one *knew*, this would seem an unlikely hiding place for a valuable jewel.

He dismounted and thought for a moment. He had no plan but to rely on the fortunate opportunities upon which thieves thrive. He would arrange a bed for the night, and a meal, then insinuate himself among the locals. The pearl was bound to be a topic of conversation, and when ale loosened some tongues, information would be revealed.

He tied his horse and entered the inn.

The interior was close and dim, but the air smelled more of spice and ale and smoky peat than it did a charnel house, for which Natto was grateful. He lowered his neckerchief and breathed deeply.

To his right, a narrow staircase rose up into silent darkness. Three wooden tables sat to his left, each with an unlit candle. They formed a half-circle in front of a soot-stained hearth, coals glowing. Before him lay a long counter topped with varnished wood; behind it, shelves held an array of tankards and pottery mugs and a few cork-stoppered bottles.

At the far end, an open doorway admitted the sounds of clanking pots and the sizzle of meat. He waited for a minute, then two, and finally rapped his knuckles on the countertop.

"Just a tick," said a woman's voice. "I'll get this off the fire and be right there."

He heard another sizzle, then a loud hiss and watched a wisp of fragrant steam wander out and disappear among the rafters.

A moment later a red-haired, red-faced young woman filled the doorway, wiping her hands on an apron. She wore a blue smock and a pair of heavy woolen trousers, her hair tied back in a kerchief. She was, to put it politely, a *sturdy* lass, fully as tall as Natto himself, and half again as broad.

"I'm afraid you'll have to wait til morning to unload your wagon," she said, shaking her head, but smiling. "My Da's just now banked down the fires."

Natto inclined his head in what might, in such a rustic place, pass for a bow. "That would be unwelcome news indeed, if I had a wagon."

The woman's smile faltered. "Everyone comes here has a wagon or a cart. How else would you carry your stock?"

"A horse with saddlebags is quite enough for me."

"In your saddlebags?" She wrinkled her nose. "First I've heard of that. What parts are you selling, then?"

Parts? Natto was unsure how to answer. "Depends on what parts you're buying." He smiled, his most unctuous and charming smile, reserved for the ladies.

"Whatever doesn't go into the pot." She stared at him. "You're not in the trade, are you?"

"What trade is that?"

She nodded, as if she had been given the answer to a question Natto had not heard asked. "Ah, you poor man. No wagon and no nose?" She pointed to the outer door. "Most can smell the plant from miles away."

"Oh," Natto said. "That. Yes, I did notice a change in the—air—as I rode in." He touched his neckerchief. "What is it?"

"Da's the renderer. Boils down what's left after the butcher's taken his cuts. Bones, skin, gristle, fat." She put her hands on her hips. "Any of that in your saddlebags?"

"No, I'm not in that line of work."

"I see. And what *is* your line?"

"Tax collector." It was the first thing that came to mind. A traveler's occupation, and it should put an end to any further inquiries, tax collectors not being the most popular fellows. "I'm on my way back to the capital. I saw your sign, and hoped you'd have a room for the night."

"Fancy that. And where might you be coming from, if you don't mind me asking?"

"I set out this morning from—" and here Natto stopped, because he had very little knowledge of the provinces.

She looked at him for a moment, then said, as if it were amusing, "Maulde?"

"Yes," Natto said quickly. "Maulde. Charming place."

The girl's mouth twitched in what Natto thought was a most unbecoming way. "Isn't it just," she said.

"Do you have a room?" he asked after a moment of awkward silence.

"I will in about half an hour. I'll need to go up and change the linens." She pointed to one of the tables. "Sit there and have a pint while I tidy up. Ale and supper's included with the tariff. May I ask your name, sir?"

Natto thought as quickly as he was able. "George," he said. "George, uh, Petin!" *There.* Now if any trouble followed him to the capital, Petin would be the one pursued.

"Very good, Mr. Petin. I have a nice front room." She named a price that was, nearly to the copper, what his purse contained. It was not a princely sum—he'd paid more for a single meal, when he was flush—but his circumstances had been drastically reduced by the purchase of the map.

He nodded, laying his coins on the counter as she drew a pint from the cask and set it on the nearest table. She put the coins in a wooden box.

"What's on offer tonight?" he asked.

"I've got a lovely pud coming off the hob in about two hours. Pearl barley, mutton, and mince."

Natto's mouth watered.

Sponda rapped on the outbuilding door. "It's me."

"Come in." Anna wiped her hands on a stained towel. She saw Sponda's face and frowned. "What's wrong?"

"Another stranger. Says *he's* a tax collector, too, just like the first."

"Did he say anything else suspicious?"

"No, but when I asked where he'd ridden from, he didn't seem to know. I suggested Maulde and he was quick to agree."

"Maulde? That's two hundred leagues from here!"

"I know," Sponda said. "Once he failed that first test, I did what you said, if another came. I told him there'd be pearl barley in the pud, and I saw his eyes go wide for just a moment."

"If he startles at the word *pearl*, he could be from Mége-Mouriés laboratory, snooping around to see if I've made any progress."

"He doesn't really look the chemist type, but I think you're right. It's been an age since we've had two guests in a week, and neither one of them a rag-and-bone man with reason to stop here."

"True. But that may be good news."

"*Why?*"

"Well, if the prize had been claimed, there'd be no need to send spies around to snoop, would there?"

"I suppose not. I gave the one we have a pint of ale and told him I needed to make the bed, then took the back stairs here. Thought you ought to know."

Anna sighed. "Take the rosehips." She pulled the jar from the shelf.

Sponda nodded. "Should I set a place for you at supper?"

"No. Save me a slice. I'll eat it cold later. I think it's best that this stranger doesn't meet me yet. But listen closely to what he says. See if you can find out what he's up to."

"I will. I told him ale comes with the room, so I'll make sure he gets full value." Sponda slipped the jar into her apron. "What if he keeps on, though?"

Anna looked around the room and laughed. "I'm a trained apothecary. And I had three brothers. I'm a wizard at concocting any number of unpleasant surprises." Her face took on a curious look. "And I just had an idea."

"What?"

"I'll tell you later, once I work it out. We're too close to claiming the prize for *anything* to get in our way."

The small upstairs room faced the road. It had a washstand with a pitcher and a chamber pot, and a narrow bed covered in a quilt that smelled like roses. Natto combed the road dust out of his beard and put on his other shirt, to make a good impression with the locals. He descended the stairs at dusk. The air now smelled of spiced meat and tobacco, and at one of the tables sat a large, ruddy man with a pipe in his mouth, his ham of a fist wrapped around a tankard.

He looked up at the sound of footsteps. "Hello, hello!" he called. "I'm Ian Cubbins. You must be the tax-man." He indicated the chair across from his with a wave of his pipestem. He called to the kitchen, "Sponda! Ale for our guest!"

The red-haired woman came out and drew another pint for Natto. "The room to your liking, Mr. Petin?"

"It's fine."

"Supper in an hour." She put his ale down and returned to the kitchen.

The man puffed on his pipe. "Do you like steamed pudding?"

"I do. It's a favorite of mine," Natto said, telling the truth for once.

"Then you're in for a treat. My daughter's won ribbons at the fair for her puddings." He lowered his voice. "It's the suet that does it. Fresh from the plant, every day."

"I see." Natto's ale caught in his throat. He liked a good suet pudding as much as any man, but until now had not really considered its origins. "You make a lot of it?"

"Aye. Hoof disease hasn't hurt *my* business none." He smiled, showing a few more teeth than Natto had expected. "You know what they say, 'All's not butter that comes from the cow.'"

"Um. Yes. You've been doing this a long time?"

"Since I was a lad. Learned from my Da, and he from his on back to—" he waggled his pipe at the uncountable years. "Yourself?"

"I'm in—revenue," Natto said. Another semblance of truth. He took money in, just not for the benefit of the government.

"Never was much with figures, me. My Sponda keeps track of the accounts, since her Ma passed." He ducked his head in a moment of remembrance then took a long and hearty swig of ale. "Ready for another?" he asked.

"Can't say that I'd mind." Natto drained his mug.

Ian was a friendly host, although his conversation ran mostly to the weather and odd facts about cattle, neither of which interested Natto. But the ruddy man saw to it that their mugs stayed full. Natto felt a familiar and pleasant glow by the time Sponda brought out their supper.

"Here you go," she said, setting the platter down. It held a golden-brown mound nearly the size of a man's head, giving off a wonderful savory steam.

Ian cut into the crust, and the gravied meat and grain spilled out, redolent of onions. He placed a generous portion onto Natto's plate. "There now. Tell me if that isn't the finest pudding you've ever had."

Natto would have replied, but his mouth was already full. He nodded enthusiastically, and half an hour later, asked for another helping of ale with his dessert.

When he was sated, Natto sat back in his chair. Sponda cleared the table, refilling his ale yet again.

"Da?" she asked.

"No more for me," her father said. "I'm off to bed. Dawn comes early." He patted her cheek and went upstairs.

Sponda filled a mug for herself. "You liked the pudding, then?"

"It was magnificent. What's your secret?"

"Well, suet and tallow *are* our bread and butter," she answered.

"Though I suppose few in the capital have had butter since the troubles began."

"True enough. It's gotten too dear for the likes of me."

"We get a bit, now and then, from farmers who still have herds, but even here it's become scarce." She looked thoughtfully at him, then nodded to herself. "Da says he doesn't miss it much," she continued. "Says he's more of a greaves and drippings man."

"They have their place," Natto agreed. He took another pull at his ale. "You should move to the capital. A cook like you would be in high demand."

"Perhaps I will, someday," she said with a hint of a smile. "Now, tell me about your journeys. We don't get many visitors, and it must be so interesting, traveling all over, in search of—" She paused to wipe an errant crumb from the table. "I'm sorry, I've forgotten what it is you said you're after."

Natto's ale-fuzzed brain almost blurted, "The French Pearl." He stopped himself, but could think of nothing else and "Hidden treasure," was what came out of his mouth.

"Treasure? Really?"

"Well, in a manner of speaking." He tried to recover. "That is to say, assets that have not been properly reported, or—" He gathered what were left of his wits. "—uncollected revenues. Very important, especially in times like these."

"Silly me," Sponda shook her head. "Here I was thinking you meant chests full of pearls and jewels and gold coins."

Natto almost spilled his ale. Was this the opportunity he had been waiting for? "Those would certainly be of interest to—to my superiors. As an innkeeper, you must hear all sorts of stories. If they turn out to be of use, there might be a generous reward."

"I see." She stood still for a moment, then smiled as if she had just remembered something. "You know, there is an odd fellow on the outskirts of town, and there are rumors—"

"Yes, yes. What sort of rumors?" Natto sat up eagerly.

"Well, I don't like to gossip," she said. "But he's rather secretive about what he does in his cottage. Strange lights and eerie noises, all times of the day and night." She leaned toward him and lowered her voice. "Some say he's a wizard."

"Really?"

"Some say."

"Where is this cottage?"

"I'll show you, after breakfast." Sponda looked back at the kitchen. "But now, I'm afraid, I've got the washing up to do and a few things to prepare before morning."

"Then I will say goodnight." Natto drained his ale and stood on his second attempt.

"I hope you sleep well," Sponda said, and again her mouth twitched. It was most unbecoming.

Anna came into the kitchen as Sponda was drying the last of the plates. She put her arms around the innkeeper and kissed the back of her neck. "How was supper?"

"The pud came out well. Yours is on the table, under the cloth."

"And the stranger?" She sat down and picked up a fork.

Sponda made a face. "He's not a spy. Just a common thief."

Anna raised an eyebrow, her mouth full.

"While I was out talking to you he opened the cash box. Nicked back what he'd paid me, and three coppers besides."

"Ah." She swallowed. "I'm a little relieved, though. Why do you think he's *here?*"

"It wasn't just chance. He's looking for something. Every time I said the word *pearl*, he jumped out of his britches."

"Really." Anna sat quiet for a minute, then smiled. "In that case, I think we ought to give him one."

Natto spent a restless night. He was up several times to relieve himself, not uncommon after an evening of drinking, and every time he crawled back into bed, his bare legs itched like the devil. Chafed from two days of riding? He was miserable, and thoughts of the mysterious wizard flittered through his head as he tossed and turned.

At first light he heard the father rise and lumber down the stairs in his hobnailed boots. Natto buried his pounding head in the pillow and tried vainly to fall asleep, but gave up after another hour. He used the chamber pot again—it had become rather full—and put on his trousers. Downstairs, breakfast was laid out on the counter: tea and oatcakes with jam. They were plain fare, hearty and filling, and he had two helpings.

He hadn't seen the red-haired woman, so when he'd finished, he picked up his plate and cup and took them to the doorway. "Miss?" he called.

He heard the noise of a door shutting at the back of the kitchen, and a moment later she appeared, pulling off a heavy cloak. "Sorry," she said. "I was out back, um, checking to see if the hen was laying." She saw the dishes in his hands. "Here, let me take those for you."

"Can you show me the odd fellow's house?"

"What? Oh, yes, him." She glanced toward the back door, then hung her cloak on a hook. "Give me fifteen minutes to put away the breakfast things." She gestured to a skillet and a mixing bowl. "Did you pass a pleasant night?"

"Not really," Natto said. "A lot on my mind, I guess. My duties and all."

"Sorry to hear that. Care for a fresh cup of tea?"

"Thank you, no." He rubbed his temples, which throbbed from lack of sleep and what his acquaintances called ale-head. Perhaps a hair of the dog that bit him? It was still part of the tariff, even if the coins hadn't stayed in the till. Stupid cow hadn't noticed. "I don't suppose it's too early for a pint?"

She smiled. "My Da's been known to breakfast on it himself. I've just washed up the tankards. Go and have a sit. I'll bring you one."

Natto went and stretched his legs in front of the fire. In another minute he had a drink in front of him.

"By the time you're done with that, I'll have the kitchen tidy, and we'll take a walk outside," Sponda said.

The first ale of the day always seemed to have a special tang to it, Natto thought. And it was just what he needed. By the time Sponda came out of the kitchen, fastening her cloak, he felt ready to take on the world again.

"There's a nip in the air," she said. "You'll be wanting your coat."

And the amulets on it, Natto thought, if the rumors turned out to be true. He climbed the stairs, and once in his room started to unbutton himself, but the chamber pot was far too full. He put the lid on and shrugged into his coat.

"Pardon me," he said from mid-stairs, "But the—um—pot—is a wee bit full and I'm afraid I need to—" He felt his face turn red.

"I'm a country girl. I understand," she said. "I'll empty it when I get back. In the meanwhile, you can use the stables. Aim for the straw, if you please."

Natto mumbled his thanks and went outside. The smell of the rendering plant hit him like a blow. He felt the oatcakes stir. He pulled his neckerchief up, and went to the stables. When he came out, Sponda stood bareheaded in the middle of the street, looking down the road, her hand up as if she'd been waving. But she merely tucked an errant strand of hair back into her braid.

"Better?" she asked.

"Much," he said, his voice muffled by the cloth over his mouth. "How do you stand the smell?"

"I've lived here my whole life. You'd get used to it, after a time."

Natto found that highly unlikely.

They walked down the road until Sponda stopped and pointed to a building twenty yards on the other side. "See that smoking chimney? That's his cottage. Name's An—drew. Andrew Barnes."

"Thank you," Natto said. He squared his shoulders. "I think I can take it from here."

"Of course. You have your duties." She nodded, then walked back in the direction of the inn.

He waited until she was gone, then crossed to the same side of the road as the cottage so that his approach could not be seen from its windows, feeling rather clever for thinking of that. He slunk along a rail fence until he reached the one-story hovel. Its yard was bare mud, strewn with rocks. A bundle of feathers was nailed to the front door.

His knees trembled as he eased around the corner and peered in a grimy side window. He saw a small room, barely furnished with a single chair and a table in front of the hearth, where a low fire burned. The only other light came from a candle at the center of the table. Around the base of the candlestick lay an array of small objects—a key, a bone, a few coins, a black box, a bundle of herbs.

Natto drew in his breath. Wizard's goods, if ever he'd seen them. Beside the table, standing in shadow, was a bespectacled man, slender as a girl, with a thick mustache, his hair in a dark tail, as had been the fashion in the capital a few years back. He wore a long purple robe with a matching skullcap. As Natto watched, he picked up the bone, muttered some low words, then replaced it in a different position.

Clutching the amulet on his coat, Natto felt the hair on his arms and the back of his neck prickle with fear. He held his ground and watched as the wizard practiced his arcane rites.

After what seemed like an endless time, the wizard picked up the square black box, half the size of a man's fist. He muttered some incomprehensible syllables, then slowly opened it and removed a velvet pouch. He undid the drawstrings, muttering incessantly, and tipped the contents into his hand.

It was a pearl, a magnificent jewel, fully as large as a gooseberry.

Natto gasped, and quickly put his hand over his mouth, lest his position be revealed. He drew his head back a few inches.

But the wizard had not heard. He stood for several minutes, tipping his palm toward the candlelight, rolling the sphere so that its color shifted with each movement—white, then silver, lavender, pink, pale green, white again—as if he had captured a rainbow, transformed again and again in the flickering light. Finally, with a small sigh, the wizard replaced the pearl in the velvet bag, and the bag into its box.

He looked around the room, his glance passing over the window without pause, then stepped over to the hearth. He set the box on the mantel and slowly tugged loose a brick waist-high on the right side. Behind it was a dark opening, into which he put the box, muttering all the while. He replaced the brick, returning the hearth to its original appearance.

Stepping back to the table, he reached into a pocket, and in one fluid motion tossed a handful of sparkling powder toward the candle flame. The room filled with a blinding, blood-red flash.

Natto jumped back, sightless for a moment. When the spots in his vision had cleared, he peered into the tiny room again.

The table was bare. The wizard was gone.

Was he? Natto waited for a minute, five, ten, then broke into a jig. He had done it! He had found the pearl! In two days' time, he would be a wealthy man. He walked cautiously around the cottage, nerves quivering, but the yard was also empty. He circled one more time, to be absolutely sure, then put a hand on the latch.

Nothing happened. His hand didn't burn, there was no fire, no demons. He went inside. The room was dim, lit only by the coals, but it smelled like sulfur. He made the sign of warding and touched the amulet, kissing his fingers and murmuring the only prayer he knew. Then he walked to the hearth and ran his hands down the bricks on the right side.

It took him a few tries to find the loose one; he pulled it out with a grating sound, loud as a trumpet to his own ears. He stood motionless for a full minute before daring to reach into the hole, but encountered only the smooth leather of the box. He opened it, felt the round weight of the velvet bag, and tipped the pearl into his hand.

Even more beautiful up close. He gazed at it for a moment, then roused himself. There would be plenty of time for admiration once he was away from this wretched village. He replaced the pearl and bag and slipped the box into the pocket of his coat.

It took all his will to stop himself from whistling on the way back to the inn. Even the stench from the rendering plant seemed less odious.

Sponda was behind the counter, a ledger and an inkwell in front of her. She looked up from her accounting. "Were you successful?" she asked, smiling. "Did you find treasure?"

"What?" Natto nearly jumped out of his boots, then remembered his presumed errand. "Alas, no. The man is an eccentric, to be sure, but there was nothing to collect, tax-wise."

"Sorry," she said. "I seem to have sent you on a fool's errand."

"It is a frequent part of my job. I'll be heading back to the capital as soon as I gather up my things." He turned toward the stairs.

"Wait," she said. She put down her pen. "The least I can do is wrap up some bread and cheese for your journey. Perhaps one last ale—for the road?"

It *was* a long ride, and his wineskin was nearly empty. "Thank you. That's very kind." He sat at one of the tables.

She fussed a bit with the tap, then set the tankard onto the wood in front of him. "I'll make you up a lunch." She went into the kitchen.

When she heard the door open, Anna looked up from the chest in the corner of her laboratory. She folded her academic robes—the purple of St. Zatar's—and replaced the horsehair mustache in the box with her other disguises. Her family had been fond of theatricals, and although St. Zatar's had admitted women for some years, there were still traditionalists who disapproved; she had often found it easier to navigate the campus as a gentleman scholar. She closed the lid of the chest and turned around. "Did he fall for it?"

"Hook, line, and sinker," Sponda said, laughing. "What *was* the thing he found?"

"Just a sphere of camphor, dipped in a few coats of *essence d'orient*." She saw the blank look on her lover's face. "It's a mixture of carp scales and varnish." She pointed to a piece of linen spotted with lustrous patches that shone like a rainbow. "Wouldn't fool a jeweler for a moment, but *he* was delighted."

"How do you know?"

"I stayed to watch. Once the flash powder hit the candle I had plenty of time to scamper up to the loft and hide."

"You're the most clever girl I've ever known." Sponda gave her a hug. "He's headed back to the capital. When he tries to fob off that 'pearl,' he'll get his comeuppance."

"But we won't get to see it. Where's the fun in that?"

Sponda stared. "You're up to something."

"I am. You put the powder in his ale this morning?"

"I did."

"Then it will be an interesting afternoon," Anna said. "What are you making for supper?"

"Biscuits and drippings."

"I do love your biscuits."

"It's the buttermilk," Sponda nodded. "It makes them sing in your mouth without you putting a name to any particular flavor."

Anna stared at her. "That's it!" She jumped up and began jotting notes into her journal. "That's exactly what my spread lacks. Buttermilk will add a creamery flavor, it will keep for ages, it can't spoil—" She threw down her pen and flung her arms around Sponda. "Now who's the clever one? I'm going to make a new batch this afternoon. We'll try it at supper, and if it passes the taste test, *we'll* be on our way to the capital!"

They capered around the room for a minute in a most unscientific way.

Anna finally stepped back. "I must get back to work. But when your Da comes in, send him back here. He'll play along, won't he?"

"Da loves a good prank as much as anyone."

"Good." Anna turned to her well-stocked shelves and handed Sponda a metal canister.

"What does *this* one do?"

With a wicked grin, Anna told her.

When Natto had finished his ale he went up to his room. As he lifted his rucksack, the two pints he'd consumed that morning began to vie for his attention, too urgently to make it to the stables. He looked down and saw the empty chamber pot was back under the washstand.

With a sigh of relief, Natto opened his fly and aimed at the pot, closing his eyes for a moment as the pressure inside him was released in a long and satisfying stream. He shook himself off and opened his eyes to do up the buttons of his trousers, then shrieked in surprise.

His piss was blue.

He began to shake. It had been too easy, getting the pearl. He should have known there'd be a spell. He grimaced as he looked down at himself, but saw no difference on the outside.

"Is something wrong?" Sponda called from the bottom of the stairs.

"Yes!" Natto cried.

"I'll be right up."

"No!" He stared at his open fly. "I'll come down." He did up his buttons, then put the lid on the chamber pot and took it downstairs.

"Is there a problem with the pot?" Sponda asked. "I just cleaned it."

"I know, but—" And here Natto stopped cold, because although he was not a man of courtly manners, there were some things that weren't proper conversation with a woman, even if she was just the renderer's daughter. "Hell," he said. "Look."

She took off the lid. "Oh dear. Not again."

"Again?"

"More than once." She tilted her head and looked at him. "When you were at the wizard's house, you didn't eat or drink anything, did you?"

"No, nothing."

"Hmm. Touch anything, other than the seat of a chair?"

"Well, I might have—"

"That's it, then. He's got protections everywhere. He whisks them off when he knows there'll be company, but you took him by surprise."

"Will it go away?"

"Usually does. Unless—" She stopped and lowered her eyes. "I don't mean to be bold, Mr. Petin, but did you notice any other changes in your—your manhood?"

Natto shook his head. "No. And I did look."

"Well, *that's* good. One poor fellow had his turn black on him. Within a day it had shriveled like an old carrot. Nothing the doctor could do, by then." She took the pot and set it on the floor, replacing the lid. "'Course he deserved it. He was a black-handed thief. And a *stupid* thief, if you ask me, stealing from a wizard."

"Only a fool," Natto said in a small voice. He felt the blood drain from his face and barely made it to one of the tables before he sat down with a thump. "Might I have another ale? It was, as you can imagine, a bit of a shock, seeing—" He stared at the pot as his voice trailed off.

"Of course. Best thing for it. The more you drink, the faster you'll get rid of it." She went behind the counter and busied herself with the tap. "Oops. I'm sloppy this morning." She held the tankard up by its rim and wiped it off with a rag, removing the cloth with a flourish when she set the ale down. "That ought to help."

"Thank you." Natto gripped the mug in both hands and downed half of it in one mighty gulp. "I'll finish this and be on my way."

Sponda shook her head. "You can't ride, not in your condition."

"Really, I must return to the capital." Natto felt as if the box in his coat pocket were burning a hole through the wool. "Urgent business."

"What if complications set in, out there—?" she gestured toward the window and the desolate country beyond.

"Hmm. Perhaps one more night might be prudent. The same tariff?"

"Three coppers more," Sponda said. "It's the week-end."

"Oh." He withdrew his purse and counted out all the coins from the day before.

Sponda glanced at the cash box, then put the coins into the pocket of her apron and smiled. "I'll even make another pudding. Dessert, this time. Let me see, how about spotted dick? Oh, dear. Perhaps not tonight." She thought for a moment. "I know. I'll make you a Pond. It's my Da's favorite."

"Sounds delicious." Natto drained his ale. "I think I'll have a little lie-down." He bent to pick up the chamber pot, but she held up her hand.

"I'll rinse it and bring it to you. Only way to tell if the ale is doing its job is to start afresh." She refilled his tankard, wiping it off with the same cloth before pushing it into his hands. "There. Take that up with you."

Natto did. He drank it sitting on the edge of the bed until she brought the pot. Once she was safely downstairs, he took off his pants and, handling himself gingerly, produced a steady blue stream. He looked down. *That* was still its original color, at least. He bit back a moan and crawled under the covers.

He tossed and turned for a while, bare legs itching again, but had had so little sleep the night before that he eventually fell into a fitful slumber, full of disquieting dreams. When he woke, late afternoon light slanted through his window. Cooking smells wafted up from the kitchen, and his stomach growled. The growling set off another urge, and he stood, stretching. Standing over the chamber pot in his loose shirt, he reached down and gripped his—

Natto screamed.

It was black. So were his hands.

He stood in panic for a moment, then felt a warm dribble run down his leg. Blue.

He began to weep.

Eventually he dressed and trudged downstairs.

"Well, well. You're still with us, then?" Ian called from his table by the fire. He had a mug and a basket of roasted chestnuts, the floor littered with papery skins.

"I'm not on my way home, if that's what you mean." Natto pointed to the tap. "May I?"

"Help yourself. Sponda's up to her elbows in flour, and I'm not of a mind to move."

Natto drew a mug of ale and perched on the very edge of his chair. "Is there a doctor nearby?"

"Why, are you ill?"

Without a word, Natto held out his hands, the palms and fingers stained black.

"I see." Ian stared, then cleared his throat. "Is it only the hands, lad?"

Natto shook his head.

"Your johnson too?"

When Natto nodded, the older man huffed. "You *do* need a doctor, and soon." He clasped Natto's shoulder. "But you're in luck. He's already on his way. Coming after supper to take a look at my aching foot." He tapped his boot on the floor. "It's just a touch of the gout, but Sponda worries."

Natto drank his ale. "Does your doctor have any experience with my—problem?"

"Aye. More than most." He smiled and reached for a chestnut.

It was only the two of them for supper. Sponda stayed in the kitchen, seeing to the pudding. Natto didn't think he had an appetite, but the biscuits were light and flaky and the drippings rich, and he found himself mopping his plate.

"Save some room. Sponda's Pond is the queen of puddings." Ian lit his pipe.

"I look forward to it." Natto excused himself and went upstairs. He had been drinking steadily, which made his predicament seem somewhat foggy and distant, but every twenty minutes nature's calling jarred him back to his desperate reality. Ian was sympathetic and tried to keep his spirits up by telling stories of a life in rendering, which had to do with unidentifiable lumps, and why you shouldn't confuse soap and candle tallow. Natto listened numbly, released by a knock at the door.

"There's the doctor now," Ian said and went to let him in.

The doctor was a tall, thin man with spectacles and a Van Dyke beard. His graying hair was pulled back into a tail. He wore a suit of brown worsted and carried a black leather bag. "Ian, good to see you!" he said in a reedy voice.

"Doctor Reynard. Good of you to come. You're just in time for dessert. Sponda's made a Pond."

"Excellent. No one makes it better than she." He set his bag on one of the empty tables.

"It's done!" Sponda called from the kitchen. She came out bearing a platter on which sat a caramel hummock, the top sunken, the crust glazed and crackling along the edges. The steam smelled like a summer's day.

"That," Ian said proudly, "is our Pond." He picked up a knife and a large spoon. "Watch close now. This is the best part." He sliced into the pudding, revealing a whole lemon in the center and releasing a glorious oozing stream of golden syrup. It flowed until it had formed a pool of rich sauce that filled the platter like a moat. "See," he said. "Now it's an island in its own pond. Doctor?"

"Please."

Ian cut a generous slice and ladled the sauce over it.

"George?"

"What? Oh, yes, thank you."

When everyone had been served, Sponda said, "What do you think, Da?"

"The crust is splendid—our good suet—and oh, my dear, the sauce! Lemon and sugar and sweet butter. It may be the best you've ever made."

Sponda clapped her hands in delight. "Do you really think so?"

Natto dug in eagerly. "Oh my god," he said, true reverence in his voice. "This is—this is—it's spectacular."

The doctor took a bite. "Is that butter I taste?"

"What else could it be?" Sponda laughed.

"I thought you said it was scarce." Natto scraped his fork through the last of his sauce.

"It is," Sponda replied with that odd, twitching smile. "But we make do."

"You do, indeed," said the doctor. He smiled at her, then pushed his empty plate aside. "Now, Ian, about that foot?"

Natto sat patiently while Ian's foot was examined. It didn't *look* any different than an ordinary foot. Dirtier, maybe. But the doctor tutted and poked, then dug into his bag for a jar of salve.

"Thanks. What do I owe you?"

"Let me see, with the salve, it's," he tapped a finger on his beard. "Twenty silver crowns."

"I have it right here." Ian pulled a cloth bag from his pocket.

"Twenty crowns!" Natto blurted.

"That's the usual rate," the doctor said. "I see that you're surprised. I imagine a doctor's visit is much, much more in the capital."

Natto had no idea. He'd never been to a doctor in his life. And a good thing, too. It cost a bloody fortune.

"George has a bit of a problem, if you don't mind," Ian said.

"Certainly." The doctor turned to Natto. "What's the trouble?"

"I—it—never mind." He would just have to wait until he got to the capital. A doctor's visit might cost more there, but it wouldn't matter. He'd be able to afford it.

"Don't be daft, lad," Ian said. "You need help. You—" he looked at Natto and snapped his fingers. "Ah. I think I understand. Excuse us for a moment." He pointed to the door. "George?"

Natto hesitated, then followed him out into the street, pulling his neckerchief up as he did.

"You get used to it," Ian said. He leaned against the wall of the building and lit his pipe. "Are you short of funds, lad?" he asked in a kindly voice.

"At the moment. I just need to get back to the capital. I'll see my own doctor there," he lied.

"You won't make it to sunrise, as fast as that's spreading."

"*What?*"

Ian shook his head, slowly and sadly. "George, you seem like a good fellow. Let me ask the doctor to put your treatment on my account."

"You'd do that?"

"It's a sorry world when you can't rely on the kindness of strangers."

Foolish old man, Natto thought. "Thank you," he said aloud.

"'Course I'd need some collateral," Ian continued. "We may be country folk, but I wasn't born yesterday."

"What sort?"

"That mare of yours is a fine animal and I could use another horse until the loan's repaid."

"That seems reasonable." Hah. Natto laughed to himself. He'd get the salve or ointment or tincture, whatever it was, and be saddled and gone hours before first light.

"Good. Now what about the rest?"

"Rest? What do you mean?"

"Well, around here, horses aren't so dear. Ten crowns is a good price. But that leaves another ten unaccounted."

Natto's brain raced. What else did he have to offer? He came up empty, just as his bladder reminded him that it was not. He stepped toward the stable. "The ale," he said.

"Oh, me as well. It's the only bad part about drinking, I say."

They did their business over the straw. Ian looked over and sucked air through his teeth in a startled hiss. "Good god, lad. You didn't tell me it was that far along. It's a miracle you're still alive."

Natto heard a squeak come out of his mouth. "It could *kill* me?"

"Aye and it's an ugly, painful way to go." Ian buttoned up. "You *need* what the doctor has." He put an arm around Natto's waist. "Tell you what. Let us help, and I'll find a way for you to work off the other ten crowns."

Here? Not on your life, Natto thought, then reconsidered. He had no intention of paying the man back, so it didn't matter if it was ten, twenty, or fifty crowns. As soon as he had the medicine, he'd scamper. It wouldn't be the first time he'd left town owing money. "Yes, thank you. You're very generous."

"Good lad."

The doctor was alone when they returned. "Sponda's in the kitchen," he said. "It's just as well. She told me what she knows, and it's nothing a woman needs to see."

"I'd like to put George's treatment onto my account," Ian said.

"I can do that." The doctor hesitated. "But, Ian, I must warn you. If Sponda is correct, the curative costs much more than a common gout-salve."

"I understand," Ian said. "I'll do whatever it takes."

Natto moaned. If he got in *too* deep, Ian might come after him. No. He smiled. Ian would come after *Petin*. Natto sat down and held out his hands.

"His johnson, too," Ian added. "Black as night."

"I see," said the doctor. "Blue urine?"

"Yes."

"How long?"

"Just since this morning," Natto said.

"That's good. If you'd waited until tomorrow, there would have been nothing I could do." The doctor opened his bag and took out an amber bottle with a cork stopper, then laid a mortar and pestle on the table. "How much do you know about medicine, Mr. Petin?"

"Not much."

"That's all right. I'll explain it in layman's terms." He clasped his hands behind him. "You see, the four humors of the body are each governed by a particular mineral compound." He stopped and looked at Natto. "Understand?"

"I think so."

"Fine. Now a blood disorder calls for iron. Lungs react to salt, and the stomach and intestines to charcoal. The bladder—and its related organs—respond only to calcium." He paused in his recitation. "Still with me?"

Natto shrugged.

"However, when it comes to a specialized ailment such as your own, the minerals themselves also become more specific. The *only* known cure is a compound of crystallized calcium carbonate, powdered and dissolved in an acetic elixir."

"And you have all that?" Natto asked. His head spun with every word.

"This is the elixir." He held up the amber bottle. "It's a formula of my own devising. Extremely difficult to distill in the proper proportions."

"You're a lucky man," Ian said. "He's one of the few doctors in the realm that keeps a supply on hand."

Natto felt anything but lucky. "What about the other part. The calcium bit?"

"In a separate vial," the doctor said. He rummaged in his bag, pulling out bottles and jars, frowning more and more. "Oh dear," he said. "It appears to have fallen out on the ride here."

"What?" Natto said in a panic. "Then how will you—?"

"I'll have to improvise." He tapped his beard again. "It doesn't *need* to be laboratory grade," he muttered. "I suppose any pearl would do."

"Pearl?" Natto's mouth was suddenly dry.

"Yes." He picked up the mortar and pestle. "I crush it in here, then add it to the elixir."

"*Crush?*"

"Crush, pulverize, grind up." The doctor waved his hand. "For *that* component, technique is largely irrelevant." He placed the mortar on the table. "Once you've downed the mixture, you'll be completely cured in twenty-four hours' time."

Natto shook his head. "I changed my mind. I'll just wait and see what happens."

"Mr. Petin. Do you not understand the gravity of your condition? Waiting is simply not an option."

Natto sat very still for a long time. Without the pearl, he had nothing. But even he had to admit that nothing was better than dead. With a deep, painful sigh he reached into his coat pocket and—

His pocket was empty. He tried the other one. Empty as well. With a great, gulping sob he laid his head on the table.

"Now, now, lad," Ian said, patting his shoulder. "It's not as bad as that. If you need a pearl to save your life, well, I couldn't look myself in the eye if I just stood by."

Natto raised his head.

"It's been in my family for—a while now. I'd reckoned on it as Sponda's wedding present, but—" he smiled. "I think she'll understand." From the pocket of his trousers he pulled out a small black leather box and handed it to the doctor. "Will this do?"

Natto gasped as the man opened the box and rolled the gooseberry-sized pearl out onto his hand. "Perfectly," he said. He dropped it into the mortar with a delicate *plink* and before Natto could say a word, crushed it into powder with a few deft motions.

"No. No. No." Natto moaned, but it was too late.

The doctor opened the amber bottle and tipped in the powder. The mixture fizzed and bubbled over the glass lip before settling. "There you are," he said. "Drink up."

Natto drank. The vile, acrid liquid burned his throat and when he belched, a few seconds later, it stank of fish and turpentine.

"Have some ale," Ian said. "To wash the taste out. And don't you worry about the pearl. It *was* a family treasure, but I can add it to the rest you owe me." He patted Natto on the shoulder. "Rendering is a fine profession. You'll work your tab off in no time at all."

When the soporific that Anna had added to the elixir had taken effect, and the man who called himself Petin lay snoring and drooling on the table, the others retired to the kitchen.

"I thought that went well," Ian said. "I picked his pocket clean as a whistle. He never felt a thing. 'Course he *was* a bit distracted." He cut himself a slice of Pond. "What was the black stuff?"

"Silver nitrate. Sponda wiped it on his tankard." Anna peeled off her beard, and began to remove the bits of spirit gum beneath. "It's one of my brother Roger's favorite pranks. Invisible until light hits it, then the stain lasts a good long while." She set the metal canister on the table. "I'll leave it with you, in case he needs another dose."

"Does it make the blue, too?"

"No, that's methylene. *That* you dissolve in his ale." She gave him the jar.

Ian looked at the chemicals, then sighed. "I can't believe you'll be gone in an hour," he said to Sponda.

"We have to take both horses before he wakes up."

"I know, but I'll miss you, girl. Every day."

"Me too, Da." She gave him a long hug. "But I'm not leaving you all alone. Now you'll have an assistant to keep you company."

"What do they say about small favors?" He kissed her cheek. "How long will you be in the capital, do you think?"

"Weeks," Sponda said. "Maybe months. We'll have to see what happens."

"This stuff of yours, you really think it might win the prize?"

"It has every chance," Anna said. "Even you couldn't tell the difference in the Pond tonight."

"That wasn't butter?"

"It was not." She smiled.

"I'll be swoggled. That was really your—" he stopped. "What are you going to call it?"

Anna patted her journal. "I've thought of dozens of possible names. The one I like best is a variation on the Latin word for 'pearl.'"

"Because of the way the suet fat looks when it melts?"

"Exactly. So I'm calling it *margarone*."

"That's a pretty fancy word for fake butter," he said.

Sponda laughed. "You'll get used to it."

WOODSMOKE

Every childhood summer is special. School is out and freedom beckons. Then comes a magic summer. A lake or a woods, a place far away from the everyday, a best friend, and songs that will forever resonate beyond ordinary frequencies. In memory, the sun will always be high in a cloudless blue sky, the evening light liquid and golden, the nights full of stars. There are many kinds of magic; each of them brings unanticipated change, opening doors whose thresholds can only be crossed once.

For Patricia Ann Maas that summer was 1963, and it began on the second Sunday in June.

Session One

> There's a long, long trail a-winding into the camp that
>   we love,
> Where the friendships are enduring as the skies above.
> Where nature is our refuge, and every tree and each rock
> Is a messenger of welcome, calling us to Camp Wokanda.

Camp Wokanda was only a two-hour drive from the city, but it felt like a pilgrimage. After the houses and the supermarkets and even the drive-ins had fallen away, Patty Maas sat in the back seat of her father's Buick, not quite holding her breath, waiting for the first of the landmarks that marked the boundary between her world and her parents'.

Lunch at the Green River diner, a cheeseburger and a Lime Rickey. The rusting car on a pole, thirty feet in the air, that marked the turn onto State Route 41. After that the flat fields became wooded hills and in another fifteen minutes, angling off to the right, Old Creek Road. Her father muttered about the undercarriage as he slowed down on the rutted, gravel surface.

Five miles now. Patty sat on her hands so her excitement wouldn't broadcast itself, and watched the land roll by her window. Trees arched over the road, closing it in like a cool, dark tunnel. Creeper vines covered fence posts and rocky outcroppings jutted from dense foliage as the hills steepened on both sides.

Finally she saw Slantin' Sal, the sandstone monolith canted over the road. Patty leaned out as they passed, looking for Wokanda wishing sticks. Sure enough, deep in the shadows she could see four twigs propped up against the stone. All was well.

When the car entered the shade of the enormous rock, she felt two things happen. One, the sudden coolness—and her own excitement—made her arms go all goosebumps. And two, in a transformation invisible to her parents, Patty Maas began to disappear. Patty was a reasonably good girl, a B-plus sixth grader who dutifully, if not enthusiastically, went to Sunday school, and whose bedroom and handwriting could both be a lot neater.

By the time they reached the camp gate, the back seat held a grinning, fearless adventurer known—to everyone who mattered—as Peete.

It was Peete's fifth time at Wokanda. Before, she'd come for a one- or two-week session, but this year she was staying for the entire summer. Her parents didn't really approve. Camp was uncivilized, and they feared—with good reason—that the veneer of ladylike manners they had managed to apply to their daughter during the school year would slough off in an instant.

But Gene Maas had been offered an extended foreign business trip, wives included. They'd made a half-hearted offer to take her along; she'd seen the relief in her mother's eyes when she chose Wokanda. They would golf and have cocktails and sightsee, and she would chop wood and eat s'mores and sleep under the stars. Everyone was happier.

Her father parked in a wide, mowed field. The counselor at the registration desk was new this year, and didn't know Peete. Part of her wanted to crow, "I am back! Why don't you cheer?" but it would have been awkward for her secret identity to be revealed right then.

"Name?"

Her mother spoke first, "Patricia Maas. M-double-A-S."

The girl looked down at her list. "Wow. You're going to be here all summer? That's unusual."

Peete smiled. She liked being unusual. "What cabin am I in?" She wouldn't be twelve until the end of the summer, but please, please put her in Red Hawk, the unit for junior high girls, where they got to sleep in real teepees.

Inside the fabric of her shorts, she wrapped her fingers around her pocket watch, her most prized possession. She had bought it with her allowance, saved up for months, and had told no one. It was not a girly watch, gold and tiny, or a Daddy watch on a fat leather strap, which her mother would have forbidden. It was a secret watch, tucked into the hobbit pocket of her cutoffs, a splendid, heavy object, with a steel case, a black face, and numbers that glowed pale green in the dark.

The counselor looked at her list. "You're in Sassafras. Up in Ki-Oat."

"Huh?" Peete knew every trail at Wokanda, but had never heard of that cabin. "Where's *that?*"

"The other side of the lake, back beyond the dining hall." The girl pointed to the opposite hillside. "It's new. Do you have a suitcase?"

"In the trunk," Mr. Maas said. It was the first time he'd spoken since complaining about the gravel road.

"Great. Leave it at the sign that says LUGGAGE." The counselor handed him a label that said *Maas - Sassafras.*

"Can't we drive up?" her mother asked.

"Not with a car, ma'am. A golf cart takes bags up to the remote sites."

"Oh. I see." Mrs. Maas drummed her fingers on the side of her floral handbag. "So we'd have to *hike* to see Patty's cabin?"

"It's only a ten-minute walk up to the dining hall, then another ten on the Ki-Oat trail."

Mrs. Maas looked down at her shoes—yellow leather flats with green daisies on the toes. "They might have mentioned that in the instructions," she said in a scold.

"It's okay. You guys can just leave me here." Peete tried to keep the delight out of her voice. Every other year they'd insisted on going into her cabin, sitting on the bed, even talking to people, as if *they* belonged here.

"Are you sure?"

"I am." For a moment, Peete allowed Patty to resurface and masquerade as the daughter her mother had always wanted. "I'd hate for you to ruin those pretty new shoes," she said.

"Oh, sweetie." Mrs. Maas beamed. "That's so thoughtful of you." She turned to her husband. "What do you think, Gene? Shall we abandon her here?"

He shrugged. "Too hot to hike, that's for sure." He looked at his watch. "Besides, if we go now, the game'll still be on when we get home."

He dragged her footlocker to a small pile of suitcases, wiped his forehead with a handkerchief, then reached into his wallet. "Here's thirty bucks for postcards and stamps and whatever else they sell in the store here. That ought to hold you." He gave her a peck on the cheek and a swift hug.

Her mother wanted a longer hug and said to behave and watch out for poison ivy, brush her teeth, and remember to write. After a second kiss, she added that they'd miss her, and did she have Uncle Ed's phone number, while they were traveling?

"I'll miss you too," Peete lied.

Then they were in the car, driving back through the gate, waving until they disappeared around the curve of the road, a plume of dust marking the last traces of Patty for the rest of the summer.

Peete reached into her knapsack and put on her tattered, beloved baseball cap. She began to whistle, kicking her high-top sneakers in the dirt and swinging her sleeping bag as she walked to the lake bridge and the trail up to her new unit.

Wokanda had two hills that surrounded Lake Kiowa, a teardrop-shaped body of water about the size of two football fields, with a cattail-filled marsh at the wide end, and a footbridge at the other. On its west shore lay the camp office and nurse's cabin, the dock and swimming area, and Cabin Row, where Peete had always stayed: a dozen wood-framed, screened buildings named after local fauna—White Dove and Bear and Porcupine. Behind them, a narrow trail led up the wooded slope to the fabled Red Hawk unit.

In previous summers, Peete had not spent much time on the second hill, except for meals in the Dining Hall, or visits to the tiny Nature Cabin. The rest of that side of camp was hiking trails, some staff cabins, and the unit where the Kits, the counselors-in-training, lived. And now it was hers. She began to swagger a bit. At Wokanda, it didn't matter that she was only eleven, or that she was a girl. Here, she was Peete, as bold and daring as Zorro, Daniel Boone, or any other TV hero.

Outside, if boys were around, girls became invisible, and weren't allowed to do anything fun. But since *every*one was a girl here, they got to do it all: build a fire or raise the flag or use a hatchet to split wood. Arms were muscled and tan and everyone wore blue jeans. Even the counselors, adult women, could still throw a baseball and run as fast as the wind, and didn't spaz out when they got a splinter. Nothing like her mother's friends. No one at camp got her hair done or wore nail polish or nylons. Peete could—almost—imagine being old, if she could grow up to be like that.

Behind the Dining Hall, a newly painted sign that said COYOTE pointed to a freshly raked path. She stopped and thought for a minute, then said, out loud, "Oh. Ki-Oat."

The shady path curved through an unfamiliar part of the woods. Ten minutes later, Peete was astonished to discover that Ki-Oat was not a cabin but a cluster of four tree houses. Her first reaction had a touch of disappointment, because everything looked so new. She could smell the freshly sawn lumber, and the nails were still shiny. On the outside, she lived in a suburb, in a modern ranch house, and she'd always loved the history and tradition of Wokanda's cabins, former campers' names carved into wood crackled and textured by decades of hot summers.

Excitement took over again as soon as she discovered that entry into the tree house marked SASSAFRAS started with a climb up a sturdy ladder nailed to the trunk of a huge old oak, then through a trapdoor!

She pulled herself up into the little cabin in the sky. The oak grew right through the center, its topmost branches hidden by a corrugated translucent ceiling. The walls were waist-high, their upper halves open to the air, with rolled-up bamboo blinds in case of rain. The square room held four iron cots with thin, striped mattresses, each with an empty orange-crate nightstand.

No one else was there yet, so Peete got first pick. She threw her stuff onto the bed on the far side of the tree and lay down with a bounce that squeaked all the cot's springs. She was home. The hot summer sun filtered through the forest, dappling the floor in overlapping puddles of light. She could smell pines all around, hear branches rustling in the breeze and the *tunk* of a paddle against the side of an aluminum canoe out on the lake. The outside world was already far away.

By late afternoon, the other three beds were occupied by girls named Jenny and Brenda and Linda, who were all best friends. Peete had come with a buddy her first year, but Laurie didn't like bugs and mud and never came back. It was okay, flying solo, but watching the three girls giggling together did make her feel like the odd man out.

"Ki-Oats!" called a voice from the tree house up the slope. "Fire Circle, five minutes!"

Peete climbed back down the ladder. The unit was a flat clearing about twenty yards across, with the fire circle in the center. Six large logs circled end-to-end served as seating around a shallow rock-ringed pit. The three campers' tree houses— Sassafras, Maple, and Red Oak—lay in a line to the right, with the staff's, Gingko, fifteen feet up the hill. Near the path was a picnic table, a battered wooden bookshelf filled with coffee cans of tools and craft supplies, and an iron pump, the dirt at its base already dark and puddled. Behind it, at a reasonable distance, was an outhouse, its door marked with a painted crescent.

She sat on one of the logs and sighed with contentment. Woods on all sides, a thousand shades of green, moss like velvet carpet, shadows long and narrow in the late afternoon sun. At the edge of the clearing, over a patch of blackberry canes, the wings of dozens of tiny flying creatures sparkled as they flitted in and out of a shaft of light. Around her she heard the crunch of sneaker-clad feet over leaves and pine needles, the sharp snapping of twigs, a distant woodpecker rapping *onetwothreefour.*

The circle filled with a dozen girls in t-shirts and shorts. The ones who'd come in pairs chattered with their friends until a college-aged girl stepped into the center of the ring. "Welcome to Ki-Oat!" she said in a loud, cheerful voice. "I'm Miss Jeep, and this is Miss Soapy," she gestured to her partner. "Your counselors."

Soapy—the Miss was only used for introductions and formal occasions—was short and had bright red hair and a round face. Jeep wore a flannel shirt hacked off at the shoulders, had dark hair in a thick braid, and was already very tan.

"Dinner's in a hour—yes, we can still hear the bell way up here—so let's introduce ourselves, and start making some plans." Soapy pointed to the first girl.

"I'm Sara," she said.

They went around the circle. When it was her turn, Peete grinned and said, "I'm Peete." She got a few quizzical looks, but she was used to that, being a *kid* with a camp name, the only one of her kind.

Session Two

Make new friends, but keep the old,
One is silver and the other gold.

Miss Bucky's bugle sounded "Reveille" at 7:30 a.m., the staccato notes echoing across the lake. Peete woke, poked her head out of her cozy, flannel-lined sleeping bag into the chilly air, then burrowed back. She didn't like mornings, but she loved breakfast—hot cocoa and cinnamon toast—so she waited for the big cast-iron bell to ring the fifteen-minute warning before she actually got up, threw on a sweatshirt, zipped up her jeans, and found her sneakers. Then she scrambled down the ladder, stopped at the pump to finger-comb some water through her sleep-tousled hair, and headed down the path.

A hundred campers stood in line or huddled in groups on the wide stone veranda of the Dining Hall. Counselors waded through the throng, pushing open the swinging screen doors to get their mugs of coffee. At 8:30 on the dot, the bugle sounded "Soupy," the doors opened wide, and a stampede of hungry campers rushed to find seats in the long, high-raftered room.

Inside, it was dim and cool, smelling of creosote, dishwasher steam, and oatmeal. A fieldstone fireplace stood at each end, and ten bench-lined tables jutted out from the log walls, a counselor at each head and foot. Girls rushed about, looking for their special favorites, hurrying to get a seat next to her.

Peete stood for a moment, scanning the room for Initial People. That was how she thought of her own chosen ones. They seemed a little more than three dimensional, standing out in any crowd, the sight of them sending a little thrill through her. In her mind, their names shone in capital letters, illuminated, like in an old Bible, or the first page in a fairy tale. Miss Lucky, the camp director; Miss Juniper, canoeing and waterfront; and most of all, Miss Nibs.

Nibs was just about everybody's favorite. She was tall and had short, dark curly hair and was always smiling. Outside, she was in medical school, studying to be a doctor. At camp, she was the head of the Kits. All of that meant that at every meal there was a big push to sit at her table.

As usual, Peete ended up at Jeep's table, along with four other Ki-Oats. She stood, waiting to sing grace:

> *If we have earned the right to eat this bread, happy*
> *   indeed are we.*
> *But if unmerited thou giv'st to us, may we more thankful*
> *   be.*

The moment the song ended, the room filled with the tumult of a hundred girls sitting down, chairs and benches scraping, paper napkins rustling, silverware clattering. Food was served family style, a big Melmac bowl of hot cereal, a platter of toast, a pitcher of hot cocoa.

At the end of the meal were the morning songs, rousing, get-your-blood-pumping tunes: playful songs with moving and clapping, tricky rhymes, and tongue-twistery speed tests that Peete sang loudly and enthusiastically. Every activity at Wokanda—except swimming—involved singing. Peete was not a great singer, but she loved being part of the chorus of voices that reverberated through the room. Outside, no one ever sang, except at church. But here, everyone did, all the time, and it made her whole body happy.

"Peete. Got a sec?"

She turned around. Nibs stood on the path above the dock, her whistle on its lanyard around her neck, her pith helmet on her head. *She remembers me!* Peete thought with a secret thrill. *She remembers my camp name!*

For two and a half weeks, three meals a day, Peete had run to get a seat at Nibs's table, but had always gotten beaten by older, faster girls. That didn't matter now. Nibs was talking to *her.*

"Sure," Peete replied, trying to sound casual. "What's up?"

"I need a favor."

"Anything." Peete meant it. She'd walk through poison ivy *and* blackberry thorns for Nibs.

"Great. Come with me."

Peete grabbed her towel and followed Nibs up the path to the flagpole circle and the small cabin beside it, which housed the nurse's station and an office with a phone.

A girl with blonde hair in two braids sat on the bench outside.

A new batch of campers had come in on Sunday, but Peete hadn't seen her in the Dining Hall.

The girl stood up when she saw Nibs. She was taller than Peete by a couple of inches and kind of gawky, with long skinny arms and legs. She had blue eyes, and her face was angular and freckled.

Nibs put a hand on the new girl's shoulder. "This is Margaret Wendover. Her parents are overseas, so she's going to be in Ki-Oat all summer, too."

"Oh. Okay." Peete wasn't happy about that. She liked being the only camper who didn't have to go home. She tried to smile.

"I was hoping you could be her buddy, show her the ropes," Nibs continued. "If anyone knows this camp, it's you."

"That's true," Peete agreed and smiled for real, so big her cheeks stretched, because *Nibs* recognized her skills.

"There's an empty spot in your tree house this week, so she can move right in." Nibs turned to Margaret. "We'll get your bags up there after lunch."

The girl nodded. So far she hadn't said a word.

Peete wondered if there was something wrong with her. What *was* she wearing? Most girls arrived in camp clothes—blue jeans and t-shirts—but every week there was at least one who was all dressed up, like her parents thought it was a party, or church. Still, Peete had never seen anyone, anywhere, in an outfit like this one.

Margaret wore black pants that looked almost like pedal pushers, but were floppier, and ended way above her ankles. Over them she wore a loose white shirt with half-long sleeves. Peete wasn't even sure that "shirt" was the right word. The garment didn't have a collar or any buttons, just an open V in the front. Weirdest of all, she was wearing a pointy straw Chinese hat, even though she looked kind of Swedish. Only her brand-new, very white Keds were normal.

If it was a costume, Peete had no idea what she was trying to be.

"Is she foreign?" Peete asked Nibs.

"Peete!"

"Sorry," Peete said. "I figured if I'm going to be her buddy, it's something I should know." She turned to the girl. "Do you speak English?" she asked slowly.

"I do." Margaret looked down at the ground, then most of the way up before she spoke again. When she did, she was smiling, just a little bit. "And French. Also Latin, a little German, and I'm becoming reasonably fluent in Lao and Khmer."

Peete whistled. She had never even heard of the last two. "You probably won't need those here." She stuck out her hand. "I'm Peete."

"I thought this was a girl's camp." Margaret frowned, ignoring Peete's hand.

"Oh, it is," Nibs said. "It is. The only guy around is Henry, the caretaker."

"I spell it different," Peete said. "Three Es. Like a pirate. It's my camp name. Like Nibs, er, Miss Nibs." She pointed to the name carefully painted on the counselor's pith helmet.

"Does everyone here have another name?"

"Just staff," Nibs said. "Peete's a bit of an exception."

Peete grinned.

"Swimming should be just about over." Nibs looked at her watch. "Why don't you go introduce Margaret to the rest of the Ki-Oats."

"Sure thing."

Nibs went into the office, the screen door banging behind her.

"What is your real name?" Margaret asked in a soft, low voice as they walked down to the lake.

"You don't ask that." Peete shook her head. "First lesson of camp etiquette."

"Why not?"

"It's like a secret identity."

The girl looked blank.

"Like Superman and Clark Kent?" Still nothing. Peete sighed. Definitely something off about this one. "Like fairy tales? Not a good idea to say your true name?"

"Oh!" The girl's face lit up. "I understand." She looked thoughtful. "I've never really felt like a Margaret. May I be called by another name?"

"I guess," Peete said. She crossed her fingers. *Don't let her be a copycat and think* she *can have a camp name.* "Like what?"

"Maggie?"

"Oh, sure." Peete was relieved. Just a regular old name.

"Splendid. My family doesn't use nicknames." She shrugged. "They're Methodists. Missionaries, in fact."

"Where *are* you from?"

"This year, Vietnam. A village outside DaNang. We move frequently."

"So why did they send you here?" Peete asked. "It's a great camp—the best—but it's kinda far."

"My mother came here when she was a girl. My grandmother, too, a long time ago."

"Really?" Wokanda had opened more than fifty years ago, but Peete had never met anyone whose camp lineage went that far back. She had a *lot* more questions, but they'd reached the dock. "Hey, Jeep, Soapy!" she yelled. "Meet Maggie, the new kid in Sassafras."

Because it was Nibs that asked, and because it made her feel important, Peete devoted herself to being Maggie's buddy. From Reveille to Taps she kept up a running commentary, giving her a tour of Wokanda: the Dining Hall, the path down to the lake, where to watch out for poison ivy, and even the gestures for singing "Do Your Ears Hang Low?" Peete knew she'd have to teach Maggie a lot about camp, but was surprised at how much of *outside* she had to explain. The girl knew *nothing*. Her family didn't have a TV, so she had never heard of the Flintstones, or the Rifleman, and she didn't know what Dr Pepper was. She had never even eaten pizza.

After a hot and sweaty afternoon hike on the second day, Soapy sent them all to Egypt, the shower house. "You can hang your towel there," Peete said, pointing to a row of hooks.

Maggie looked around. "Where do I change?"

"Here." Peete pulled off her t-shirt and tossed it onto one of the benches.

"No," said Maggie. "That won't do." She crossed her arms over her chest. "I would like some privacy."

"Why?"

"Because in my family, we are not naked in public."

"Oh. Right. Missionaries." Peete thought for a minute, then pointed around a corner. "The shower in the back has a curtain. Will that do?"

"I suppose it will have to."

Maggie spoke carefully and listened politely—she was the most polite girl Peete had ever met—and only every now and then stopped Peete to ask a question. At first she was so silent she nearly disappeared in Peete's wake. At lunch on her third day, one of the older girls said, "Look, it's Peete and Re-Peete!" then laughed at her own wit. Maggie looked down and folded her napkin in her lap. At dinner, Peete was on her way back from the kitchen window with a pitcher of the Kool-Aid–like beverage called "bug juice," when she heard a Kit say, "Hey, look! Peete's not here, but I can still see Peete's shadow!"

Peete thought that was pretty funny. Maggie said nothing.

The next morning, a few minutes after Reveille, Peete poked her head out of her sleeping bag and said, "Okay, Maggie, today—" She stopped. Maggie's bed was not only empty, it was made, the comforter smoothed and tucked, her white cotton nightgown neatly folded on the pillow. Peete shrugged her sweatshirt on over her PJs and climbed down the ladder.

Maggie and Jeep sat on a log, holding mugs, a little fire blazing in the pit. Next to them was a battered metal pot, steam drifting off its surface.

"Morning, Peete," Jeep said.

"Hey. Are we cooking out today?" No one had mentioned it.

"Nope. Biscuits and gravy in the Dining Hall."

"Then why the fire?"

"Maggie made tea." Jeep lifted a mug. "Want some?"

"No." Peete sat down on another log. The heat felt good in the morning chill. "Nice fire."

"Thank you," Maggie said.

"*You* made it?" Peete about fell off her log. She hadn't gotten around to teaching Maggie anything about fires yet.

Jeep nodded. "Only one match, too."

Peete frowned and said nothing. A one-match fire was like a camp hole-in-one, a feat that she had not yet mastered.

"In our village, much of the cooking is done outdoors," Maggie said. "It's a necessity, not a luxury."

"Speaking of luxuries," Jeep said, "we were just talking about ways for the group to spiff this place up a little, make it more homey."

"The only table is way over by the pump," Maggie said. "It would be useful to build one right by the fire circle, for preparing food."

"*Build* one?" Peete asked. "Out of what?"

"Branches," Maggie said, in a tone that made it seem obvious. "And vines, if the right sort grow around here."

"Easier to use twine," Jeep said with a laugh. "There's plenty of that in the pole barn." She looked at Peete. "You can tie a bowline knot and a half-hitch, can't you?"

"Not really." Peete was all thumbs when it came to most handicrafts.

"Your cabin didn't learn any lashing last year?"

"Huh-uh."

"That's all right," Maggie said. "I can teach you."

You—you can teach me? Peete started to sputter, but the breakfast bell rang just then, and she had to run to get dressed.

The Ki-Oats spent the morning tramping around the woods gathering sticks. "Not too thick," Jeep said. "Think broom handles." Which was harder than it sounded, because unlike the hardware store, nature wasn't organized by size. Coming from a neighborhood of trimmed hedges and neatly mowed lawns, Peete usually liked the forest chaos, but not this morning.

Wood-gathering was Peete's least favorite camp chore, even worse than KP. By lunchtime she was so sweaty she felt like her face was going to slide right off her head and she had bug bites all over both legs. She couldn't swat the mosquitoes because her arms were full of sticks. And worst of all, Maggie had gotten to stay in the unit and use the hatchet *and* the axe to prepare the biggest branches.

By the time the lunch bell rang, the new table was lashed between two trees, and was amazingly sturdy for furniture made out of sticks. Everyone was talking about it, and what a good idea Maggie'd had. Peete kicked at pebbles as they walked to the Dining Hall, wondering just how much longer buddy duty had to last. But she was glad they were together when Nibs called out, "Hey! Want me to save two seats?"

"Sure thing!" Peete yelled back. Nibs's table! At last!

Lunch was Peete's favorite, ham salad sandwiches and potato chips, with cherry bug juice, made with well water and icy cold. Peete gulped down two glasses, barely noticing the awful iron-water taste.

Nibs mostly talked to Maggie, asking how she was liking camp, getting settled in? Peete had tried to answer for her, because Maggie talked so slow, like she had to think about every word, but Nibs shot her a look, and said, "Maggie?" Peete

213

consoled herself with seconds on ham salad, and then was sorry when they sang "Grand Old Duke of York," which had a lot of jumping up and down.

For once, rest hour was a welcome relief.

Session Three

Oh, Father Time's a crafty man, and he's set in his ways.
And he knows that we never can make him bring back
*   past days.*
So Wokanda, while we are here, let's be friends firm and
*   true.*
We'll have a gay time, a happy play time, for we all love
*   to play with you.*

Peete was not the tallest Ki-Oat, or the strongest, or even the most skilled. But she fancied that she was the cleverest, perhaps the bravest. She saw herself, by turns, as a pioneer, an Indian warrior, an outlaw for whom a dare was a challenge and a scabbed knee was a badge of honor.

She assumed that since Maggie was a minister's kid, she was probably none of those. She kept a Bible in her orange crate, and, like a few other girls, knelt down on the wooden floor of the tree house to say her prayers every night. Peete had Maggie pegged as a goody-goody, just another pale blond girl who thought camp was a tea party, and fretted over a little dirt. The kind who liked KP, because it reminded them of home. Sure enough, Maggie volunteered for dish duty, made her bed every single morning, and even borrowed Soapy's iron to press her odd white shirt after washing it.

Within a few days, Peete discovered she had underestimated her new bunkmate. Maggie's family had moved a lot, to very strange places, and she adapted to camp quickly. She was surprisingly strong, with broad shoulders and ropy muscles in her arms, from carrying water from her village well. She had lived outdoors most of her life, was used to walking long distances and getting dirty or wet, and wasn't afraid of bugs or snakes. Not at all.

"I've had scorpions in my *shoes*," she said one morning, casually lifting a spider off her towel. She tossed the creature back into the woods. "They're venomous. This is nothing."

She might not know the names of all the trees in *these* woods, but she knew how to navigate by the sun and carve a whistle from a sapling branch with a few deft strokes of her pocket knife. Her grandparents had been in vaudeville, and she could do magic tricks—bending coins, and making balls disappear into thin air. "It's not real magic, just prestidigitation. That's Latin for *clever fingers*," she explained one afternoon. "You only see what I want you to see."

Clever. Humph. Peete grumbled when it became was clear that her role was not as Maggie's instructor or protector, but her equal. Since most of the other girls came to camp with a friend, Jeep buddied the two of them for activities, which made Peete grumble more, until she noticed that, with Maggie's help, she'd gotten much better at knotcraft and orienteering, and that was okay.

At least when they went down to the lake—once a day, twice if the thermometer hit a hundred—Maggie was a lowly Guppy. She didn't know how to swim at all; there were crocodiles in the rivers where she lived, and parasites that could wiggle up your pee hole and eat you from the inside out. She would only wade in up to her waist, and hold her nose to duck underwater. Peete was a Mermaid, the best group of all. She rolled her eyes at the name, but it meant she didn't have to wear a life jacket in the canoe, and could do cannonballs off the deep side of the dock.

———

Peete walked out of the Dining Hall after lunch on Wednesday, annoyed that swimming was cancelled, because a storm was coming, and there might be lightning. She could feel it. The morning mugginess was gone, and the tops of the trees waved back and forth against a no-longer-blue sky. The air smelled like the well water, old and cool, iron and leafy earth.

The younger campers stayed in the Dining Hall to do crafts. Most of the Ki-Oats went back to the unit to read or write letters; Peete wasn't in the mood. She wrote a dutiful postcard every Friday, and received a cheery but equally dutiful letter from her mother about as often. The only good mail had come the first week, a bundle of comics she'd sent to herself, the day before she left. Comics were perfect for a rainy afternoon, but she'd read them all. Maybe she'd go to the Nature Cabin and check on the clay bowl she'd made. If it was dry, she could take it up to Ki-Oat and paint it.

The Nature Cabin was a one-room log structure, the kind Peete imagined Abraham Lincoln growing up in. It only got direct sun in the late afternoon; the rest of the day it was shadowed and cool. Its shelves held books about birds and trees and geology, along with some Nancy Drews and other abandoned summer reading. Handmade posters with glued-on Wokanda leaves and twigs adorned its walls. Two windows and a narrow porch overlooked the lake fifty yards below.

Peete's bowl sat on the table, along with half a dozen others. She poked it with a finger. Still kind of damp. The air was so humid that crafts took forever to dry. Rain wasn't going to help.

The sun went behind a cloud, and the room grew almost flashlight dark, at two in the afternoon. A silver sliver of lightning streaked down the sky on the far side of the lake. Peete opened the door to the little porch and counted, one-one-thousand; she got to four before a rumble of thunder sounded. She stepped out and was startled to see Maggie sitting on the edge, her legs dangling out into the air, her head bent over a book. Maggie looked up at the sound of the wood creaking.

"Oh. Hello. I didn't know anyone else was here."

"I came to see if my bowl was dry," Peete said, then stood with her mouth open. Out here, the view of the oncoming storm was spectacular. The whole sky was roiling with massive dark clouds, purple at the horizons. "Wow," she said.

"It is rather amazing, isn't it?" Maggie closed her book. *A Wrinkle in Time.*

"Good book," Peete said. She'd read it that spring, not even for school.

"I'm enjoying it." She put it into her lap. "Sit, if you like."

Peete hesitated, then sat a few feet away, legs crossed Indian style. She leaned back on her arms and turned her face to the sky. Lightning flashed and forked, illuminating the scene like the bulb of her father's camera, leaving pale turquoise afterimages that seemed to float through the air. One-one-thou—the thunder was huge and immediate, rolling blocks of sound crashing into each other, so loud she could *feel* it.

The lake dimpled with the first drops of rain, bright round spots that spread in concentric circles, overlapping until the surface seemed to be boiling, bubbling. Raindrops hit the cabin's tin roof like individual drumbeats, the tempo faster and faster until the whole world was noise, the frenzied applause of a huge, unseen audience.

"Perhaps we should go in?" Maggie had drawn her legs up.

Peete shook her head, changed her mind. "Yeah, prob'ly."

They were damp, but not soaked when they sat down on the cabin floor; with the door to the porch closed, the room was so dark it felt like night. A *crack!* right above them shook the walls. Peete felt her skin prickle, excitement mixing with the possibility of danger, like a roller coaster ride, like a close call.

"Can I ask you something?" she said after a few minutes.

"I suppose."

"My dad says President Kennedy is trying to start a war in Vietnam. Is that why you're here? Did your family have to leave?"

"No, although we have seen a few soldiers in DaNang. But—" Maggie hesitated. "—but that's not why."

"So—?"

The storm hammered on the roof, rain streaming down the windows. Across the lake, Cabin Row was blurry abstract shapes. After a minute, Maggie asked, in a whisper, barely audible above the sound of the rain, "Have you gotten your period yet?"

"No. Ugh." Peete made a face. "But Dr. Turner says now that I have some hair—there—it could happen any month. Is that what yours says?"

Maggie looked puzzled. "I've never needed to see a doctor."

"Never? Come on. You were *born*, weren't you?"

"I was. In a village in Burma, on the second of June, 1951. But I was delivered by a midwife. Mama said they planned to travel to the hospital in Rangoon, but I was a few weeks early."

"What about a physical, for camp? Didn't you have to get shots?"

"For this?" Maggie snorted. "Every two years the Red Cross inoculates my brothers and me for malaria and typhus and half a dozen other diseases just so we can get our passports stamped."

"Wow. You have a passport?"

"Of course." Maggie shrugged. "Otherwise I am unable to fly."

"Right. But what does any of that have to do with why you're here?"

"Well . . ." She was silent again. "My—my mother thought that if I began to bleed, camp would be safer than the village."

"Huh?" Peete stared. It was so dark now that Maggie's face was just a pale oval, and Peete couldn't read her expression. "I don't get it."

"When a girl starts to bleed, she's old enough to be a wife."

"C'mon. You're twelve!"

"It's different there. The Xo Dang are a primitive hill tribe, and Mama was afraid that—how did she put it?—that the flower of my young womanhood might—" She looked down at her lap. "—might inflame the men."

"Inflame? What does that mean?"

"Peete. Don't you know anything?"

"I know lots of things," Peete said, stung. "Lots and lots."

"Do you know what men do to women?"

"Sure," Peete said, trying to sound worldly and experienced. All she really knew was from the little birds-and-bees book her mother had made her read. It said nothing about inflaming.

"All right, then. That's why I've come to live with my grandmother and go to school in the States."

"I guess that makes sense," Peete said. She stared at a poster about animal tracks. Behind her she heard the patter of raindrops on the full canopy of summer leaves high up on the hill, an oddly dry sound, like rice on a taut canvas awning.

"My turn?" Maggie asked.

"For what?"

"To ask why *you* don't go home, like the others."

"I—" Peete groped for the reassuring heft of her pocket watch, holding on to it until her voice steadied. "I don't want to."

"Why not?"

"It's better here. I'm Peete." She looked out at the rain. Maybe it was dark enough that Maggie couldn't see *her* face, either. "I'm somebody." She had never said that out loud before.

"Are you not Peete at home?"

"No."

"Then who are you?"

Peete had explained, that first day, that it wasn't polite to ask someone's real name. That didn't mean campers didn't try to find out. Peete had overheard another counselor call Soapy "Lisa," and knew that Nibs was really Emily Nelson, and that, outside, she lived with Miss Lucky—Rebecca Luciano—

because Nibs had accidentally left her mail on the table one day after lunch.

"Promise you won't tell?" Peete asked.

She waited, holding her breath, until Maggie said, "I promise."

An even longer wait while Peete worked up her courage. "Patty." She sighed. "At home, I'm just Patty."

"I see. How did Peete come about?"

"My last name is Maas. M-double-A-S."

"Yes, it's on your trunk."

"So, outside, I'm Patty Maas. And in second grade, a kid thought he was real clever and called me Peat Moss. *Peat Moss, Peat Moss,*" Peete said in a sing-song voice. "So I punched him."

"If you didn't like it, why did you adopt it?"

"After I hit him, no one messed with me." Peete smiled. "Even *sixth* graders knew who I was. I kinda liked that."

"I can see," Maggie said. "And it fits you. You're not a Patty. Not at all. But why are you here for the entire summer?"

Peete watched the rain on the windows. It had slowed to a drizzle. The din had separated into smaller, individual sounds: the eaves drip-splash-dripping onto the wet sill, the flat, irregular patter of water falling from leaf to leaf. Lightning flickered far away and she counted to six-one-thousand before she spoke again.

"My dad's on a business trip. Brazil. They said I could come with them, but I would've hated it."

"Why?" Maggie asked. "I find travel fascinating."

"Not with *my* parents." Peete picked at a hangnail. "They don't get me. I think my dad really wanted a boy." She shook her head and after a moment said, softer, "And my mom really wanted a girl."

"You are a girl."

"Not a *girl* girl. My whole life, my mom's wanted me to be like Shirley Temple—" She looked at Maggie. "You know who that is?"

"I'm not entirely ignorant of American culture."

"Then can you picture me in shiny black shoes and a dress with petticoats?"

Maggie chuckled. "Hardly."

"See. But that's the kind of girl—excuse me, young *lady*—that my mom believes I'm going to magically turn into one day."

"Then she is a fool," Maggie pronounced. She reached over and squeezed Peete's hand. "I am glad you're Peete, and I'm glad of your company this summer, shiny shoes or not."

"You too," Peete said. She felt her face grow warm. It was not a bad feeling. They sat on the floor, drips punctuating the silence, watching the mist rise up off the lake as the sun reappeared. Birds began to call again, and a few minutes later, "Gray Squirrels! Listen up!" sounded clear across the water as counselors herded their charges into activity

"I guess we should head back," Peete said.

"I suppose."

But neither one of them moved, not until they heard a babble of voices and the sloppy percussion of rain-booted feet on the muddy trail outside.

Session Four

The call of the fire comes to us through the shadows that
    fall at the close of the day.
Its flames bring us peace and a calmness of spirit that
    drives all our troubles away.
We are thankful for days and the joys that they give us,
    for nights and the rest that they bring.
May we go on believing in this love we're receiving, just
    now 'round the fire as we sing.

Each session, Maggie and Peete got a pair of new bunkmates. The last half of July, they were Barb and Lily, who had known each other since they were in diapers. Like most of the Ki-Oats, they were twelve, but Lily already wore a bra, not even a training bra.

After lunch on Friday, Peete and Maggie climbed in and found her sitting on her bed, staring at a thin piece of paper. Right on top of her orange crate was a box of Tampax. Peete had never seen a *camper* with one of those.

Lily saw her staring. "I think my period's prob'ly gonna come next week, and my sister says you can't wear pads when you swim in a lake."

"Why not?"

"Fish can smell blood, and they'll wiggle under your suit and bite you. Down there."

Peete had never heard that one. "Is that true?"

"I dunno." Lily shrugged. "Cindy likes to tell me stuff that turns out to be crap. But still—"

"Yeah. Ick." Peete made a face. "Have you used one?"

"Not yet. I bought them the day before I left—my mom doesn't even know I have them—but I can't figure out the instructions." Lily held up the piece of paper. "I was hoping to ask someone here."

"Nibs is going to be a doctor," Maggie offered. "She would know."

"No, gross," Lily said in a touching-worms tone of voice. "She's a dike."

Peete frowned. "What's that mean?" *Every*one liked Nibs.

"She's a lezzy." Lily looked at Peete and shook her head. "You know, a girl that likes to touch other girls?"

"Oh, sure." A lot of people did that here. Peete didn't know it had a special name.

"She can't be," Barb said. "*My* sister says it's against the law for a camp to hire those people."

"C'mon, she even looks like a guy."

"She's just got short hair." Barb tapped her fingers on the box of tampons. "Why don't you ask Soapy?"

"Yeah, she's engaged, so she's okay. But, still, I feel weird about it. You know—" Lily let her voice trail off.

All three of the other girls nodded.

"Can I see?" Peete held out her hand. She was pretty good at figuring out diagrams and stuff, and she'd always been curious what was in those little boxes. Her mother had only explained pads, and mostly talked about the pink girdle thing you had to wear with them.

She stared at the paper. Maggie leaned over from her own bed, and Barb and Lily stood next to the tree.

"Make any sense to you?" Lily asked.

"Uh-uh." Peete turned the paper sideways, squinted at it, turned it around again.

"What is *that?*" Maggie said, pointing to the diagram. "I don't think I even *have* one of those."

Barb laughed. "That is *exactly* what I said."

"She did," Lily agreed. "Cindy said it's a cross section, like in a biology book, to show where your insides are, if you were cut down the middle."

"That's not very useful." Peete shook her head. Nothing about periods made any sense. After a minute she refolded the paper and handed it back to Lily. "Good luck."

"Yeah. Thanks." Lily stuck it in her pocket. "Maybe nothing'll happen until the end of the session."

"You could ask Juniper about the fish, when we go to the lake tomorrow," Maggie said, sitting back on her own bed. "It's probably an old wives' tale."

"I hope so. Maybe she'll—" Lily was interrupted by Soapy's whistle and a shouted, "Ki-Oats! Fire Circle! Two minutes!" and they all jumped.

"Tonight's the council fire," Jeep said when everyone was assembled, "and we need to write a Ki-Oat song. So let's toss out some ideas."

Twelve girls chattered while Soapy wrote on her clipboard.

Peete thought of some great rhymes for Sassafras, but no one would let her sing them. At the end of an hour, they had a pretty good tune that they practiced again and again until everyone knew the words by heart:

> *We are the Ki-Oats!*
> *We all love root-beer floats.*
> *We live in trees, not boats.*
> *So everyone take notes:*
> *Sassafras has a lot of class,*
> *And there's no syrup in Maple.*
> *Gingko's a tree that's hard to spell,*
> *But at Wokanda, Red Oak's a staple!*

Peete liked almost everything about Wokanda, but the Friday night council fires were special. The whole camp spent the afternoon getting ready. The Kits made torches—sturdy branches whose ends were wrapped with Kotex, wired in place, then soaked in a bucket of kerosene. Campers learned new songs. Both bath houses had lines of girls waiting to take showers, so Soapy shaved her legs under the pump. Right before dinner, everyone changed into her best—or at least cleanest—clothes.

The staff all wore blue shorts and white shirts or blouses and a few of the counselors wore their ceremonial gowns: calf-length buckskin or brown cotton embroidered with Indian symbols and strung with long ropes of colorful beads, earned over decades of service to the laws of camp fire. Maggie put away her ordinary shorts and t-shirts and wore her floppy black pants and buttonless white shirt. Dinner was a feast—fried chicken or pork chops with mashed potatoes—and everyone was on their best behavior, including Peete.

Some Fridays she just rinsed a few days' dirt off in the lake rather than line up for the showers, but she always appeared at dinner in blue shorts and a white, button-down shirt, her hair actually combed. Council Fire was sacred, the only ritual she had ever felt bound to, a devotion of her own choosing.

The council fire circle lay at the end of a trail that wound gently up the hill from Cabin Row, off-limits every other day. At dusk, girls lined up according to age, Chipmunks first. The Ki-Oats were near the end, their seniority bested only by the Red Hawks and the Kits. It was still light when they began gathering, but the sun had sunk behind the hills by the time the first voices started the processional song: *We come, we come to our council fire, with measured tread, and slow.*

Up on the trail, spaced every twenty feet, counselors stood in the dark forest, holding flaming torches to mark the path, their faces flickering yellow-orange, light and shadow. Like the guards at Buckingham Palace, they maintained a solemn decorum, but as Peete passed by, Juniper nodded and Jeep winked.

The path ended in a flat clearing midway up the hill. Campers filed in and sat on three rows of knee-high logs that curved around a fire pit, easily six feet across. A waist-high log-cabin-and-teepee arrangement of dry wood and tinder was laid and ready to be lit. At the far edge of the circle, flanked by two blazing torches, Miss Lucky sat on a massive stone throne, Miss Nibs and Miss Nancy, the camp nurse, on flat rocks at either side.

Peete and Maggie and the other Ki-Oats stepped into the circle, singing in a slow cadence with everyone else. *We come, we come to our cow-own-cil fire.* Maggie had a beautiful voice, high and clear. It cracked a bit on some of the notes, but almost everyone choked up Friday nights. The singing continued until all were seated and the counselors had come in from the trail. It was full dark by then; to Peete, the girls across the circle were only pale faces above even paler shirts.

Miss Lucky stood and lifted a fiery torch. She called forward the first of four Kits, and lit each one's torch as the circle waited in silence. Then, in unison, each Kit thrust her flame through the logs of one side of the "cabin" and the great fire blazed up, filling the circle with light, sparks soaring twenty feet into the black sky. The colors of leaves and clothes and beads suddenly returned, and each face became distinct and familiar. As the flames danced, the circle of girls began to sing:

> *Burn fire burn! Burn fire burn! Flicker, flicker, flicker,*
> *flicker, flame!*
> *Whose hand above this blaze is lifted, shall be with*
> *magic touch engifted,*
> *To warm the hearts of lonely mortals, who stand without*
> *their open portals . . .*
> *Burn, Fire, Burn!*

"Now let's hear what you've all been doing this week," Miss Lucky said. "Chipmunks?"

A tiny girl stood and read an account of the seven-year-olds' adventures from a trembling piece of paper. The older the campers, the more creative the presentations: a poem, a counselor with a guitar and a song written about that week, even a little skit. After each offering, the circle resonated with the camp equivalent of applause—palms pounding on the surfaces of the sitting logs.

At intervals, the whole circle sang together—not the bouncy songs, or the hiking songs, or the silly after-lunch songs. These were hymns to the joys of the woods and campfires. In the flickering darkness of the council fire ring, Peete sang with a different voice, a voice she did not know how to use in the outside world. She sang as if the words came from inside her, as if she were singing the truth. An even deeper part of her resonated when a few strong singers added a descant line that wove through the melody like a faint scent of woodsmoke on the breeze. Joy in a minor key.

By the end of the ceremony, the littlest campers were limp with exhaustion, and were taken off to bed. Counselors held guttering torches as everyone else filed down the hill in silence to sit on the shore of the lake, below Cabin Row. The staff walked to the little bridge that crossed the narrow neck of the lake and lit candles, the tiny flames reflected in the dark still water. Then they began to sing the hallowed songs of Camp Wokanda, songs of friends and memories and leaving.

Peete had quietly moved away from the other Ki-Oats and sat by herself against one of the porch supports under the Red Fox cabin, invisible for once. She hugged her knees to her chest and closed her eyes, letting the voices wash over her, through her, into the deepest, most secret part of her.

There are notes that can shatter glass, and notes that will make the bravest warrior's eyes sting, resonating at an emotional frequency nothing else touches. In the darkness, serenaded by her tribe, fearless Peete began to weep. She let the tears run down her face and did not wipe them away. The songs were lullabies, a comfort she couldn't admit she needed, a comfort no one on the outside would offer once she left the shelter of Wokanda.

"Peete?" It was Maggie, somewhere up the slope.

Peete did not answer for a minute. Then she croaked a rusty, "Here."

Maggie threaded her way through the seated crowd, stepping nimbly to avoid crushing outstretched hands, and slid down to the ground next to Peete. "Wow," she said. "That was really something. Boy." She glanced at her silent friend. "Why are you crying? You're not going home yet."

Peete said nothing. After a minute she sniffled and wiped her nose with the back of her wrist. "I dunno. These songs always get me."

"Love songs often have that effect," Maggie agreed.

"They're not *love* songs." Peete felt a little surge of annoyance and disappointment. She'd hoped Maggie would understand.

"But they are." Maggie scooted over until their knees touched. "Listen. They're singing about how much they love the woods, and this camp, and everyone who belongs here."

"Maybe."

"Truly." She eased an arm around Peete's shoulder. "I'm glad my grandmother came here so I get to share this with you."

Peete leaned against her in answer. On the bridge, the chorus began its farewell, echoed by Miss Bucky's bugle, sounding "Taps" from the Nature Cabin's porch:

> *Day is done, gone the sun,*
> *From the lake, from the hills, from the sky.*
> *All is well, safely rest.*
> *Friends, goodnight.*

Betwixt and Between

> *Woodsmoke curlin' lazy round a pine-log fire,*
> *Leaves are rustlin' in the evening breeze.*
> *Night sounds floating clear across a still lagoon,*
> *Purple shadows cast by forest trees.*
> *Camp days are full of memories.*
> *They ne'er will be forgot, our days here they will not.*
> *Sleeping together 'neath the trees,*
> *Makes lasting friendships never to be broken.*

Every other Saturday morning was busy with Ki-Oats packing, retrieving items from Lost and Found, making last-minute trips to the store for souvenirs, and teary goodbye hugs. The tree houses looked bare and empty without the bright colors and vivid stripes of bathing suits and towels hanging from the wooden sills.

Peete and Maggie stayed out of the way until lunchtime. Maggie had gone to the store to see if they'd finally gotten some airmail stamps. Peete had painted all four orange crates as a surprise for their next bunkmates and was up in Sassafras putting the finishing touches on them—Indian symbols copied from a book.

She stepped back to admire her work, paintbrush in hand. "Now, *those* are some nice-lookin' crates!" she said aloud. She flung her arm in the air in triumph, which was short-lived as the bright red paint from the brush arced onto Maggie's light blue comforter.

"Damn," Peete swore.

She carefully put the brush down on an old envelope and grabbed her towel, but dabbing at the streaks only smeared them. "Double damn." She looked at the label on the paint can. Water-based. "Okay. Okay. So it'll wash out," she said to the comforter. She folded it and the towel into a manageable bundle, then carried it down the ladder and went to find Soapy.

"Aw, for the love of Mike, Peete. I'm too busy this morning to deal with the blunder fairies," Soapy grumbled. But she took the laundry and added it to the pile of luggage on the cart heading down the hill. "I'll wash it and put it on the line to dry, but then I'm going into town, so you'll have to bring it back up."

Peete said she would and returned to Sassafras. Ten minutes later, Maggie's head appeared through the trapdoor. "No stamps yet, but Cynthia sent a letter and enclosed some photos."

Cynthia was a bunkmate from two sessions back. She had brought her Brownie camera and was forever snapping pictures. "Of what?" Peete asked.

"A rather nice shot of the two of us, at our fire circle. She made a copy so we could each keep one. She says—" Maggie stopped and stared at the thin white sheet covering her cot. "What happened to my bed?"

"Uh—blunder fairies?" Peete tried.

"I do not believe in them." She crossed her arms over her chest and gave Peete her sternest look.

"All right. Me. I'm sorry. I got excited, and the paint kinda flew wrong."

"I see." Maggie stood very still for a minute, then uncrossed her arms. "Well, since it did need washing, I suppose I can forgive you." She handed Peete one of the snapshots and laid the letter down on her own orange crate.

Lunch was sloppy joes, another of Peete's favorites, and they sang an extra lot of songs after—farewell songs, and thank-yous to the cooks, and "Happy Trails to You." Then they walked down to the meadow where a stream of parents' cars were arriving from outside, and said goodbye to the Ki-Oats who were turning back into ordinary girls, one by one. By late afternoon, Peete and Maggie were the only campers left. Juniper let them take out one of the canoes and they drifted around the little lake until the waterfront counselor waved them in. "Dinner in fifteen," she said as they put away Maggie's life jacket and the paddles.

The Dining Hall seemed cavernous and empty with just a dozen Kits and a handful of staff. Most of the counselors had the night off and had left in a caravan of cars, heading out to the pizza place in Green River. Dinner was a smorgasbord of leftovers from the last days' lunches and dinners, so Peete got ham salad *and* sloppy joes in the same meal and was very full and happy when they walked out with the Kits, singing at the tops of their lungs as they walked up the path to their units.

> *Were you ever on the horn, where it's always nice and*
> *   warm?*
> *See the lion and the unicorn, riding on a donkey!*
> *Hi-Ho, way we go, donkey riding, donkey riding,*
> *Hi-Ho, way we go, riding on a donkey!*

As campers, Peete and Maggie weren't allowed to be by themselves in the unit at night, so Jessie—a Kit who was debating whether her camp name should be Toodles or Pelican—walked back to Ki-Oat to stay until Soapy and Jeep got back from town. They built a fire and made cocoa. Jessie taught them a rummy game called Tonk, and they played for pebbles until it got too dark to see the cards.

The Kit hadn't thought to bring a sweatshirt, and after shivering for fifteen long minutes, she made them swear on their honor as Ki-Oats that they would go straight to bed, and left for the comparative warmth of her own cabin.

Bed. Yes, they would. But not quite yet.

Peete and Maggie sat at the fire ring, a small circle of warmth and light surrounded on all sides by total darkness. Unseen crickets chirped, and they heard the deep chorus of frogs far out in the marshy end of the lake. The flickering light cast ever-changing shadows on the trunks and ladders of the tree houses, the fire crackled and popped, and when Peete added another log, a shower of sparks shot up ten feet in a sizzle of tiny pyrotechnics.

They lay down on the wide log, head-to-head, whispering softly, looking up at the stars and the Milky Way. Peete stared, trying to take it all in, to memorize the sky for later, when the glow of the city would obscure everything but the moon. She gasped when a shooting star streaked across the whole sky and closed her eyes, still seeing a thin glow. When she opened them again, headlights shone through the trees far down the hill.

"Time to go," Maggie said. She raked a stick through the coals, sprinkling them with water from the fire bucket until no tell-tale red glows were visible. Peete rinsed the cocoa pan and put it back on the table.

By the time they were done, they could see the gleam of a flashlight bobbing down the path and hear Soapy and Jeep singing, then laughing, then shushing each other in loud whispers.

"I'll bet they've had a few beers," Maggie said over her shoulder as she climbed the ladder into Sassafras.

"You think?" Peete started to giggle and bit her lip until she was up and in and could use one hand to cover her mouth. They knelt on an empty bed and stared out across the darkness until they saw the lantern wink on in Gingko, then go out a few minutes later. Peete looked at her watch, glad the hands glowed in the dark. "It's after midnight. I guess we should get some sleep."

"It's not a bad idea." Maggie padded over to her bed in sock-clad feet. "Gosh, darn it," she said under her breath.

"What's wrong?" Peete whispered.

"My comforter. It's still down at the laundry."

"I forgot." Peete slapped her own forehead. "I'd go get it, but I'd have to use the flashlight, and some people are prob'ly still awake."

"We were supposed to be asleep hours ago."

"I know."

"It's awfully cold tonight." Maggie looked down at the thin sheet and hugged her arms around her body.

Peete thought. "My sleeping bag makes a pretty decent quilt. If I unzip it, I could put it over both of us."

"Oh." A long pause. "All right."

"You change while I put on my PJs and we'll be toasty in a jiff." Peete skinnied out of her jeans and pulled on her pajamas, then unzipped the flannel-lined bag. She gathered it in both arms and dumped it onto Maggie's cot. "Here, help me spread it out."

In her white cotton nightgown, Maggie looked almost ghostly in the darkness. The two of them smoothed the bag over the sheet. By the time they were done, they were both shivering.

"Climb in," Maggie said. "I wake up earlier."

Peete scooted under the covers, her back to the wall of the tree house. Maggie followed, and in a minute they lay front to back, Maggie on the outside of the cot. The bed was narrow, not designed for two. They wriggled a bit, spooning around each other, knees bent, until they began to warm up and got as comfortable as they could.

"Can you breathe?" Maggie whispered.

"Uh-huh. I'm glad your hair's braided." Peete scooted a fraction of an inch. "I don't know what to do with my arm."

"The up one, or the down one?"

"Up."

"Put it around me," Maggie said, and Peete did.

Maggie felt skinny but warm under her thin cotton gown. Peete could smell her shampoo and the coconut scent of Coppertone and the slightly chemical odor of Off. Together they smelled like summer, and now summer smelled like Maggie. Peete had the sudden urge to lean in and kiss the back of Maggie's neck goodnight.

After a moment, she just snuggled half a fraction of an inch closer. "G'night, Mags," she whispered. That was new, a nickname that had come out of nowhere. But it seemed perfect. A not-for-outside-name. A just-for-us name.

"Sweet dreams," Maggie whispered back.

Peete felt Maggie's breathing slow, and in a few minutes, knew she was asleep. She lay in the darkness with her arm around her friend for a long time. She wasn't sleepy and didn't want to move, to break the spell. She was happy, different happy, in a way she had never been before, and her stomach kept doing little flip-flops that felt nice. Better than nice.

She was glad they were in a tree house, glad no one could see in, accidentally or on purpose, or surprise them in the morning. When she did fall asleep, she felt as warm and safe as she ever had, as if she had finally found the place where she completely belonged.

Sometime around dawn—light enough to see shapes and colors— she was aware of Maggie stirring, then stretching, then slipping out of bed. Peete lay with her eyes closed, listening to the sound of a sweatshirt zipper, the creak of the trapdoor opening, the soft thumps of a pair of no-longer-white Keds hitting the ground at the base of the tree.

She rolled over onto a warm, Maggie-scented spot. When she woke up again, the sun was higher than it should be. Had she missed Reveille? She sat up and was startled to see her own bed, a few feet away.

Oh.

Peete got dressed and climbed down the ladder, feeling oddly shy and uncertain, as if she had awakened a stranger, a subtle shift in her Peete-ness that she did not yet understand. Maggie and Jeep were at the fire ring, having tea, the way they had most mornings for the last month.

"G'morning," Peete said.

Maggie turned and lifted her mug, smiling. "I made you tea. Lots of milk and sugar." She'd never done that before.

"Sure, why not?" Peete nodded. "Thanks."

"Shhh." Jeep put a finger to her lips. "Soapy's sacking in this morning."

Maggie and Peete looked at each other and struggled not to laugh.

"What?" Jeep asked.

"Nothing." Peete picked up the mug of tea, warming her hands.

Maggie shook her head. "We heard you singing."

"When? Oh—Um, we were—" Jeep stammered, her face reddening through her tan.

"Have you ever seen a Vietnamese village celebrating Tet?" Maggie smiled.

"Nope. What is it?"

"New Year's. First there's a lot of rice wine and beer, then there's a lot of singing, and the next day a couple of elephants are wandering loose—and a lot of people sleep in."

"Busted," Jeep said. "No elephants, though." She took a long swallow of tea. "Can I count on the two of you to keep mum about all this?"

"We will breathe a word to no one." Maggie looked at Peete. "We're very good with secrets."

Session Five

Take the hand of a comrade, seek the pine where it
*   stands,*
Follow on as she leads you in happy gay bands.
Know the lure of adventure in the star-dusted night,
Know the quick beat of dawning in the pale morning
*   light.*

Once a week, the kitchen packed sack lunches for the Ki-Oats and the unit went on a three-mile hike—an hour's walk, two hours to sit and eat and explore, an hour back to camp. Jeep and Soapy tried to pick different destinations, but the choices were limited by time and geography, and by the fifth session, Peete and Maggie had been to them all so often they could have gone blindfolded.

The old barn at the top of the cow pasture had a dramatic view of the rolling hills and the surrounding countryside, and was great for hide-and-seek. Fun, but almost like staying in camp, because the trail led from the end of Cabin Row. Peete's favorite hike took them out the gate and onto Old Creek Road, unpaved and just unfamiliar enough to feel like an adventure.

Girls walked in groups of twos and threes, some holding hands. When Maggie linked arms with her, Peete looked around, self-conscious. Lily's scornful voice echoed, uninvited, in her head—*girls who touch other girls*—but no one paid any attention and they ambled on. Even when the road was shaded, winding through deep woods with outcroppings of rock, Peete felt a warm glow.

They crossed two narrow bridges before turning onto a shortcut, a trail edging a narrow ravine that seemed almost primeval, with deep green moss and ferns growing in every crevice, sounds of water tumbling over boulders in the creek below. A faint breeze wafted up, smelling damp and cool, like the memory of a cave. A carpet of soft, dark-brown leaves covered the forest floor. Last year's summer. Fallen logs disintegrated back into the soil, still log-shaped, but now formed of Lego-sized blocks, reddish and spongy. Peete touched one with a finger and it crumbled apart, exposing a fat spotted salamander, black beetles and roly bugs skittering in all directions.

At the far end of the trail, the ravine met the road again. Soapy blew her whistle, and they stopped for lunch in a shady glen known as the Fountain of Youth. The fountain itself was an old iron pipe jutting out of a mossy wall of rock, edged with rounded stones, like a kind of shrine. The water spilled into a tiny pool, then trickled down to the creek. A battered tin cup always hung from a hook imbedded in the rock. Peete wondered who was in charge of it. Did the camp replace it, or the county?

Not that it mattered. By the beginning of August, an hour of hiking, even in the shade, was a hot and muggy exercise, and the girls quickly lined up for a mouthful of the icy water, so full of minerals it *had* to be good for you.

When they'd eaten their bologna sandwiches and tiny bags of Fritos, the other Ki-Oats went exploring. Peete and Maggie each drank another cup of water, then sat on a flat rock, their backs to the cliffside, throwing twigs into the creek, watching them wind among the rocks and pools, then disappear. Maggie tipped her conical hat down to shade her face. She only wore it on hikes; it was still an oddity, but very practical for the summer sun.

"Do you think there really is one?" Peete asked as she peeled her orange.

"One what?"

"Fountain of youth."

"I doubt it," Maggie said. She thought for a minute. "The historic one is thought to be somewhere in Florida, but that seems unlikely, given how many old people live there."

"True." Peete spit out an orange pip. "It would be neat if this one was."

"Why?"

"Then we'd never have to go home."

"Perhaps. This is quite wonderful." Maggie looked out over the creek before she continued. "But I'm not certain I want to be twelve for the rest of my life."

"Beats growing up." Peete made a face. "Shaving your armpits?"

"Hmm. Good point." Maggie nodded. "Plucking your eyebrows."

"Foundation garments."

"High heels."

"See?" Peete spit out another seed. "Why is it such a big deal, 'becoming a woman'?" She made quote marks with her fingers.

"It doesn't sound all that appealing, does it?" Maggie put the last of her orange peels into the paper sack.

"Nope." Peete sighed and slid down the rock to lie on her back. "So it would be neat if the fountain was real. If I drank enough of it, I could stay like this forever." She looked up at Maggie. "You'd have to drink it too. It wouldn't be any fun if you got all grown-up and left me behind."

Maggie lay down beside her. "All right. We'll drink together." She rested her head on Peete's shoulder and they lay on the rock without speaking until Maggie made an annoyed groan.

"What?"

"All this talk of drinking water," Maggie said, standing up, "Has made me need to—use the facilities."

"Okay, I'll stand guard." Peete sat on the edge of the rock while Maggie climbed down the bank. She walked a few yards downstream until she was half out of sight, her back to Peete, then crouched down, her feet on two rocks, and pulled down her pants. She could pee outdoors easier than any girl Peete had ever known. It didn't run down her leg or soak her sneakers or anything. Peete envied that. Maggie said it was because in most of the places she'd lived, in Asia, toilets were just holes in the ground, and you *always* had to squat, so she'd had lots of practice.

Soapy's whistle blew. Maggie waved over her shoulder, to show that she'd heard, and headed back a minute later. Peete reached down and pulled her up onto the rock. They stood in the sun for just a moment, inches apart, so close that Peete could smell oranges on Maggie's breath. Then the whistle blew again, the moment passed, and they rejoined their unit.

"Care to try the fountain of youth, madam?" Peete said as they passed the pipe.

"Why certainly." Maggie laughed. "You never know." She filled the cup and winked at Peete.

The Ki-Oats walked back single file on the narrow dirt shoulder, facing any cars that might come by. Old Creek Road was quiet and rural, not on the way to anything important, but occasionally a farmer's truck would putter around the corner, tires crunching, or the postman waved from his van, on his way to Wokanda with the mail. After half an hour of walking, they stopped again, at Peete's very favorite spot—Slantin' Sal.

The huge rock canted over the road at a precarious, forty-five-degree angle, and the shade beneath it was black in contrast to the sunlit gravel. Sal's surface was covered with lichen and moss in a dozen shades of brown and green, and a handful of small saplings grew from its top, thirty feet above. It was not part of a hillside, but stood majestically alone among the trees and underbrush and grasses, the queen of the forest.

Standing in Sal's shadow, decades of Wokanda girls had carved their names and initials into the soft sandstone, and higher up, faint and worn with age, were the markings of the pioneers who had used it as a landmark when they first settled the region. Local Indian legends called it a sacred spot, a place of great power, and generations of campers had been told that if you made a wish while placing a hickory twig under Sal—helping to hold her up—it was sure to come true.

The Ki-Oats foraged through the woods at the verge of the road until each girl had found a suitable twig and propped it against the base of the massive rock. A few just left a stick and rolled their eyes, too sophisticated for mumbo-jumbo, but others placed their twigs carefully, murmuring under their breath. Peete spent a long time looking for the perfect twig, and an even longer time standing at the side of the rock, formulating her wish.

"Gotta go," said Soapy, pointing at her watch.

"Gimme a sec?" Peete replied. "I'll catch up."

Soapy looked hard at Peete. "Special wish?"

"Kinda."

"Okay, two minutes," Soapy said, "But any longer and you're on KP for spaghetti night." She blew her whistle. "Ki-Oats? Forward, march."

Peete waited until they had all disappeared around the bend before kneeling down and placing her twig at the very edge of Sal's shadow, away from the others. She reached into her pocket and curled her fingers around her watch. Then she closed her eyes and whispered to the ancient stone.

Session Six

Remember the times you've had here, remember when you're away.
Remember the friends you've made here, and don't forget to come back some day.

*Remember the hills and woodlands, the sky and lake
    so blue.
For you girls belong to Wokanda, and Wokanda belongs
    to you.*

Late on the next-to-last Wednesday afternoon of the summer, while the rest of the Ki-Oats were on a hike to the cow pasture, Peete and Maggie sat at the picnic table in the unit. The leaves of the trees behind them, a few now veined with yellow, were backlit like stained-glass windows, illuminated by the sun just over the west hill. They were working on a surprise for Jeep and Soapy, a souvenir to remember them by. *Not that they're likely to forget* us, Peete thought, putting the lid on the can of blue paint.

"My grandmother's house is only half an hour from the city," Maggie said, setting her paintbrush down. "Perhaps you could come and spend a weekend, before school starts."

"That'd be great." Peete smiled; her lip trembled. She didn't want camp to end, to have go back to her old life. To Patty. A sleepover wouldn't be quite the same as waking up with Maggie under the trees every morning, but at least it was something to look forward to.

"I'll write her and ask." Maggie looked around. "Do you have the glue?"

"Nope, it's in the craft bin."

"Ah. Do you need anything?"

Peete shook her head and Maggie started to stand, then said "Ow!" and sat again, holding her belly.

"Are you okay?" Peete asked.

"I don't know." Maggie's face was sweaty, even in the shade, and her freckled face was paler than usual. "I feel like my insides just got all twisted."

"Stomach ache?" They'd had chili for lunch.

"No." Maggie winced. "Farther down. Down—there."

"Oh. *Oh*." Peete's face flushed as she realized what was probably happening. "Do you want to lie down or something?"

"I do." She bit her lip and hugged herself. "But I'm not certain I can manage the ladder up to my bed."

Peete thought, hard. Soapy and Jeep were at least half an hour away. The only unit close by was the Kits and—"Nibs!" she said out loud. "She's almost a doctor. She'll know what to do."

Maggie nodded without a word.

Peete pushed the craft supplies to the far end of the table. "Just lie down here. I'll go get her." She was surprised at how calm her voice sounded; she was pretty scared on the inside.

Running on the trails was against the rules, because there were roots and rocks and no one wanted a broken ankle. But Peete ran anyway, as fast as she could, her high-top sneakers kicking up puffs of dust.

She was out of breath when she reached the Kits' encampment. Eight of them sat around their own picnic table, reading Red Cross Lifesaving manuals. They all looked up when Peete came crashing through the bushes. "Where's Nibs?"

"In her cabin."

"Thanks." Peete pounded up the steps of the little wooden hut and paused to knock on the screen door. You didn't just barge in on a counselor's space. "Nibs!" she shouted.

Nibs opened the door. "Peete? What on earth?"

"It's Maggie. I think she's getting her—" Peete paused for breath and for the words to squeeze themselves out. "—her, you know, her period."

"First time?"

"Yeah. It hurts a lot," Peete said. "And Jeep and Soapy are up at the old barn."

"Gotcha." Nibs nodded. "Let me get a first-aid kit."

Peete wasn't sure how that would help. Maggie wasn't *injured*. Okay, there might be blood. Peete wasn't real clear about all the details. Besides, the book her mother made her read only said some girls might feel "mild discomfort." Mild? Maggie was *hurting*, so maybe the book had been wrong about everything else, too.

Heading back on the path with Nibs—not running, just walking faster than usual, like they had a purpose—made Peete feel a tiny bit better.

"It's scary, I know," Nibs said. "A big change. But I'm sure Mother Nature has a plan."

"Mother Nature hurts that much?"

"Sometimes. Ever had a bee sting?"

"Yeah. I guess." They reached the Ki-Oat clearing. Maggie lay curled on her side on top of the picnic table.

Nibs knelt down. "How you doin', kiddo?"

"Not so well."

"I can see. Show me where it hurts the most."

Maggie splayed her hand below the waistband of her pants. "All over, down there."

"Are you bleeding?"

"I don't think so," Maggie said. "I haven't looked, but nothing feels wet."

"Some girls just get a few spots." Nibs sat on the bench. "Or not. Everyone is different." She put a hand on Maggie's forehead. "You're a little clammy. I think we should get you to the nurse's cabin for a lie down."

"I don't think I can walk that far." Maggie's voice was barely a whisper. "Can't I stay here?"

"Better to be near a real bathroom." She gently patted Maggie's shoulder. "I'll go get the cart and drive you down."

Maggie nodded, and Nibs loped back down the trail.

Peete sat down and held Maggie's hand. There wasn't much else to do.

"I'm sorry," Maggie said after a minute.

"For *what*?"

"For leaving you behind."

"It's okay," Peete said.

"Really?"

"Of course." Peete wasn't sure that was true. As much as they'd joked, she'd known this was going happen to both of them, a rite of passage they'd share, eventually. Maggie had just gone first. But she felt an odd sadness, like being on the other side of an invisible doorway. She reached into her pocket, curling her fingers around the comfort of her watch.

Maggie whimpered, her voice so small and scared that Peete just wanted to wrap her arms around her and not let go until it was all better. Then she heard the putt-putt of the cart's motor, halfway up the path, and instead pulled her watch out, its metal case winking in the sunlight. "Take this." She pressed it, warm and solid and reassuring, into Maggie's hand. "It helps." She tried to smile. "Not that I ever get scared or anything."

"I couldn't. It's your favorite thing in all the world."

"Not anymore." Peete took a deep breath and said out loud what she had not quite let herself know until that moment. "I love you." She brushed her lips against Maggie's hair.

Maggie smiled, a tiny smile against the larger pain. "I—"

The cart's horn honked as it passed the big oak, and Peete sat up. Nibs parked next to the picnic table and jumped out. "Ready, kiddo? Lean on Peete, take it nice and slow."

Maggie sat up and swore, really swore, a word Peete was surprised she even knew. "Sorry," Maggie said.

Nibs looked worried, not mad. "I think we'll let that one go."

One arm around Peete's shoulder, the other around Nibs, Maggie shuffled over to the cart, biting her lip. She slumped onto the wide seat.

Peete climbed into the empty cargo space and reached over the seat to put her hand on Maggie's shoulder.

"Hold on tight." Nibs turned the ignition key. "It's going to be a bumpy ride."

She drove slowly, but the trail was rutted and uneven, and Maggie cried out a couple of times, her eyes closed tight, her face gray. The gravel road down from the Dining Hall to the other hill wasn't much better, but in five minutes they had pulled up next to the bench in front of the small log cabin where Peete had first met Maggie.

"I'll get Nancy Nurse," Nibs said. "Sit tight."

Nancy Nurse had been at Wokanda since Peete's first summer. She wore a crisp white shirt and khakis, a stethoscope around her neck. She was older than the other staff, a little gray in her short dark hair, and spoke in a quiet, kind voice. "Hey there," she said. "You look like it hurts pretty bad."

Maggie just nodded.

"Well, I've put the kettle on, and there's a comfy bed with a hot water bottle and a couple of Midol waiting. You'll feel better in two shakes of a lamb's tail."

They helped her into a small room, cleaner than any place else at camp. Under an open window with blue checked curtains billowing gently in the breeze were two cots with white sheets and patchwork quilts. Maggie lay down on one, a little gasp when she had to fold from standing to lying, then she curled on her side, her breath ragged and shallow.

Nancy Nurse frowned. "Em?"

"Nasty cramps, I think," Nibs said. "But there's a lot of complicated plumbing in here." She patted her own stomach. "I figured you'd better take a look."

"Is Maggie okay?" Peete asked.

"I'm sure she'll be fine," Nancy Nurse said. "A lot of girls are hit hard the first time. Let's just eliminate anything else."

"Food poisoning?" Nibs asked.

"Doubtful. I'd have a dozen girls in here already if it was bad chili. I'd like to rule out appendicitis, though."

"Good idea." Nibs looked at her watch. "I need to get back to my unit." She put a hand on Peete's back and edged her toward the door. "Let's give Maggie a little privacy."

"No," Maggie said, soft but clear. "I want Peete to stay."

The two women exchanged glances. Nancy Nurse nodded.

"In that case, I'll send a Kit up to Ki-Oat," Nibs said. "Soapy and Jeep need to know what's going on."

"Thanks." Peete sat on a chair at the end of the bed.

"Now, Maggie, I need you to lie on your back, just for a minute," Nancy Nurse said. "I'm going to pull your shirt up and ease your pants down a little and see if I can figure out what's got your knickers in such an awful twist."

"Do you have to?"

"She's kinda shy," Peete explained.

"Honey, I've been nurse at girls' camps for more than fifteen summers. There's not much I haven't seen. Roll over?"

After a minute, Maggie did. Nancy Nurse exposed her stomach and lay a hand gently next to her belly button, which was an outie, Peete noticed. "Okay so far?"

"Yes, ma'am," Maggie said softly.

"Hurt here?" The nurse pressed on her right side.

"Not really."

"Good. Here?" She pressed a few inches lower.

"A little."

"How 'bout here?" She moved her hand to just above the rucked-down waistband of Maggie's panties, and Maggie let out a cry that was almost a scream.

Peete startled, then reached over and held one of Maggie's sock-clad feet. "What did you do?"

The nurse ignored her. "Oh. Oh. Shh, now shh, sweetheart," she said to Maggie, sounding as if she were talking to a small child. "I'm not going to poke anymore. I promise."

"What's wrong with her?" Peete asked. "What's happening?"

Nancy Nurse stood up and shook her head. "I don't know. It's the wrong location for her appendix, but if it's cramps, they're the worst I've ever seen. I'm going to phone the doctor in town. You stay here." She pulled the quilt over Maggie's shaking body and walked into the other room.

Peete heard the sound of the dial clicking around again and again. She got up and sat on the edge of the bed, lowering herself carefully so the springs wouldn't bounce. She picked up Maggie's hand. "I'm right here," she said.

"I'm scared."

"Me too."

From the other room Peete heard half a conversation. "—Sullivan, the nurse at Camp Wokanda. No, a camper. Margaret Wendover." A pause. "Twelve." Another pause. "Menarche. But her lower abdomen is rigid, and she's in an unusual amount of pain." A longer pause. "Just aspirin and Midol." A rustle of paper, the scritch of a pencil. "Half an hour. Thank you." The receiver clunked back into its cradle.

"Sing to me," Maggie said.

"I can't really—"

"Please? One of the special songs?"

Peete hesitated, feeling awkward. But if it would help Maggie feel better—? She started very soft and low, her voice shaky.

> *Green trees around you, blue skies above.*
> *Friends all around you, in a world filled with love.*
> *Taps sounding softly, hearts beating true,*
> *As campers sing goodnight to you.*

Peete found her true voice and sang sweet, soft Friday-night love songs to Maggie until the doctor's car pulled up. He was a tall, balding man with glasses, wearing a coat and tie and carrying a heavy leather satchel. He talked to the nurse in low tones in the other room, then came in sounding hearty and in control.

"All right, young lady. Time for you to leave. I need to take a look at your friend."

Peete started to protest, but the doctor shook his head and pointed to the door, then closed it behind her, just as the bell rang for dinner.

"Go on up and eat," Nancy Nurse said. "You can check back in an hour."

"I'm not hungry."

"Probably not. But there's nothing you can do here." She smiled, but had the same look on her face as the doctor. "Dining Hall. Scoot."

Peete sighed and went out the door. But she did not go down to the bridge that led to the other hill. The window of Maggie's room was visible from the main path, so she ducked around the corner of the nurse's cabin and crouched below the window of the office with the phone, hidden by the wide trunk of an ancient pine. She waited and listened. All she could hear from the other room was the murmur of the doctor's voice and, once, Maggie—a yip of pain or surprise, followed by a single insistent word, "No!" Peete wanted to rush in, but just gripped the edge of the sill and listened intently. Nothing more from Maggie, just doctor murmurs.

After what seemed like a very long time, she heard the sound of the door shutting, heavy footsteps entering the office. She eased herself up until her eyes were level with the sill and peered in the window.

"I'm confused, Miss Sullivan," the doctor said. "This patient was one of your campers?"

"Yes, all summer. Maggie was born overseas. Her parents are missionaries. Why?"

"Maggie?" He looked puzzled. "An odd nickname."

"Not really. It's short for Margaret."

He frowned. "Why on earth would anyone—even a mission-ary—name their son Margaret?"

Peete stared, her mouth open, her fingernails digging into the bark of the tree.

A very long silence, then Nancy Nurse said, "I don't under-stand. Hasn't she just gotten her menses?"

"*She* hasn't gotten anything. His testicles have descended.

It's rather unusual, as late as puberty, but not unheard of. Unfortunately, there was torsion in the spermatic cord. Quite painful. Otherwise, he's a healthy, normal young man."

Outside, Peete leaned against the cabin's rough log wall and felt like she was going to throw up. He *had* to be wrong.

"That's impossible," Nancy Nurse said.

"I assure you, it's not." He cleared his throat. "I gave him a mild sedative. A bit of a shock. It appears even he was unaware of his true nature."

"How could—? Wouldn't she—he—" She let out a harsh sigh. "Did the parents *lie?*"

"I rather suspect they don't know." The doctor sat down. "In very rare cases, the external genitalia are—ambiguous—at birth. The baby looks like a girl, so it's raised female. When the child comes of age, however—" He took off his glasses and wiped his forehead. "I've only read about it in medical journals, you understand. It simply wouldn't happen in a modern *American* hospital."

"But wouldn't there be a—" Nancy Nurse broke off in mid-sentence.

"Penis? Yes. It's extremely small, of course, almost entirely hidden, but appears to be functional. With luck it will grow in the next year or two." The chair scraped as he stood up. "I was able to relieve most of the torsion manually, and he's resting comfortably, but he should be under observation for a few days."

"Of course. I'll keep a close watch."

"He can't stay here." The doctor frowned. "This is a girls' camp. Most inappropriate. Are there relatives locally?"

"A grandmother. She lives a few miles outside the city."

"Fine. Have her meet me at the hospital in Green River. I'll drive him there myself. Let me call and make arrangements for a bed."

Peete watched him pick up the phone, each click of the dial sounding like a lock being snapped shut. She straightened up and walked slowly around the cabin, moving as if the air was thick, as if she were dreaming, until she was under the open window with the blue-checked curtains. She stepped onto the log wall and climbed up, resting on the sill, then sliding down onto the floor.

The room looked exactly the same as it had fifteen minutes before, but everything in the world had changed. Peete stood and watched her friend sleep, breathing gently, color returned, no longer in pain. But no longer a Ki-Oat. No longer a Wokanda girl. Not part of the songs. Not now. Not ever again.

After a minute she reached out and touched the pale hand lying on top of the quilt, the silver glint of a pocket watch just visible between curled fingers.

Blue eyes opened, unfocused and lost, brimming with tears. "Peete?"

"Mag—" the name teetered, then broke on Peete's tongue. "No. No. What do I—?" Her voice cracked into a sob. "I don't know your real name."

"Neither do I," said the boy in the bed.

THE SCARY HAM

In the early '90s, my father's brother gave him a Christmas present, a ham. Not the kind in a can, but a full-sized southern-style ham. A Smithfield ham. They are supposed to be aged a bit before serving, hanging for six months or a year in a dry Virginia smokehouse.

My father hung his in a damp Ohio basement.

For twenty years.

It hung in a corner of the room that held odds and ends, boxes and plastic bags of foam peanuts. When I was a kid, and we had a cat, it was the room that held the cat box and cat litter.

One day around 2005, I was helping my elderly father clean out a closet in the back hall. "Where do you want me to put these boxes?" I asked.

"In the basement, in the room to the right of the stairs."

"The scary ham and cat-shit room?" I asked.

He stared at me. "Why on earth would you call it *that*?"

I shrugged. "It's where we used to keep the cat box, and it's where the scary ham is."

"It's not a scary ham," he harrumphed. "It's a Smithfield ham. You're *supposed* to hang it."

Not for twenty years, I thought, but I did not say that out loud.

The ham was covered in some sort of netting, which was covered in many, many layers of mold and mildew. It loomed over the room. It made people gasp in horror.

I tried to point some of this out to my dad, but he just scoffed. "One of these days, I'm going to take it out to my club—" (He was the sort of pillar-of-the-community man who *had* a club.) "—and give it to the chef. He'll know how to prepare it. I'll have a dinner party for my friends. It'll be a gourmet feast."

"Dad," I said. "Your friends are all in their eighties. They will *die.*"

"Nonsense," my father said. "It's a *Smithfield* ham."

My father died in the spring of 2008, at the ripe old age of 86, leaving behind three daughters, a house, and the ham.

After we'd taken care of all the urgent and important tasks that come with losing a parent, my sister Mary and I looked at each other and said, "What are we going to do with the ham?"

"Do you want it?" I asked.

"God, no!" She made a face. "I'd have nightmares. Do you?"

I shook my head. "But we can't just throw it out."

After a minute, Mary said, "I think we should have a Viking funeral. We'll go out to a lake and put it on a raft and set it on fire."

"We don't have a lake."

"We'll take it to a park, then."

"We are fifty-year-old women. We can't just set a toxic ham on fire in a public place. We'll get caught. We'll get arrested."

"Okay, so how about we take it to Dad's club and leave it on the 18th green and *run?*"

"People know us. We're 'Jack's girls.' We'll get even more caught."

"You are no fun," she said.

The ham remained hanging in its room in the basement.

Meanwhile, there was probate and there were lawyers and banks and insurance and real estate people to be dealt with, because my father was a good Republican church-going Ohio businessman. And as the oldest daughter, it fell to me to meet them at the house and deal with appraisals and paperwork.

They were very professional, most of them women a bit younger than me, in nice suits with power scarves and sensible heels. They were proper and respectful. And at some point in the middle of one of those visits, I would say, in my most polite hostess voice, "Would you like to see the ham?"

There would always be a pause, a slightly disconcerted look, and then they would smile and say, "Why certainly," although they had *no* idea why I wanted to show them a ham.

So I'd turn on the light and lead them down the creaky basement stairs, and stop at the bottom. I'd open the door on the right just enough to reach in and turn on the light, and then I'd fling it wide open, and say, with pride in my voice: "This is our ham!"

Every time, the woman would *leap* back and emit a sound between a strangled squeal and a full-out scream.

I began to enjoy those visits.

It was a scary ham.

I must add here that my father bought the house in 1951, and died in 2008, so there was 57 years' worth of household stuff from basement to attic. And no one in my family throws things away, so I spent that summer clearing out my childhood, and my parents' entire lives, and a fair amount of several ancestors' worldly goods. It took months.

Dad had died in April, and by the end of the summer, I'd gone through every closet, cupboard, cabinet, drawer, and box that I could find. I'd shipped home the few pieces of furniture I wanted, innumerable cartons of photos and memorabilia, and filled two large dumpsters. It was time for an estate sale and getting a crew to clean out the house and put it on the market.

The ham was still hanging in the basement.

Every month or so I called Mary and asked about whether she wanted me to set aside various things, what she wanted to do with Mom's wedding dress and Dad's army uniform, questions that I couldn't answer by myself. And near the end of each call I'd say, "What about the ham?"

"A Viking funeral!" she'd say. And I'd sigh and say no.

(I should clarify. I had two sisters, both younger. One had Down Syndrome, one is an English professor. I tell many stories about my family, and it's not always easy to figure out which sister I'm talking about. In this case, it's the professor.)

Before Labor Day, Mary flew to Ohio for a week to sort through the last of the stuff, say goodbye to the house we grew up in, and load Dad's minivan with furniture and boxes and drive back to Colorado.

On the second-to-last-day of her trip, I said, "The ham. We have to deal with the ham and we have to do it today or tomorrow." I gave her the big-sister stare. "Do not mention Vikings. We are not lighting it on fire."

"Poophead," she said. "But we *have* to have a funeral."

"Absolutely."

And so it began.

For my entire life, there had been a large gilt-and-white box that sat on a shelf in the family room, full of random snapshots. It was the sort of decorative box that one's midwestern family has. We'd sorted through all the photos, and the box was going into the estate sale, but—

It was just the right size for the ham.

I put a bandana around my face and cut the ham down from its mooring in the basement ceiling. Mary went out and bought a length of red velvet. We draped it across the box and laid the ham out in state.

It looked better in the box. Like a mummified Egyptian baby. A small baby, maybe a few months old, wrapped in moldering cloth, resting on red velvet.

We took the box out to the backyard and set it in the shade of the towering elm tree. It looked rather sad and forlorn. We needed more accessories.

In the process of cleaning out the house, I had found many, many things whose existence I had never been aware of. There were cupboards that had been forbidden when I was a kid, and which I had no reason to look into on visits as an adult, and there were corners of the basement and attic that were just too deep in other clutter to have ever been visible.

At some point during the summer, I had found a trio of stuffed monkeys. Not taxidermy, just toys. Stuffed animals. Because I had two sisters, many items had come in threes—Christmas stockings, Easter baskets, matching beach towels. So three girls, three monkeys.

Except that I am the oldest, and I sell vintage toys on eBay, and I could tell that *these* monkeys significantly predated me. And they were very grubby and well-worn. Maybe well-loved, but I had no idea by *whom*. I had never seen them before.

But there they were, and they seemed to go with the ham, so we arrayed two of them around the gilt box. (The third one was too far gone to display.)

I had also discovered a hunting horn, about four feet long, the sort one might use to open the Derby or announce the release of the hounds. Never seen *it* before, either, but after four months, I was taking that sort of thing in stride. I took the horn out to the backyard and attempted to play "Taps".

I have very little musical ability, and no experience with actual instruments, so I did not come close to succeeding, but I did make loud noises, and at one point played what *might* have been a bit of the Ohio State fight song. Appropriate enough for a Columbus ceremony.

To complete the array, we had a shoebox full of used birthday candles. I do not know why my mother saved them. Even in an emergency, a used birthday candle will burn for, what, like an eighth of a second? But she had saved hundreds of them, so we doused them with lighter fluid, put the shoebox in front of the ham, and set the candles all on fire.

Between that and the hunting horn, it *was* sort of Viking-ish.

Soon we noticed that a few neighbors were peering over the fences that surrounded my Dad's suburban backyard, to see what that horrible noise was, and stood, staring, at the flaming box and the decrepit monkeys and the very, very dead ham.

We waved. *Nothing to see here.* I stopped playing the horn. We ran the hose over what was left of the box of candles, wrapped the ham in its red velvet shroud, and got into the car. We drove to a local park. No raft, no more flammable materials, but there was a creek, so we figured we'd toss the ham into the water and say something nice about it.

A lovely little park, in the town we grew up in. We thought we'd just saunter down to the creek and have a ham toss and that would be that. But it was late in the afternoon, in August, on a Saturday, and about 400 families were having a picnic. We didn't know all of them—it had been a long time since Mary or I had lived there—but we knew some. And we walked through their sea of plaid blankets and plastic tablecloths, cradling what looked for all intents and purposes like a dead baby.

We smiled at people. I kept pointing to the bundle in my arms and mouthing, "Just a ham. Just a ham." If anyone heard me, I doubt this was reassuring.

We finally got to the woods, and to the creek. Mary said a few words in Episcopalian, and I unwrapped the ham for the last time.

I swung once, twice, three times, getting enough momentum to actually get it up and out over the water, then let go. The ham sailed a few feet, then sank like a prehistoric stone thing. Very fast. No bubbles, just a great *bloop!* and then nothing.

Requiescat in pace, perna formidilosa.

We folded the red velvet into a triangle, like a flag, left it by the creek, and went to have a few beers.

On Monday, Mary drove home. I spent another ten days finishing up the odds and ends at the house, checking the newspaper every single day to see if there were any reports of fish floating belly-up downstream, or people in Circleville dying of a mysterious plague.

No news was good news.

As far as I know, the ham is still there, at the bottom of the creek. Perhaps unchanged. I doubt that it was edible, by any sort of creature, and I'm not sure any substance could dissolve it. After I'd cut it down from the basement ceiling, I tried to carve into it, to see how far down through the mold and mildew I'd have to go before I hit recognizable ham-like meat. I never found out. I broke three knives trying.

It was a very scary ham.

More Praise for *Wicked Wonders*

The stories collected in Ellen Klages's *Wicked Wonders* are the best kind: ones that deliver charm and delight the first time, then open further and compound their meanings on each consecutive read. As I devoured the collection, I kept saying, "This one is my favorite. No. This one." And then I turned the page to find even more.

This magic has its origins in the fact that, in *Wicked Wonders*, a different universe hides almost in plain sight within each beautifully rendered familiar setting. From a cafe that subdivides infinitely in "Mrs. Zeno's Paradox," to "Echoes of Aurora," where the unseen becomes manifest, to the terrifying, tantalizing mystery in "Singing on a Star," and the glorious heart of "Woodsmoke," each story is equal measures whimsy and joy, love and sorrow, compounded by clear-eyed hope.

Honestly, Klages captures this essential thing in her notes for "Mrs. Zeno's Paradox," when she describes politenesses around foods and a physics parallel, saying, "I . . . fumbled my way through a layperson's guide to quantum physics, took two aspirin, and re-read Dorothy Parker." She captured my imagination as well with that description, as with all her stories.

This is a keeper collection, one to return to for inspiration and delight. A fantastic achievement.

—Fran Wilde, award-winning author
of *Updraft, Cloudbound,* and *Horizon.*

257

AFTERWORD
WHY I WRITE SHORT FICTION

Imagine holding a small carved bowl, its weight and shape and size a perfect fit for two cupped hands. The grain of the wood flows with the bowl's curves, the interplay of light and dark pleases the eye, the texture is silken against your skin. You turn it, admiring the craft, the artistry, the attention to detail.

"It's lovely," you say, handing it back to its creator. "Now when are you going to make something real, like furniture?"

Now imagine the bowl is a short story.

Why do so many readers—and writers—consider short fiction to be some sort of training wheels? As if writing a short story is just a way to wobble around until you find your balance and center of linguistic gravity and are ready for the big-girl bike of a novel?

Sigh.

Short stories are my favorite art form. A good one is compact and complete, a telling little slice of life, capturing a moment in time that—for the character—defines her, changes her, is the tipping point for all that will follow. Picture yourself walking down a street at dusk, passing by an open front door. Perhaps you see a family at dinner, arguing. Perhaps you see a brief kiss. Just a sliver of a stranger's life before you walk on. That house will never be the same for you.

When I write, I try to capture one of those pivotal moments. If I succeed, I have shifted the reader's view of the world, just a little. The character is not the only one to experience change.

That is my job, shifting perceptions, one story at a time.

The trouble is, I don't like writing.

But I love having written.

At the beginning of a story, I have only the glimmer of an idea. A line of dialogue, a character, a setting, a time period. I think about it. It settles in my brain, nestles—or nettles—like a tickle or an itch. It often sits like that for a very long time.

My process is messy and nonlinear, full of false starts, fidgets, and errands that I suddenly need to run *now*; it is a battle to get something—anything—down on paper. I doodle in sketchbooks: bits of ideas, fragments of sentences, character names, single lines of dialogue with no context. I play on the web as if Google were a pinball machine, caroming and bouncing from link to link to tangent, making notes about odd factoids that catch my eye.

I am a writer, and writers are magpies. Ooh! Shiny! Some of those shinies are distractions, but others are just the right size or shape for me to add to the jumble of flotsam and fragments that I am slowly building into a mental nest where I will—I hope—hatch a story. I gather scraps until that amazing moment when a few of them begin to coalesce into a pattern.

My father once told me that I have a mind like a lint trap—I pull stuff out of everything, and a lot of it just clings. Many of my stories crystallize around some vividly remembered detail: the smell of the basement in the house I grew up in; the way the light slanted across the lawn of my best friend's house when it was time to go home for dinner; the incendiary, sticky texture of the hot vinyl backseat of my mother's Ford convertible against my bare, damp legs.

Layers of tiny, precise detail accrete. Like a coral reef, or knitting a scarf out of strips of whimsy.

Eventually, I have to put some words onto paper. Readers expect stories to have words, in some sort of coherent order. But this is a painful chore, and I avoid it, procrastinating desperately until the deadline looms too close to ignore.

I try. These words are awful. Boring, clichéd, stilted. I can no longer write a coherent sentence. I despair.

Of course, first drafts always suck. I know this, and I forget it every time. (In the back of my mind, I still believe that Hemingway sat down at his typewriter, wrote *A Farewell to Arms*, and then sauntered off to have lunch.)

About my first drafts: I write longhand. Bold ink, wide-lined paper. I cannot create on a keyboard. I scribble images, crumple pages, toss them across the room. I make some pictograms, cross them out, draw big loopy lines that tether sentences to marginal notes as if they were zeppelins. Eventually, I get a keeper, a few words, a paragraph that is strong enough to anchor other prose. Another sentence crawls out of the ooze and onto dry land, grows legs, begins to explore new territory, and I follow.

I struggle until I watch my hand write that one sentence that makes the hair stand up on my arms, that makes my eyes sting, that lets me know that I've found a bit of truth that will be the story's center.

Then the words finally begin to come.

In torrents.

I fill page after page of blue-lined sheets, the pile growing until my hand aches and I look up and discover it is dark outside and I don't remember if I had dinner.

Many of these words are not useful. They are irrelevant ramblings and too-long, too-boring dialogues in which characters just chat. There are huge paragraphs that are exposition to rival world's fairs.

But they are words, and too many is so much better than too few.

Once I have a handful of pages filled with my nearly illegible scrawls, my mood begins to brighten. Now I have material to transcribe, which feels like a very reasonable, manageable task. All I have to do is type up what's already there, become my own amanuensis, taming the chaos into orderly lines of print.

I can do that.

I get out the keyboard, and settle into my comfy chair.

(Note: Although I have taken typing classes—twice—it is *so* not one of my skills. I type slowly and with only a few of my available fingers, and even then it is tedious and full of errors and I spend a lot of time backspacing.)

But this gives me ample opportunity to edit as I enter my own data. I begin to lose myself for hours at a time. Fidgets gone, concentration narrowed and focused, the characters are beginning to breathe, the shape of the story becoming visible. I can see where the holes are, what is needed—and what is no longer needed: redundant, bloated, or sloppy.

As the larval story forms in front of me on the screen, I find myself grinning. I am happy. At last I get to play the writing game, winnowing and pruning and reducing. Thesaurus, the word lizard, is my boon companion, clarifying and capturing just the right nuance, the perfect shade of meaning.

I work with the rhythm, the meter, sentences gliding into one another, paragraphs cascading, narrative connective tissue forming. I revise and change, smoothing the rough edges, reading aloud, finding the places that clunk, that trip, that make me wince with clumsy repetition.

I love this last stage of a short story. I feel like Julia Child making a sauce. I reduce and reduce, intensifying the "flavor" of the prose. I become obsessed, the rest of the world a vaguely annoying interruption. Dishes pile up, emails go unanswered, vegetables turn to protoplasm in the fridge.

I'm almost there. I back up every fifteen minutes, and if leave the house, the story is on a thumb drive in my pocket.

So close. (As is the deadline, usually.) I wake up eager to open the file, read from the top, running my metaphysical fingers over the almost-polished surface, catching the last few splinters, until I can find nothing that does not belong, nothing that is not necessary, until it is all of a piece, a silken run from beginning to end.

When do I know a story is finished? When the last line feels inevitable. Not predictable (I hope), but the moment when the door to that stranger's house closes, leaving the reader satisfied, but also musing and pondering.

Then I read it aloud one more time, catching a few last clunks, and hit SEND.

I am done! I do the Dance of Completion, open a bottle of wine, flop onto the couch, watch TV with no guilt.

Done!

Or not. I always reread a story again a day or two later, partially because I want to reassure myself that I really can still do this, and partially because it's like a new puppy and I just want to pat it now and then.

In general, I think, I am pleased. I like this story. Well, mostly. There is that one sentence—

No, Klages. Back away from the story. But I can't.

Once, after a story was sold, and the contract signed, I spent an hour taking out a comma, putting it back in. Moving a word from the beginning of a sentence to the end, then back to the beginning. I frequently drive editors crazy, even at the copyedit stage, making just one more squirrelly change that I am sure affects the delicate balance of the entire story—and that I'm equally sure no reader will ever notice.

My editors are very patient.

But every word counts. I endure my own chaotic, hyperactive, wretched process so that I can get to that place where the words dance for me—and me alone—before I let it out into the world.

AFTERWORD

Perhaps the words do not dance to a song you have heard before.

And that is why I write.

10 FACTS ABOUT ELLEN KLAGES

(Three of these are not true. See if you can guess which.)

1. Ellen was born in 1954 at Mt. Carmel Hospital in Columbus, Ohio.
2. She once smoked a joint with Lily Tomlin.
3. She was the Minister of Propaganda for a nudist colony.
4. She was a Sunday School teacher.
5. She has never eaten human flesh.
6. When she rents a car in a new city, she tunes the radio to the country station.
7. She has a collection of Chicken-of-the-Sea tuna items.
8. She was once a bouncer at a pinball arcade.
9. She writes her first drafts on a manual typewriter.
10. She used the F-word (carefully footnoted) in each of her high-school term papers.

STORY NOTES

Mrs. Zeno's Paradox (2007)

Years ago, when I worked in a downtown office, there was a table by the coffee machine where people would set out food to be shared: leftovers from parties, donuts from a meeting, Girl Scout cookies—goodies free for the taking. My desk was across the hall. I'd watch one of the men walk by, stop, pick up a cookie or a donut, take a bite, walk on. A few minutes later, one of the women would come by. Inevitably, she'd stop, look, and say (usually out loud), "Oh, I shouldn't." She'd pause for another moment, then cut the donut, cupcake—or slice of pizza or pork bun—in half. Didn't matter *what* it was; if it was divisible, she would cut it in half.

This story is my homage to that table, and to every lunch or dinner I've ever attended where the offering of the dessert menu prompted one of my friends to say, "You want to split something?"

One afternoon I started thinking about halves, and halves of halves, tiny fractions, and just how small could a piece possibly get? I looked up measurements, found microns and angstroms, fumbled my way through a layperson's introduction to quantum physics, took two aspirin, and reread Dorothy Parker. I borrowed Annabel and Midge from her brilliant 1941 short story, "The Standard of Living," and channeled her dry wit to find just the right voice for this odd short-short.

Friday Night at St. Cecilia's (2007)

Looking back, it seems that most of my childhood was spent playing games. I come from a card-playing family. Canasta, Cribbage, Russian Bank. We played for blood. (Ask my sister Mary; she still has the scars.) But after school, and on rainy Saturday afternoons, at home or visiting my friends Neats, or Bean, or Goat, I played board games for fun. Monopoly, Sorry!, Risk, Clue, Lie Detector, and Park and Shop; everyone's rec room had stacks of well-worn boxes.

Over the years, pieces went missing, and when I wasn't looking, most of the games disappeared from the cupboards in our family room as my mother donated them to the church rummage sale or the annual Junior League Bargain Box. So when I discovered eBay, that most perilous of addictions, I began buying a few of them back for my own (sort of) grown-up house.

The ones I played were mostly from the 1960s, some of them editions of games that had been around since before I was born. The originals are even better. The 1949 Clue game is a beautiful thing—the tiny pipe is actually made of lead, and the British drawing room suspects are on cards in muted lithographic tones. The earliest versions of Go to the Head of the Class have wooden pieces with line drawings of "characters" called Butch and Sissy in place of the brightly colored cardboard Cowboy Joe and Sis that I grew up with.

I bought reference books about board games, rediscovering old favorites and stumbling upon others that I hadn't known I coveted; their intricate boards and clever spinners and timers and gimmicks called to me. The shelves in my dining room began to fill up. Friends hinted about 12-step programs.

Hah, I told them. I am a writer. I am allowed to have strange obsessions, as long as I eventually weave them into my fiction. And so, for your entertainment—and my redemption—enter Addie and Rachel.

Echoes of Aurora (2009)

In 2008, I was invited to be a Guest of Honor at WisCon, the feminist science-fiction convention held in Madison, Wisconsin. I'd be doing a public reading the first evening, and Aqueduct Press asked me for an original story to go in a limited-edition chapbook, along with stories by the other GoH, the brilliant Geoff Ryman.

No pressure.

I wasn't writing that fall. My father had died in the spring, and I'd spent five months cleaning out the house I'd grown up in—fifty-seven years' worth of family stuff—and I was grieving and exhausted.

I said yes, not knowing whether I could pull it off. Having a deadline did give me a bit of structure, at a time when I felt like I was in freefall.

I am crap with titles. The files on my computer have placeholders like "Map Story," or "Game Bitch." The final title is usually the last thing on my fictional to-do list, and I'm rarely thrilled with it. There are exceptions; this is one of them.

My friend Elise Mathessen, an incredibly talented jeweler, had made a necklace of unpolished opal chips. I don't bedizen myself often, but this piece *called* to me. Elise offered an Artist's Challenge in trade. She would give me the string of opals (at a steeply discounted price), in exchange for one of my photographs and the promise to write a story using the necklace's name: Echoes of the Aurora.

So, for once, that's where I started.

An out-of-town friend came to stay with me in sunny October, the perfect time to visit San Francisco (rainy winters; chilly, foggy summers), and we spent a day doing touristy things, seeing parts of the city I forget exist, because they're not part of my day-to-day life. I took her to Fisherman's Wharf for sightseeing and good seafood, and we ended up at the Musée Méchanique, a warehouse-like space filled with old arcade machines from the early twentieth century. We got a roll of quarters and entertained ourselves with Mutoscopes, Strength Testers, and Fortune Tellers.

In 2000, I'd moved back to Ohio to be nearer my elderly father and my sister Sally, who had Down Syndrome. They were in Columbus, in the old family house; I got a house in Cleveland, an easy two-and-a-half hour drive away. I moved in April. Summer was hot and green and full of thunderstorms and fireflies (none of which occur in San Francisco). I was content, and oddly at home after a self-imposed exodus of nearly forty years.

September and October were a revelation.

When I was growing up, Fall just meant that school was starting, I'd have to wear a jacket, and there'd be piles of leaves to leap into and scatter. No big deal. And I'd lived my entire adult life in San Francisco, which is beautiful, but where the four seasons are not dramatically delineated.

They *are* in northern Ohio. Suddenly the green-dominated landscape of summer became an orange and yellow and red world. I'd turn down one street, and gasp at the brilliant yellows of the huge oaks that fronted every yard. I'd drive into the country and thrill to the sight of a scarlet hillside of maples as I rounded a curve.

The room where I slept had two walls of windows, and every morning I'd wake to a slight variation in the colors and shapes of the branches outside. I took dozens of pages of notes. I was entirely besotted by autumn.

The last piece of this particular mosaic came from a trip to a cave in southern France in 2001. Not Lascaux—it's closed to the general public—but Pech Merle, in the Lot River valley, about half an hour from the city of Cahors. A mile of caverns, deep underground, the walls covered with paintings. Horses and deer and mammoths. What really got me were the hands. A human being spit pigment onto that wall, 25,000 years ago. I can't really relate to mammoths, but the hands looked *just like mine*. That made the long-distant past feel so immediate, so *real*.

When I finish a story, my last step, after endless editing and fussing, is to read it aloud. I find the remaining bumps and rough patches that way, find the sentences that are awkward, or do not fit together. But this story is unique. It is the only one I've ever written *specifically* to be read aloud. From the first lines, I crafted it for my own (performance) voice, my own speaking cadence and rhythm.

Singing on a Star (2009)

This story came out of my oldest, strongest memory.

I'm in bed, in the yellow bedroom of my parents' house. (I moved out of that room when my sister Mary was born, when I was three and a half, so I'm younger than that.) It's dark, and I'm listening to a Disney record narrated by Sterling Holloway, the story of a little taxi, sad and desperate, set in a seedy, Damon Runyon city. A Will Eisner city. *The Naked City*.

Vivid, inexplicable images, outside the realm of any possible nursery-school–age experience: a tangle of concrete struts arching over alleys, soot-stained brick, corrugated metal garbage cans, neon over a distant doorway, jazz filtering out. And they are inextricably bound to that yellow bedroom, which is as accurate as carbon dating in my family.

All my life those images have sat in the back of my mind, dimly lit and seductively creepy. Where did they come from? I'd occasionally ask someone my age if they remembered a Disney record called *The Depressed Little Taxi*. Ha. No. At flea markets, antique sales—and much later, on eBay—anywhere there was an accumulation of late 1950s children's records, I thought—*What if*—and looked. I never found a single trace of its existence.

Then one night, in the wee hours, I was playing on my laptop, a glass of wine at hand, tired, but not quite ready to sleep, following one interesting link to another. I typed "Sterling Holloway" into Google's search bar; it is his voice that is even more evocative, that instantly conjures my pre-school room, shadowed with loss and regret.

I went from site to site to site to site and, at two in the morning, on YouTube, I may have found it. It *was* Disney, but an animated cartoon, not a record. If it was *the* source, I knew it would permanently overwrite the elusive images that had lived, for fifty years, on the borders of fantasy, dream, and memory, and I would lose—forever—that sense of noirish magic.

I had to watch it. I had to find out.

But I had to write the story first.

Gone to the Library (An earlier version was published as "A Practical Girl" in 2009)

For eight years (1992-2000), I worked at the Exploratorium, San Francisco's pioneering museum of science, art, and human perception. I was in the editorial department, headed at the time by noted science-fiction writer Pat Murphy. Along with Pat and Dr. Linda Shore, I cowrote three (nonfiction) books of hands-on science, full of experiments that kids and their families could do together.

I got to play with all sorts of fun stuff as we sifted through what worked, what didn't—what had "wow value" and what was *meh*. My desk at work (and my counters at home) were always covered with balloons, string, jars of borax, bottles of Mrs. Stewart's bluing, plastic straws, and other random paraphernalia.

For our third book, *The Brain Explorer*, (nicknamed, in-house, "meta-cognition for ten-year-olds") we deconstructed puzzles and brain teasers. One chapter was about variations of tic-tac-toe. It's not the world's most exciting game, but it's significant because it's a "finite two-person game with perfect information," and (because *all* possible moves could be programmed) was influential in early computer development.

One of the variations used the numbers 1 through 9, instead of Xs and Os. If you get three numbers in a row that add up to 15—you win! But there was a trick. If you went first, and put a 5 in the center square, you'd win on your next turn—no matter *what* the other person did.

That took the fun out of it, which is why it didn't make the final cut for the book.

But in the process of playing around with it, I discovered magic squares, grids filled with numbers in a pattern that makes all the diagonals, columns, and rows add up to the same "magic" number. In the case of a tic-tac-toe grid of nine squares (3x3), that number is 15.

There is only one 3x3 magic square.

There are 880 different 4x4 magic squares.

There are more than 275 *million* different 5x5 magic squares, and the numbers get mind-bogglingly large for the squares after that.

I lived and breathed magic squares. There are at least half a dozen books about them. Like most math books, I find the introduction and the first chapter fascinating; the material in chapters two and beyond makes my head explode. I am very, very good at arithmetic. I can add and multiply in my head (which turns out to be a useful skill when I go out to dinner with friends). I am, alas, lousy at *math*. (And music. I just don't have that sort of brain.)

Since then, I have wanted to use magic squares in a story, but they're not particularly practical bits of math. Trying to find a context, I read a bunch of books about the history of mathematics and computers, laughed at imaginary numbers (not the numbers themselves, just the nomenclature), and settled on Princeton in the 1950s as an appropriate setting to include both Grace Hopper and ENIAC.

Then I sat back and read John Cheever short stories for a week, for style and tone, and set about trying to Vulcan mind-meld many disparate parts into a single, entertaining whole.

Goodnight Moons (2011)

I was having a beer with editor Jonathan Strahan in the hotel bar at the Denver Worldcon in 2008. He told me he was editing an anthology of stories set on Mars in the near future, and did I want to write one? It was not my first beer of the evening, so I said yes immediately.

"It has to be set in the future," he said. "And *on* Mars."

I nodded. Sure. Piece of cake.

Except it wasn't. I struggled for months.

Almost all of my previous work had been set in the past, in the mid-twentieth century, on a very recognizable, not-really-alternate Earth. I find the past infinitely interesting. I love research—so much easier than writing—and I love history and finding artifacts in the nooks and crannies of old houses at estate sales.

I am not as enamored with the future. It's too amorphous and unpredictable. It could be *anything*. I like to peer around the corners of the past, looking for the undiscovered bits—or at least the overlooked ones—while at the same time I am comforted by its orderly nature: it has already happened.

But, under the influence or not, I'd said yes to the future.

I thought idly about the story for six months. Jonathan would email me periodically to ask about progress and remind me of the deadline, and I would assure him that the story was coming along nicely.

I had not written a word. I had not figured out characters or even a glimmer of a plot. I began to contemplate a mystery, set on Mars during a dust storm. I thought about darkrooms. What would be *invisible* under red light? Or visible in a different way? I used the red lenses from a pair of 3 D glasses and set up a few experiments.

My kitchen was littered with pieces of white paper with words and shapes drawn in red ink and red marker, with blobs of Hawaiian Punch stains, drops of my own blood (scratched mosquito bite, not a self-inflicted wound). Nothing really worked, not in the dramatic, Aha! way I was seeking. Nothing to build a story around. The deadline continued to approach.

I went out to lunch with my friend and former Exploratorium colleague, Paul Doherty, who has a PhD in physics from MIT; pretty much a rocket scientist. Over sandwiches we talked a lot about red light, red light shifts, etc., but there was still no Aha!

Then I mentioned a sliver of a fragment of an idea, the only other plot-like thing I'd been able to come up with—what if a woman astronaut got pregnant on a Mars-bound flight? What would happen to her? To the baby?

Aha!

We talked for another hour, both throwing out ideas and *what-ifs* as fast as we could until we noticed we were the only people left in the restaurant.

Paul loaned me a couple of books about space physiology, and

I went home, confident that I could now scribble out a workable story in a couple of days. Sigh. Draft after draft just fell flat. I had interesting facts, I had a plausible plot, but nothing was coming together. I reread Ray Bradbury's *Martian Chronicles*, and read *Little House on the Prairie* for the first time. I ate a Mars bar.

One night after a glass of wine (maybe two), I grabbed a large black pebbled sketchbook and a marker and wrote a loopy first-person, stream-of-consciousness poem-ish thing. Descriptions and imagery and a few wisps of dialogue. It was all there, in very embryonic form, from start to finish.

It took me a few days to knock it into sentence-and-paragraph prose, and another week to polish and tighten it. When I was done, I had a fairly complex story in less than 3,000 words. Lean and spare, and packing a pretty good wallop. As writerly satisfaction goes, it doesn't get much better than that.

Short stories don't get reviewed much, and the few critics who mentioned this one thought it was "touching" and "cute" and had a tender ending. Made me wonder if they'd actually read it. Some saw it as a feminist story; I think it's the opposite. It's my Heinlein story: a woman is denied her right to choose by her husband and public opinion.

On the other hand, after I did a reading with a panel of other writers, including Will Alexander (who won the National Book Award a few months later), Will mentioned "Goodnight Moons" on his blog, and I treasure his reaction:

"Every beat in the story made us all laugh until we finally noticed ourselves quietly crying."

Yeah. I meant to do that.

Household Management (2012)

I was trying to write a story for Ellen Datlow and Terri Windling's anthology, *Queen Victoria's Book of Spells*. Nineteenth-century stuff—not really my thing—but I thought it'd be fun to stretch. I was reading *The Poisoner's Handbook*, a fascinating history of crime and forensics in turn-of-the-century (19th becoming 20th) New York, and got the drift of an idea. Hmm . . . arsenic. Fascinating stuff. (Since I was a kid, reading Agatha Christie, I've always wanted to know what arsenic actually *tasted* like. I have not tried it, for the usual reasons.)

Poison led me to murder, to crime to—the great Victorian crime solver. But hasn't every aspect of that canon been done and redone and overdone? Hmm. Mrs. Hudson rarely gets more than a bit part. She deserves her own, small story.

Ellen and Terri turned it down, but it quickly found a home at *Strange Horizons*. It's short and simple, but I'm rather chuffed to have written it. I was hoping it might lead to an invitation to join the Baker Street Irregulars, but no one has come knocking. So far.

The Education of a Witch (2012)

This one's almost entirely autobiographical. Most of my stories come from bits and pieces of memories, either woven into fiction, or used as a jumping-off point. This one's almost a memoir, with one foot in reality, and the other brushing up against fantasy. Other than a judicious name change or two, it's as close an account of my preschool years as I could manage.

Writing for an adult audience from the point of view of a four-year-old is a challenge. Her world is not very big, and neither is her vocabulary, but the story itself is fairly complex.

I grew up in the suburbs, raised on Disney. I thought then—and still do—that the heroines (Cinderella, Snow White) were insipid and boring, and that the evil women—like Maleficent and Cruella De Vil—were fascinating. They had their own houses (or roadsters), they dressed for style and power, and they always entered a room as if they owned the joint.

From the moment I was able to walk and talk—despite my mother's continued attempts to dress me in pink, give me shoes with bows, or foist dolls upon me—I was never, ever a princess. They were good and sweet and obedient, and I was not. And they always ended up with a pretty boy with a sword and a title and not much else of interest.

Maleficent, on the other hand, lived in a castle by herself and could turn into a dragon. Case closed.

My *Sleeping Beauty* phase was when I was about four. (It was followed by dinosaurs, Joan of Arc, and eventually The Monkees, each with its own memorabilia.) My mother finally gave up on Princess Aurora, and tried to get me to bond with the three fairies—Flora, Fauna, and Merryweather. But it was no use. I was Team Maleficent, all the way.

I really did have a Maleficent hand puppet. (She disappeared eventually, like most childhood toys, probably lost to the rummage sale along with all the old board games.) I did not remember her cloth body being plaid, but when I went digging on eBay to try and reclaim that small bit of my youth, there she was. Plaid. I was a bit startled.

I looked at family photos from the year my sister Mary was born. (I was three-and-a-half.) I found a picture of my nursery school class. I bought a late 1950s edition of Dr. Spock's *Baby and Child Care*, the parenting bible of the time, and read about sibling rivalry and new babies and the sort of advice my mother would have relied on. I watched the DVD of *Sleeping Beauty* and took pages of disjointed, impressionistic notes. I read Shirley Jackson—"The Lottery," of course, but also the two memoirs she wrote about raising her four children, until I had a version of her tone in my head.

Word for word, line for line, I think this is the best story I've ever written. When I read it aloud, it flows like silk. There's nothing about it I would change. I'm pretty happy with everything I've written, but even so, that's rare.

PS-1: Many of my stories have "Easter eggs" for sharp-eyed readers, or small gifts for my sister and others I know well—characters named after the milkman or mutual friends. Often, I suspect, I am too clever for my own good. (I figure since I spend weeks, even months on most stories; throwing in a few bits just to delight myself seems reasonable.) My favorite clever bit in *this* story is one that no one has noticed, or at least no one has ever mentioned: the baby's name is Rose Breyer.

PS-2, An aside: I watched the DVD of the Disney *Sleeping Beauty*, which came with interesting "bonus material," including footage of the animators making preliminary sketches of the fairies, using live models. The three actresses who modeled were short, less-than-svelte women: Frances Bavier (who played Aunt Bee on *The Andy Griffith Show*); Madge Blake (who played Larry Mondello's mother on *Leave It to Beaver*, and Aunt Harriet on the 1960s *Batman*), and Spring Byington, who stared in *December Bride*, a show that I loved as a kid, although I am at a loss to say *why*. Perhaps I had nascent gaydar, even then; Ms. Byington was in a long-term relationship with Marjorie Main, who played Ma Kettle in many films. (See why I like research? I never know *what* bizarre factoids I'm going to uncover!)

Sponda the Suet Girl and the Secret of the French Pearl (2013)

As you can probably tell from the majority of stories in this slim volume, I do not write High Fantasy. No swords, hardly any sorcery. No one on horseback. But I was invited to submit a story to a high-fantasy anthology called *Fearsome Journeys*, and decided it might be fun to try my hand at a form *way* outside my customary wheelhouse. In the next weeks, *much* crumpled-up paper littered the floor of my office, and I made very little progress.

In an attempt to at least come up with character names, I scribbled pages of failed faux-Arthuriana. I drank more wine, and late in the evening, watched my hand write: SPONDA. I laughed out loud, turned to a clean page, started again. But there was something so patently, ridiculously *wrong* with the name Sponda that it began to take on a perverse attraction. ("No," I told myself. "Just no.")

I set the whole project aside for awhile and did things that were Not Writing. (That is a very large category of activities—all endlessly entertaining—containing, as it does, *everything* except the act of actually writing.)

The deadline began to approach. I looked through notes in the unsorted, disorganized box I had once, oh-so-helpfully labeled "Ideas," and found nothing that seemed relevant to a fantasy or adventure tale. Amusing, though. I pulled one out, shoved "Ideas" back under my desk, and began to read about the history of margarine, which I have always found oddly compelling.

I have a folder of margarine ads from the 1940s, most of them a cheery, bright yellow, and almost all of them have fine print that says something along the lines of "This product is sold in the 32 states where margarine is legal." (It did not become legal in Wisconsin, for example, until 1967.) Perhaps one day I will write a story about margarine bootleggers and the seedy margarine black market in the U.S.

But I digress.

The deadline was *looming* and all I had was the name Sponda and a handful of very dry statistics about margarine. I buckled down and read more about margarine's 19th-century origins (Napoleon, armies), which soon led to suet, suet puddings, and lovely old recipes; when I began to stir them all together, a narrative emerged. A tale, even.

I made the deadline. The story has a plot, a very satisfying hoist-on-your-own-petard plot, and is sort of science-fantasy, maybe even alternate history-science-fantasy, a swell genre border-crossing mash-up. I think it's pretty funny, a ripping good yarn. I'm quite fond of it. I do seem to be in the minority, though, because this is the first time it's been reprinted.

Caligo Lane (2014)

As I've said, my creative process is rarely linear. This story began with three lines jotted in my journal, while I was thinking about a story for the anthology *Under My Hat*:

The witch is a cartographer.
Her house is full of maps.
Many of them show places you know.

I ended up writing another story for that book ("The Education of a Witch"), but those three lines stuck with me. A few months later, I read China Miéville's wonderful novel, *Kraken*, and was quite taken with his descriptions of impossible origami and folding objects into forgettable space. My brain began making unlikely connections. I bought books about maps, read about origami theory, went to San Francisco's Japantown to buy colorful paper (and fumbled with it), and spent days exploring curious byways in my adopted city.

I spent two years reading about maps and origami, folding endless cootie-catchers, and filled three or four notebooks with fascinating, if arcane, facts. In hindsight, that does seem like a bit much for a 3,000-word short story.

Yeah, I like research.

As an example: Although the art of origami was not well-known in the United States until the 1950s, in the '20s and '30s, women's magazines ran articles about paper crafts, one of which involved folding paper with this same pattern. Women were instructed to create four of them. Used upside down (at least from Franny's perspective), they became lovely handmade nut bowls for a bridge game.

PS: Look for the return of Franny and her origami magic in my stand-alone novella, *Passing Strange* (2017; Tor.com).

Amicae Aeternum (2014)

This is yet another story that I agreed to write without thinking it through. Like "Goodnight Moons," it *had* to be set in the future, a time when humans were leaving Earth and setting out for other planets, and it *had* to be, unequivocally, science fiction.

I'd had a version of Corry's list floating around in my mind for more than a decade. A poem written by a cranky seventh-grade girl. If I ever wrote it down, I planned to submit it to *Asimov's Science Fiction* magazine.

But it wasn't a story.

I thought about living on Earth. I walked around my neighborhood every day, noticing ordinary, random objects, and lay in bed at night wandering through the streets of my childhood, always fertile ground.

Words flowed out of my pen and onto the paper without much hesitation, a nice, albeit rare, feeling. But the story itself still felt flat. I put down my pen and stepped away, did the dishes, watched TV, played solitaire on my iPad, came back and noodled, but couldn't figure out what it needed.

I don't remember what triggered the idea that Anna needed to be an active part of their last morning, not just Corry's sidekick and witness. Her gift turned out to be the missing piece, and the next draft of the story had heart. It resonated like a crystal bowl.

And not just for me, it seems. I'm not sure if it's my most reprinted story to date (I think that's "Time Gypsy," which has been around for almost twenty years), but since "Amicae" was published (two years ago, as I write this), it's been picked up for four "Year's Best" volumes—including my first ever sale to legendary editor Gardner Dozois (a feat I can now check off on my Bucket List)—along with a dramatized podcast and a translation (Polish). And the movie rights have been optioned. One reviewer compared it to Bradbury, which thrilled me beyond belief. Perhaps this story has legs.

Hey, Presto! (2014)

This was an odd duck in its original appearance, in *Fearsome Magics*. It is neither fearsome nor fantastic. It's about the science of magic. Stage magic. Legerdemain. Hocus-pocus.

My research into the world of illusions was engrossing. I spent far too many hours reading about how magic tricks are created, about the history of magic. I gazed at reproductions of gorgeous old posters and longed to travel back in time. (Not an uncommon feeling, for me.) I investigated the chemistry of a possibly exploding paint.

I own a handful of vintage Girl's Own Annual volumes, and "Hey Presto!" would not be out of place in one of them. It was fun to try and write in an unfamiliar style, to find just the right tone and vocabulary to make another milieu come to life.

I am too fumble-fingered to ever *be* a magician, or even manage a simple sleight-of-hand, so it was a vicarious thrill to be able to write about people who could. Like most of my heroines, Polly Wardlow is smart and plucky. She's someone I plan to visit again.

PS: Polly also returns in *Passing Strange* (2017; Tor.com). I thought my imaginary friends should meet each other.

The Scary Ham (2014)

This one is nonfiction. Not even thinly disguised. It's all true.

I'd told the story a few times after my Dad died (in 2008), and it amused my friends. In 2014, I was the Toastmaster for the Nebula Awards banquet in San Jose. We'd just finished dinner. Steven Gould, then-SFWA president, and I had worked out a running order for the rest of the evening, and we were about to begin when the folks operating the computers said there were technical difficulties.

In the ballroom of the hotel, four hundred people stared at a very large screen that was no-signal blue, and across the globe, hundreds, maybe thousands of people stared at the error messages on their computer screens, waiting for the live-streaming of the event to begin.

Minutes ticked by.

I finally put down my napkin and went to talk to Steve.

"Do you need me to vamp?" I asked.

"What?"

"You've got dead air, and you're about to lose half the audience to the bar downstairs. Do you need me to fill time?"

"Tech says it might be twenty-five minutes."

I shrugged. "I can do that."

He stared.

"I'm your Toastmaster. It's my job."

So Steve went up to introduce me. I had *no* idea what I was about to do, but I have a long background in improv, and twenty years of doing the Tiptree auction at WisCon, so I'm good at thinking on my feet. I drained my wine and listened to Steve.

He said that he'd talked to our mutual friend, Madeleine Robins, and asked her for a nugget of information about me that wouldn't show up on a Google search. I heard Steve say, "—and her father had a scary ham—" and I smiled.

I got up to the podium, and for more than twenty minutes, I told the story of my father's ham. I was in top storytelling form, the audience was laughing itself silly, and all was well.

The tech crew finally got things running, and we proceeded with the scripted portion of the evening. A few days later, I watched the video, and decided to try and transcribe what I'd said. I've always wanted to write down some of my family's stories, but I've never gotten the tone right; my performing voice is very, very different than my writing voice.

I had to fill in the first four or five minutes (the sound had been off; all I had was a silent video of me making faces and flailing my arms in dramatic gestures), and then I spent a few days editing it, adding transitions, and rewriting bits, transforming a spoken-word story into prose.

Tor.com published it online, and it was, briefly, an internet sensation. A week later, I got an email asking if the film rights were available. (To the *ham* story??) I said yes, got in touch with my agent, and a small deal was made. A short film by Carolina Posse and Sue Mroz is scheduled to hit the indie film festival circuit in the fall of 2016.

I will find it ironic if, at the end of my career, my most well-known story is one that I told off the cuff, not words that I sweated over and honed and polished, but, hey—that's show biz.

To see photos of the actual ham (and its funeral), go to: www.tor.com/2014/05/22/the-scary-ham

Woodsmoke

This is the only story in the book that has never been published before. I originally wrote it for an anthology that failed to materialize at the publisher's end. It's the third of three nested stories that will—I hope—eventually form a novel-length work. I have not yet written the first two.

When I was a kid, I loved summer camp. I felt more at home there than any other place in the world, including (maybe especially) my parents' house. I have very slightly fictionalized the setting and the songs; the characters are flights of my imagination. There is, however, quite a lot of me in Peete (and vice versa).

"Woodsmoke" captures that special time in my life. The summer was magic, but the story contains no fantastic elements. It's plain old fiction.

ABOUT THE AUTHOR

Ellen Klages was born in Ohio, but has lived in San Francisco for more than forty years. Her first novel, *The Green Glass Sea* (2006), won the Scott O'Dell Award for Historical Fiction, the Lopez Award for Children's Literature, and the New Mexico Book Award for Young Adult Literature. It was a finalist for the Northern California Book Award, the Quills Award, and the Locus Award. A sequel, *White Sands, Red Menace* (2008), won the California and New Mexico Book awards in the Young Adult category. Her story, "Basement Magic," won the Nebula Award in 2005, and her novella, "Wakulla Springs," (co-authored with Andy Duncan) was a finalist for the Hugo and Nebula awards and won the World Fantasy Award in 2014. Many of her other stories have been on the final ballots for numerous awards, and have been translated into Chinese, Czech, French, German, Hungarian, Japanese, Polish, and Swedish. A collection of her short fiction, *Portable Childhoods* (2007), was a finalist for the World Fantasy Award. In addition to her writing, she is a graduate of the Second City Conservatory, the Clarion South Workshop, and served for twenty years on the Motherboard of the James Tiptree, Jr. Literary Award. She collects lead civilians, odd toys, postcards, and other bits of whimsy that strike her fancy. Her website is www.ellenklages.com.